PUFFIN BOOKS

SCUMBLE

Ingrid Law is a writer and an artist. Her artwork has appeared in local and national art shows in the USA. She lives in Colorado with her daughter. This is her second novel.

Books by Ingrid Law

SAVVY
SCUMBLE

SCUMBLE

Ingrid Law

PUFFIN

PUFFIN BOOKS

Published by the Penguin Group
Penguin Books Ltd, 80 Strand, London WC2R 0RL, England
Penguin Group (USA) Inc., 375 Hudson Street, New York, New York 10014, USA
Penguin Group (Canada), 90 Eglinton Avenue East, Suite 700, Toronto, Ontario, Canada M4P 2Y3
(a division of Pearson Penguin Canada Inc.)
Penguin Ireland, 25 St Stephen's Green, Dublin 2, Ireland (a division of Penguin Books Ltd)
Penguin Group (Australia), 250 Camberwell Road, Camberwell, Victoria 3124, Australia
(a division of Pearson Australia Group Pty Ltd)
Penguin Books India Pvt Ltd, 11 Community Centre, Panchsheel Park, New Delhi – 110 017, India
Penguin Group (NZ), 67 Apollo Drive, Rosedale, Auckland 0632, New Zealand
(a division of Pearson New Zealand Ltd)
Penguin Books (South Africa) (Pty) Ltd, 24 Sturdee Avenue, Rosebank,
Johannesburg 2196, South Africa

Penguin Books Ltd, Registered Offices: 80 Strand, London WC2R 0RL, England

puffinbooks.com

First published in the USA by Dial Books, an imprint of Penguin Group (USA) Inc.,
in partnership with Walden Media, LLC, 2010
Published in Great Britain in Puffin Books, 2011
001 – 10 9 8 7 6 5 4 3 2 1

Text copyright © Ingrid Law, 2010
Art copyright © Brandon Dorman, 2010
Book design by Teresa Dikun and Jasmin Rubero
All rights reserved

The moral right of the author and illustrator has been asserted

Set in Schneidler BT
Printed in Great Britain by Clays Ltd, St Ives plc

British Library Cataloguing in Publication Data
A CIP catalogue record for this book is available from the British Library

ISBN: 978-0-141-32420-3

www.greenpenguin.co.uk

To Phillip,

who was always there for me,

even when he wasn't.

THE FAMILY TREE

MISSISSIPPI
(MIBS)

FISHER
(FISH)

FEDORA
(FE)

LEDGER
(LEDGE)

Chapter 1

MOM AND DAD HAD KNOWN ABOUT the wedding at my uncle Autry's ranch for months. But with the date set a mere ten days after my thirteenth birthday, my family's RSVP had remained solidly unconfirmed until the last possible wait-and-see moment. We had to wait until my birthday came and went. We had to see if anything exploded, caught fire, or flooded before committing to a long-haul trip across four states in the minivan. In my family, thirteenth birthdays were like time bombs, with no burning fuse or beeping countdown to tell you when to plug your ears, duck, brace yourself, or turn tail and get the hay bales out of Dodge.

1

I'd known for years that something in my blood and guts and brains and bones was poised to turn me tall-tale, gollywhopper weird. On my thirteenth birthday, a mysterious ancestral force would hit like lightning, giving me my very own off-the-wall talent. My very own *savvy*. Making me just like the rest of the spectacular square pegs I was related to.

My mom's side of the family had always been more than a little different. I doubted there were many people with a time-hopping great-aunt, a grandpa who shaped mountains and valleys out of land once pancake-flat, and a mix of cousins who ranged from electric to mind-reading to done-gone vanished – *Poof!* I'd even had a great-uncle who could spit hailstones like watermelon seeds, or gargle water into vapour and blow it out his ears. When Great-uncle Ferris turned thirteen, his savvy had stunned him with a sudden sunny-coloured snowstorm inside the family outhouse, toppling the small shack like an overburdened ice chest that rolled down the hill with him still inside it.

As for me, I'd been sure my birthday would treat me

better – sure I had the perfect mix of genes to make me supersonically swift. Unlike Mom, Dad was ordinary, but even without a savvy, he was still one of the best runners in Vanderburgh County. So it was practically destiny that I'd become the fastest member of the Theodore Roosevelt Middle School track team. The fastest kid on the *planet*.

Nothing worked out the way I'd hoped.

On my thirteenth birthday, I didn't get bigger, better, stronger muscles, or start racing at the speed of light. I didn't get the ability to whiz blizzards in the blaze of summer, either. But it wasn't like I hadn't got a savvy of my own.

Watches and windscreen wipers everywhere, look out! I could blow stuff apart without a touch, dismantling small things in bursts of parts and pieces: a light switch here, a doorknob there, garage door opener, can opener, Dad's stopwatch, his electric nose-hair trimmer too. After the first few episodes, I shoved whatever I couldn't fix underneath my bed. I didn't want Mom and Dad to know how much stuff I was breaking. Already,

I could see my future: no more training with Dad for the father-son half-marathon in the autumn. No track team, no more school, no friends. Rather than flinging crinkle-cut gherkins in the cafeteria, I'd be staying home to grow moss in pickle jars like my Beaumont cousins. Because if I hit Josh and Ryan and Big Mouth Brody Sandoval with ceiling panels and table hardware instead of handfuls of baby gherkins, Josh and Ryan might laugh it off, but Big Mouth Brody would tell for sure – and that wouldn't go down well at home.

Family rules said *keep quiet*. No one risked the consequences of sharing the family secret unless they had to; it was impossible to know what might happen if people found out that we weren't normal. Nicer folks might want to hire us for our skills. Less nice ones might want to put us in a freak show, or lock us up to study us and try to decode our genomes.

Well, secrecy was fine by me. The ability to bust apart a toaster wasn't something I cared to boast about. It helped that Dad was clearly in denial, while Mom believed she had everything under control. As far as my parents were concerned, I was simply Ledger Kale, doohickey-destructo boy less-than extraordinaire. And I was happy to let them think it.

So, nine days after I turned thirteen, Mom and Dad confirmed our family's RSVP and we packed our bags, preparing to hightail our way west from Indiana to Wyoming.

It wasn't long before everyone regretted the decision. As Dad pushed the minivan to its limits, trying to make it to the wedding on time, we were stalled again and again by a procession of problems along the interstate. I mislaid the muffler in Missouri, busted needle bearings in Nebraska, and sent us skidding in South Dakota, three wheels on our wagon. Helping Dad chase down our wayward tyre, I worried the whole transmission might be next.

I sank lower in my seat with each new mishap, willing my savvy to go away, ignoring my sister as she shook her head inside the oversized football helmet she'd worn non-stop since my birthday.

'Ledger!' Mom turned to face me in the van. 'If you're causing this trouble, *stop*.'

'Yeah,' Fedora piped up. 'Safety starts with *S*, Ledge, but it begins with *you*.' My sister's second-grade teacher had been a stickler for safety, and Fe carried her most memorable sayings inside her head, handing them out like toothbrushes on Halloween.

'I mean it, Ledge,' Mom continued. 'Keep it together – keep *everything* together – until we reach Wyoming.' She smiled her best bulldozer smile, the one hardly anyone in the world could stand against. Mom's savvy word-and-smile combo had been making me and my sister eat our broccoli and keep our rooms clean forever, and Dad never forgot to take out the trash, though sometimes he did roll his eyes as he stepped out of the door. Dinah Kale's savvy put her in control. She'd even stopped a bank robber once just by telling him to sit down and be still, shackling him with five words and a smile until the police arrived.

Now I could see that Mom was beginning to understand – the longer I sat trapped in the van, the more danger there was of me turning it into a unicycle. Already I could feel the itch and buzz of my savvy zinging beneath my skin. Another incident like the one with the tyre, and my parents might be forced to ship me to Antarctica, where only seals and penguins would come out to watch me run the local half-marathon.

Knowing there were some normal human things my Mom wouldn't stop me from doing, I started downing Gatorade like Uncle Ferris preparing to create a winter storm. By the time I spied the sign for Sundance, Wyoming, the closest spot on the map to my uncle Autry's ranch, there were four empty bottles at my feet, and I had to water the cactuses in a serious way.

'We have to stop now!' I announced.

'Yeah, I'm *dying* here,' Fedora chimed in, straining against her seat belt. 'My butt's going to fall off and I'm thirsty. Ledge drank everything we had.'

'Maybe a short pit stop, Tom?' Mom suggested with a sigh, casting a glance at the empty bottles. Dad nodded, his chin a lead weight. I sighed too, relieved my plan had worked. Already, the dome light above me was rattling in its fittings.

The town was as still and silent as if the ghost of the Wild West outlaw the Sundance Kid had come back to haunt the place. My imagination was full of childhood stories of stout-hearted sheriffs in clinking spurs and masked bandits robbing stagecoaches, but the streets were deserted. Not even a tumbleweed bumbled up the pavement.

Dad parked in front of a boarded-up T-shirt shop with a large red sign in its window. The sign read: FORE-CLOSURE. I knew what the word meant – the T-shirt shop was history. A spattering of similar red signs dotted front yards and buildings like a poison ivy rash. I'd seen notices just like them back in Indiana. The bank had put one up in Big Mouth Brody's front yard last year, threatening to take his home, and making my loud friend quieter than I'd ever known him.

'Make it quick, you two.' Mom's smile was all business as she gave Fedora a handful of change for a drink. Fe and I raced out of the car, making a beeline

8

past the doomed T-shirt shop towards Willie's Five & Dime.

It felt good to be out of the van. Even better to stretch my legs.

If I hadn't already been worried about my savvy, and if nature hadn't been screaming my name through a megaphone, I'd have stopped dead in my tracks in front of the five-and-dime. A fully restored thing-of-beauty motorcycle stood parked at an angle next to an empty Crook County sheriff's truck. The vintage Harley Knucklehead, powder-coated in gold paint, glinted in the sun like newly unburied treasure. Treasure I could turn pronto into trash if I wasn't careful. I was still looking over my shoulder at the bike as I rushed through the swinging door after my sister, ignoring the smell of hot dogs and convenience-store nacho cheese goo.

'Ouch! Hey, watch it, Cowboy!'

A couple of white-blonde braids, a flash of green eyes and a sheaf of papers clutched tightly in a girl's hand were about all I saw before I bolted down an aisle stocked with souvenirs and polished rocks, metal shelves

9

rattling in my wake. Even as I sped towards the back of the store, I realized the mistake I'd made in my scheming. I'd traded one potential disaster for another. If my savvy went berserk inside the five-and-dime, there'd be fallen shelves, busted roller grills, drink machine fountains . . . and witnesses.

By the time I hustled back out of the washroom, Fedora was busy sorting her change, fumbling to count out money for a bottle of orange juice and a bargain-bin magnet: a lacquered jackalope with two broken-off antlers, now just a rabbit with two bumps on its noggin.

Mom's puppet-master power still had us in its grip, though Fe, chattering away like a blue jay, was clearly struggling to resist. But the man behind the counter was barely listening to my sister. He watched the other girl inside the shop instead – the one whose foot I'd trampled. As I hurried towards the counter and saw the way the girl listened with open curiosity as Fedora babbled about fireworks and butterflies and our cousin's wedding that evening, I could feel my savvy getting itchier and twitchier. Fedora was getting ball-park close to breaking family rules herself.

'Stop yammering, Fe, and pay for your juice,' I muttered, shoving past my sister. 'Or I'll beat you back to the van for sure.'

'Ledge, wait! No fair!' Fe hollered, dropping half her change on to the floor, her need for speed rekindled. I was already moving towards the exit, but the green-eyed girl blocked the door.

'Are you sure you don't want any of my papers this week, Willie?' the girl called out as I tried to doh-si-doh around her, my urgency and frustration increasing with every stonewalled step. 'Mrs Witzel was abducted by aliens after the church bake sale last Sunday and I've got the inside scoop!' The girl held her papers high, adding to my irritation as she accidentally smacked me with them.

Willie gave a negatory grunt. 'You'd best be getting home, Sarah Jane,' he said. 'Your daddy doesn't want you using my copy machine any more, and I don't want any trouble.'

11

I reached the door just as Sarah Jane turned to leave. In seconds, my running shoes crossed laces with her green Converse low-tops, and our combined forward movement carried us outside in a Twister-game tangle of arms and legs, and a sudden frenzy of flying papers.

My bumbling stumble turned into a fast, hard fall, and I hit the pavement rolling – rolling like a boy-shaped bowling ball towards the motorcycle parked beside the sheriff's truck. My mouth filled with the taste of panic, sharp and metallic. I lurched to a stop, my right shoe missing the front spokes of the Knucklehead by a centimetre. I hadn't touched it, yet the machine began to teeter. To wobble. To vibrate and to shake.

As Fedora rushed out of the five-and-dime in a single-minded blur shouting, 'Ha! Beat you to the car, Mister Clumsy Pants!' my pulse sounded in my ears . . . once . . . twice . . . three times. Then, watching Fe race ahead and barrel down the block, every bit of savvy energy I'd been holding in for hours and miles broke loose.

From front wheel to back, the Knucklehead exploded.

Parts and pieces slammed into the side of the sheriff's truck with heavy, thudding smacks and the clang and *skreel* of metal on metal. The bike's handlebars hit the truck, smashing the windscreen with a crash before bouncing back in my direction like a boomerang. A second later, the door of the sheriff's truck fell off its hinges.

Mechanical rubble littered the pavement.

Fear thumped a hand-over-fist rhythm against my ribs.

I barely noticed as Fe reached the minivan, tossed in her helmet, then ran to join Mom and Dad in the coffee shop across the street, leaving the van's door wide open. That horrible zinging itch I'd had in the car was gone, but how was I going to hide *this*?

If the sheriff arrived now, he'd lock me up and throw away the key. If the owner of the Knucklehead found me first, I'd be ding-dong, doornail dead.

I squeezed my eyes shut tight, wishing that this whole savvy nightmare was nothing but a rotten dream. In the twenty seconds I spent down for the count, the girl

13

named Sarah Jane gathered up her papers and took off. I knew I ought to do the same, because when I opened my eyes, my disaster was still real-life real.

Jamming down the block, I slipped in through the van's open door just as Mom and Dad exited the coffee shop – blind to everything but my sister's stupid magnet, admiring it like it wasn't even broken. Maybe they hadn't noticed that the thing was supposed to be a legendary creature, not just some bunny with a lumpy head. But as long as Mom and Dad's focus didn't turn towards the mess I'd left behind me, Fe was welcome to our parents' undivided attention.

Headed out of town, my stomach twisted into a dozen different kinds of knots. I wondered if Sarah Jane would report me to the Crook County sheriff, or tell Willie what I'd done. I pictured a red foreclosure sign stapled to my forehead; at the rate I was going, I would soon be history.

Chapter 2

IT WAS DAD WHO FIRST PLANTED the idea that my savvy might be gold-medal material, despite Mom's warnings that savvy talents are unpredictable. Dad had been building his hopes since we ran our first three-legged race; it hadn't mattered that I'd tripped us three metres from the finish line. We had big dreams.

On the morning of my thirteenth birthday, I couldn't eat. My stomach threatened a sick, see-sawing rebellion, and I didn't want to remember thirteen forever as the birthday I barfed up breakfast. My thoughts were a treadmill of hope and worry as I pictured the trophies

I'd put side by side with Dad's if things turned out the way we planned.

Running, running, running, I thought. *Let my savvy make me fast, fast, fast!*

'Imagine it, Ledger,' Dad said, letting the corner of the sports section dip as he gave me an encouraging thumbs-up. 'By the end of today you'll be able to run halfway across Indiana in the time it takes your pal Ryan to tie his shoelaces.' Ryan had beaten me easily in the eight-hundred-metre run at school. Dad had taken me out for pizza after, but I knew he wished I'd won.

'Tom . . .' Mom gave Dad a warning look.

I pushed my scrambled eggs into shapes with my fork – cars and lightning bolts and frowning faces – destroying them again as I did my best to echo Dad's enthusiasm.

'Yeah!' I said. 'Tonight I'll run round the world at the speed of light and bring us back pizza from Italy.'

'Or wontons from Mr Lee's Panda Palace!' said Fedora.

'Not from the Panda Palace, Fe.' I rolled my eyes.

16

'That's right, Fedora. Mr Lee's is just a mile from here,' Dad explained. 'We're thinking bigger than that. We're thinking *savvy*-big, like your mom and your cousins. By the end of your brother's birthday, he'll be able to get us wontons from the other side of the globe!' Dad winked at me, adding, 'You can bring Ryan Manning back some salt-and-pepper squid as a consolation prize.'

'Ewww, squid.' Fedora made a face, then bounced in her chair, chanting: 'Noodles! Noodles! Bring me noodles!'

'Do you hear that, Ledge? When you get to China, grab some noodles for your sister.' With a grin, Dad folded his paper, ignoring the way Mom shook her head in disapproval. I wasn't sure who was more excited about my potential new savvy: Dad or Fedora. In my gut, I knew it wasn't me.

Fedora and I both remembered when our cousin Samson Beaumont turned thirteen three years before. It was impossible to forget the birthday party where our quiet shadow of a cousin vanished while blowing out his candles. Now my sister watched me like I might sprout eyeballs from my elbows or evaporate if she looked away. And when Dad and I went outside to wait for my supersonic savvy to kick in, Fedora wouldn't stay behind.

'You look ridiculous,' I told my sister as she followed us out of the door. Having heard plenty of savvy-birthday stories with endings more calamitous than Samson's vanishing act, Fe had dug Dad's old football helmet out of the basement.

'Better safe than sorry!' She raised her chin, rapping her knuckles against the plastic hiding her short brown hair – hair cut just as neat and trim as mine and Dad's. Just the way Mom liked.

Helmet or no helmet, there wasn't much anyone could do to prepare for a savvy birthday aside from taking basic precautions: no big parties, no friends, no sharp objects. I was surprised Mom had let me use a fork at breakfast. Allowing Josh or Ryan or Brody to come over had never been discussed.

I hated that my buddies wouldn't see me turn awesome; I would've liked to see their faces. Each of my friends had his own gig. Ryan was magic on the sports field – any sports field – and Josh was the ladies' man. Josh had even locked lips with Misty Archuleta during a field trip to the planetarium once, after giving her a necklace with a big silver *M* on it. Everyone had known about the kiss before the bus got back to school because Big Mouth Brody spilled the beans like an All-State bean-spiller.

When we were rug rats like Fedora, I'd been best at LEGO and Erector Sets; I'd even constructed a model of the Eiffel Tower out of toilet-paper tubes that my third-grade art teacher thought was artistic genius.

'The Leaning Tower of Pisa, Ledger!' she'd said. 'How beautiful!'

So much for genius.

It didn't matter. By the time my first pair of running shoes were broken in, my LEGO pieces were gathering dust and I was sitting in the back of the art room, keeping my creations to myself. I stopped daydreaming about building things and started focusing on the pavement.

Five years and six shoes sizes later, I ran round the block under the midday sun, chasing my thirteenth birthday savvy speed. Dad had made Fe Official Timekeeper, giving her a mechanical stopwatch and a whistle.

'Bricka bracka firecracker, sis boom bah! Ledger Kale! Ledger Kale! Rah! Rah! Rah!' Fe shouted her favourite Super-Rabbit cartoon cheer every time I finished a lap, hitting the reset button on Dad's watch.

'Is anything happening, Ledge?' she asked every time. 'Feel any different?'

'No,' I replied, working to catch my breath after sprinting full speed. Full, normal, *boring* speed.

'How about now, Ledge?'

'No.'

'Now?'

'No!'

'What about now?'

'NO!' I yelled at Fe, rounding the block again, my frustration and temper the only things gaining momentum. On my tenth lap, Fe hit the stopwatch and I stumbled – my toe catching on a lip of pavement forced up by tree roots, as if my own family tree were reaching up to trip me. Thrown off balance, I fell, skinning my knees, my elbows and my pride, while a limb-tingling sensation crawled beneath my skin like I'd landed on an anthill.

'You okay, Le–? Whoa!' I barely registered Dad's voice. Before he could finish his question, the stopwatch in Fedora's hand blew apart – *whiz-bang!* – the main-spring zinging me in the backside, the rest of the parts flying like shrapnel. Dad ducked and Fedora leaped back with a merry shriek. I covered my head to avoid getting razor-thin gears lodged in my brainpan.

Dad's stopwatch was my first savvy casualty. Fedora dashed home, shouting, 'Mom! Mom! Wait till you see what Ledge can do! He ran round the block ten times and *zippo*. Then – *bang-zoom!* – something savvy happened, and now he can bust things up!' Helmet bob-bing, my sister pummelled the air in a comical three-punch combination, repeating 'Bust! Things! Up!' as she shadowboxed around the house.

21

'Do it again, Ledge!' she demanded. 'Break something bigger this time! Go on . . . show Mom! Try!'

I didn't try. One look at my knees and Mom went to get the plasters, while I watched Dad sort through the mishmash of pieces he'd picked up off the pavement. The stopwatch's metal casing hung over his index finger, stretched out and bent. Looking at it made me queasy. I knew Dad would've liked to believe that the watch broke because I was too fast for it. He would've been proud if my cuts and scrapes were trophies won through a triumph of sudden super-speed, rather than tokens of my everyday clumsiness. But there had been no evidence that I'd become a single inch- or metre- or mile-per-hour faster.

When nothing else happened on my birthday but cake and presents and lights-out at ten, nobody knew what to think. Mom and Dad debated whether I'd got a savvy at all.

'Dad . . . I-I,' I stammered as he came to say good-night. I'd already climbed into bed and pulled the sheets over my head, hiding from the last hours of my lousy, bungled birthday.

'Don't sweat it, Ledge.' Dad's quick reply surprised me. 'So, it turns out you're an everyday Kale man like your dad. So what? It's not like you're defective. We can still run our half-marathon the way we planned. Only, now you won't have to slow down to let your old man catch up.' He winked, then glanced around my room, his gaze moving across long-forgotten art projects and model cars. Then he turned off the overhead light and wished me one last 'happy birthday' before pulling the door closed behind him.

Fedora had been wrong, I told myself. I didn't break stuff. That kind of savvy would be bad news a dozen ways to Sunday. It would ruin my plans to hit the new Wild, Wild Water Coaster with Josh, Ryan and Brody. I tried to imagine what would happen if I broke the longest water coaster in the world. The thought sent a prickling shiver down my spine. My bed frame shivered with me.

I reached to switch off my bedside lamp, but it rocked and shuddered into a battery of brass and sockets before I even touched it. The painting my aunt Jenny had sent me for my birthday fell from my bedroom wall with a *thwump* in the sudden darkness. But I didn't need light to remember what it looked like. Aunt Jenny had painted a boat on a stormy ocean, a boy on the deck – a boy who looked an awful lot like me, only braver.

Not defective, not defective, not defective. I chanted the words to myself until I fell asleep, praying to God that they were true.

After my Knucklehead demolition in Sundance ten days later, I was sweating bullets. Riding in the suffocating van, I closed my eyes and hunched my shoulders, trying to think of nothing. Trying to ignore the feeling of my savvy building steam again as I fought to forget my most recent awful memories: the smell of spilled motor oil; a sound like a thousand steel cans hitting asphalt; the glint of chrome and metal under the noonday sun.

'You okay back there, Ledge?' Dad's voice brought

24

me back. I opened my eyes, meeting his look of concern in the rear-view mirror. The mirror yawed and tilted . . . shook . . . then fell. Dad caught it easy. I clenched my fists. My savvy was as useless as a pogo stick in quicksand, and I wasn't the only one who could see that I was sinking.

'It's getting worse, Dinah,' Dad said in an undertone as he handed the mirror to my mom. 'I'm beginning to think this trip might've been a bad idea.'

'We're almost there, Tom,' Mom answered, her own tone less than reassuring. She turned to me and forced a smile. 'Just relax, Ledger,' she said. 'You can control things a little longer.'

'You mean *you* can control things a little longer,' I muttered, too quiet for Mom to hear. As my fists uncurled and my muscles loosened, I wondered how long this latest round of enforced relaxation would last. The closer we got to Uncle Autry's ranch, the more I hoped my parents weren't both thinking the same thing: that it might be safer for everyone if they simply left me on the side of the road.

Taking the second exit to the right and continuing straight on till nowhere, we reached Uncle Autry's ranch. I was first to the back of the van to grab my bag. But when the hatch swung open and two green eyes met my grey ones, I almost sent that rear door into orbit.

Sarah Jane was sitting in the middle of my family's luggage.

Chapter 3

FOR A MOMENT, STORIES OF MY cousin Mibs Beaumont's thirteenth-birthday stowaway journey on a big pink bus flashed through my mind. Sarah Jane didn't look any older than me. I wondered if it was a habit of teenage girls to run away and hide themselves in other people's vehicles. For my sister's sake, I hoped not.

Sarah Jane held a finger to her lips in warning. Knowing that she was one of the few people who'd seen me wreck stuff in Sundance, I threw a picnic blanket over her before the rest of my family appeared to get their bags. I'd already pinched Fedora until she promised not to tell, but I couldn't guess what this girl might blurt if Mom and Dad discovered her.

'I'll get our stuff!' My vocal cords stretched and snapped over the words like rubber bands pulled too tight.

'Ledge –' Mom began.

'No, really! I'm happy to get everything!' Untapped manners surfaced from some dark and dusty place as I herded my family away. Mom gave me a suspicious look.

'Let the boy be, Dinah,' said Dad. 'If Ledge wants to carry the luggage, more power to him. Don't forget the cooler, son. Just . . . you know, *try* not to break it?' Dad's words cut me to my trainers, but I had bigger worries. As Dad nodded towards the cooler, I jumped to block his view of Sarah Jane's green Converse low-tops jutting from behind it, hoping too that Dad wouldn't notice the girl's collection of papers where they lay next to our bags. I could see now that every sheet was a single-sided photocopy of a home-made newspaper, each with the same bold headline:

28

SELMA WITZEL ABDUCTED AFTER BAKE SALE – TRADES STRAWBERRY-RHUBARB PIE TO ALIENS FOR FREEDOM

The words sparked my curiosity. Who would have guessed that aliens liked pie? I suddenly wished aliens would abduct *me*, delivering me to some other planet where I might not feel so awkward and ham-fisted. But no, not even aliens would want me, I thought. I'd probably break their spaceship.

I shook myself to clear my head, then flipped the two-bit tabloids over. Dad hadn't noticed Sarah Jane's shoes or her cheesy papers. I watched him steer Mom towards Uncle Autry's big log house, where Fedora was already skipping up the steps to greet the rest of the family inside. As soon as the coast was clear, I yanked the blanket off our uninvited guest.

'What do you think you're doing?' I hissed, keeping my voice low. 'How did you get in here?' The girl's face relaxed into a self-satisfied smile.

'I'm a newshound, Cowboy. I go wherever I smell a story.' She swung her legs round and climbed out of the van. Then she held out a hand for me to shake.

29

'Sarah Jane Cabot's the name, but you can call me SJ – it's what my friends would call me if I had any.'

I wasn't interested in becoming this girl's friend. I already had friends. At least, I did before my savvy came along and broke my life. I reached past Sarah Jane, ignoring her hand, grabbing the handle of Mom and Dad's suitcase instead. Cussing as it broke loose. But Sarah Jane didn't notice my snub or flinch at my language. She was too busy looking around.

'So this is the Flying Cattleheart!' The girl gave an admiring whistle. Built of logs, but no mere cabin, the O'Connell home looked like the lodge of an outdoorsman prince. 'I've never been allowed up here before,' Sarah Jane added. She pulled a small spiral notepad from her pocket. Its narrow pages were warped and wrinkled, like the entire thing had been dropped overboard on an expedition for a big fish story. 'This place is triple-wow deluxe!'

I followed the girl's gaze as she looked around. We stood in a bowl of earth that had been carefully sculpted by my grandpa Bomba back when he had the strength to move mountains. The place still looked Wyoming wild, but now it was crazily patterned and moulded; like somehow Grandpa had mixed up the carved swards and jutting stones of Machu Picchu in South America with the curved, thickly sliced, stair-stepping terraces of the rice paddies in China, then coloured it in sage green, sandstone red and straw-bale gold. He'd even changed the course of a river tributary to bring sparkling, silver-blue water through the ranch.

I knew Grandpa hadn't moved so much as a flower-pot full of potting soil in years. Yet something deep inside me stirred as I imagined how cool it must've felt to create something this awesome.

A bee buzzed past me, heading for the large garden planted between the log house and the barn. The red-and-white barn was already dressed up for that evening's party. Even the windmill behind it was decorated in streamers. Another barn stood by the river, a mirror image of the first – except for the roof, which was made of metal beams and glass.

Autry's second barn was an insect conservatory –

a terrarium for giants. Inside the Bug House, a person could have seriously close encounters with stick insects as thin as straws and as long as a man's forearm, and Goliath beetles so big they sounded like helicopters when they took flight. There were butterflies too – butterflies galore. The place was a zoo. Or a nightmare.

Maybe my savvy had a bright side after all. I'd never been a fan of giant bugs, so I hadn't been inside my uncle's conservatory since I was little. My new talents gave me a less embarrassing excuse to stay away.

Taking in the scenery, the two barns and the wind-mill streamers, Sarah Jane looked ready to crash my cousin's wedding *and* take notes.

'You shouldn't be here,' I growled through clenched teeth. 'You're going to get me into trouble. How did you get inside our van?' I demanded again.

'Ask your sister,' Sarah Jane answered. 'She practically invited me in, leaving the door open the way she did. After hearing her tell Willie about the big shindig here tonight, I figured I had to come see it for myself. Weddings are big news, you know!' She gestured with her notebook. 'Weddings always sell a gazillion papers. But I barely got myself stowed before you climbed in, Cowboy.' She paused, looking me over like I was a sorry six-legged calf, not a cowboy. Resisting the urge to run, I tried not to squirm beneath Sarah Jane's steady gaze.

'That was quite a spill you took in town.' Sarah Jane flipped to a blank page in her notepad. 'I've never seen one kid cause so much damage. Can I ask you a few questions about what happened?'

'N-no! No way,' I sputtered, not wanting to discuss what had gone down in Sundance with her or anyone else. Not now. Not ever. Without looking at Sarah Jane, I wedged Mom and Dad's bag under my arm and slung Fedora's tote over my shoulder.

'You have to go now!' I grabbed the handles of the cooler, trying to carry all the bags at once, feeling like a pack mule descending into the Grand Canyon on roller skates: everything going downhill fast.

'I think I'm going to stay,' Sarah Jane replied, as if simply saying so made it flower-pickin' fine.

'Well, you can't,' I shot back.

33

'Why not?'

'Because I say so,' I answered, wishing I had a morsel of Mom's talent.

'Come on, Cowboy! I promise to blend into the background. You won't even see me. I'm *stealthy*.'

I snorted, thinking of my cousin Samson. 'Trust me, I'd see you. I actually know people I *can't* see, and you're not one of them.'

The corners of the girl's mouth fought to stay straight. 'I like you, Cowboy,' she said. 'You're funny.' Then she stopped smiling and narrowed her eyes. 'Wait. Really? Tell me more about these people you can't see.' Sarah Jane slipped a small nub of pencil out of one of her braids, licking the tip of the graphite once before pressing it to paper.

I looked again at the newspapers in the back of the van, shaking my head over the paper's title:

The Sundance Scuttlebutt

YOUR #1 SOURCE FOR NEWS OF THE STRANGE.

Sarah Jane obviously had good instincts to steal a ride here.

34

'Forget I said anything,' I answered. 'And stop calling me *Cowboy*. My name's Ledge.' As I spoke, a sudden gust of wind burst from the front door of the log house, coming from *inside* – and blowing *out*. I knew exactly who was causing the whirlwind of indoor weather.

Even outside the house, Fish Beaumont's gales were strong enough to set the windmill spinning behind the barn, making streamers flap and fly. Sarah Jane's newspapers flew from the back of the van. Her braids whipped in the wind like two lengths of rope trying to lasso her escaping stories. The screen door opened and slammed shut repeatedly, rousing a black, wolf-like dog from a patch of shade up on the porch.

My uncle's dog, Bitsy, barked once, then yawned a mouthful of teeth, wagging her tail as she caught sight of me. Bitsy was accustomed to unusual phenomena. She'd limped on to the ranch as a tiny, three-legged pup years ago and never left.

But even if it didn't bother Bitsy, the unusual indoor-outdoor wind reminded me that this wasn't Indiana. Here, I was completely surrounded by unexplainable people, the kind of people who would be real head-line news in Sarah Jane's cockamamie paper – or any other newspaper, for that matter. We weren't an ordinary family. And this wasn't going to be a normal wedding. Thinking of the family rules, I turned to Sarah Jane.

'Tell me what it's going to take to make you leave.'

Chapter 4

CONVINCING SARAH JANE TO LEAVE COST me ten dollars, three candy bars, two Captain Marvel comic books and my backpack. If she were the newshound she claimed to be, and weddings sold a gazillion papers, I wondered if Sarah Jane would really stay away. I almost wished we could trade places. I would've been happy to let someone else sit through the marriage ceremony in my place.

But Fisher Beaumont's wedding didn't completely reek, or make me yawn my face in half the way I had expected. Family and friends gathered in a glade above the ranch's main buildings, surrounded on three sides by towering ponderosas.

Two tall birch trees grew in the centre of the open space, their branches laced like fingers to form an arch. The bride and groom stood beneath the trees, flanked by a pair of ancient juniper stumps that twisted like sawn-off pillars. Each stump supported a basket of flowers blooming in super-fast motion – seed to sprout to flower to seed again – while one hundred humming-birds hummed overhead. Aside from looking like the back-drop to one of Fedora's animated princess movies, the effect was kinda cool.

My knee bobbed up and down mechanically. I tugged at the necktie Mom had made me wear. If Sarah Jane had doubled back to sneak a scoop, she was certainly getting an eyeful of odd. Substantial amounts of *strange*. An entire paper's worth of peculiar.

But despite my nagging Sarah Jane worries, I actually liked watching the bride. She was pretty. And she could float.

Really float.

38

Fifteen centimetres off the ground float.

The earth's pull didn't trouble Mellie Danzinger the way it did the rest of us. My cousin Fish was marrying a girl from another savvy family, just like Grandpa Bomba did when he married Grandma Dollop long ago. There were unusual families like ours from California to Maine, making double-doozy weddings like this one happen now and then.

Fish's swirling gusts of wind ruffled the gauzy stuff of Mellie's dress and veil as she hovered in her own small, anti-gravity pocket of the world. But when the minister opened the Beaumont family's big pink Bible, Fish pulled his bride down to earth with a cock-eyed grin.

Fish's hair looked like it had been hit so many times by powerful blasts of wind that it was starting to grow in further and further away from his face, like dry grass trying to grow on a wind-scoured mountainside. I supposed that Fish, at twenty-three and all grown up, was old enough to get married. But my cousin still seemed way too young to be going bald already like his poppa.

'That poor kid's got his mom's bloodline and his dad's hairline,' Dad chuckled softly next to Mom.

'What's Dad laughing at, Ledge?' Fedora whispered, jabbing me in the ribs with her elbow. As tense and tight as a coiled-up watch spring, I resisted the urge to jab back. I knew I'd be the one to get in trouble if my sister started whining.

Sitting with the rest of the guests in the glow of summer-evening sunlight, I jumped every time a twig cracked or an insect thrummed. When I wasn't watching the bride, I was scanning the edge of the glade or turning to look over the heads of the people behind me, searching for the telltale glint of prying green eyes.

'Ledger! Stop fidgeting,' Mom whispered in my ear as I shifted uncomfortably against the hard, moulded plastic of my seat, beginning to feel exactly which parts of me had got banged up outside the five-and-dime. If I hadn't been worried about Sarah Jane the Snoop, I might've dozed off like Grandpa Bomba, whose colourful, overstuffed armchair stood out amid the sea of smaller plastic ones.

40

'It's nearly over, Ledge,' Mom breathed. And with a quick flash of her savvy smile, she added, 'Sit still for twenty minutes, then you can run free.' The commands that came with time limits had always been the worst; the more specific Mom got, the harder she was to ignore.

I was stuck. Staring forward like a statue. Frozen in a savvy-powered time-out that did nothing to improve my mood, or my nervous jitters. Fixed in place, I could feel my own savvy start to build. Like an itchy foot inside a winter boot, it threatened to drive me mad.

After the I-do's, but before the final just-kiss-the-bride-already smooch, Fish's youngest sister, Gypsy, stood up in front of everyone. Gypsy Beaumont hadn't changed much since I'd seen her three years before at her brother Samson's savvy birthday. She was twelve now, almost thirteen like me. But Gypsy still looked like one of my sister's dolls after six months' play and make-believe: tangled curls pulled into a sizeable rat's-nest puff on top of her head, cheeks pink, shoes gone missing.

41

Gypsy stepped lightly, carrying an old glass jar towards one of the stumps, oblivious to the sharp meadow grass and prickly pine needles under her bare feet.

I recognized the jar Gypsy set down next to the fast-forward flowers. I could see the faded, antique, red-and-yellow *Peter Pan Peanut Butter* label easily from where I sat. It had to be the oldest peanut-butter jar ever. But there was something far more interesting inside this jar than a smush of crushed-up nuts. This was one of my grandma Dollop's jars, the jar she and Grandpa had had at *their* wedding – practically a family heirloom.

Gypsy gave the white metal lid half a twist. Instantly, music rose from inside the glass. Trumpets, violins and whatnot filled the glade, crackling with the static of a classical radio broadcast captured over fifty years past. Every note had been caught inside that jar, pulled from the air by our grandma Dollop, then canned the way other grandmas might can string beans or salsa. Only Grandma had known how her savvy held the music inside those jars, but she wasn't around any more for us to ask.

I wondered what Sarah Jane would think of Grandma Dollop's jar if she saw it. I tried to turn to look for her again before remembering that I was still stone for ten more minutes. All I could see was the ceremony in front of me, the trees, the stumps and Grandpa Bomba swaying his wobbling head to the music.

As the canned orchestra continued to play and I continued to stew, a woman in a floppy, flowery hat turned in her seat in front of me. Great-aunt Jules had small, squinty eyes and arms so round her watchband cinched her wrist as tight as the twist in a balloon animal.

'Such a lovely tradition, my sister's wedding jar. So many of us have used it. I can't wait for the days when my own grandchildren ask for it.' She dabbed her squinty eyes with a tissue. 'Dolly sure did have a savvy to hold on to!' Then Aunt Jules stopped sniffing. Tilting her chin in my direction, she eyed me like some sorry reject from the savvy factory.

'Is it true nothing happened on this one's birthday, Dinah dear?' she whispered loudly to my mom. It took all the strength I had not to say something rude. Dad gave a soft snort, covering it over quickly with a cough.

'That's nothing you need to trouble yourself with, Aunt Jules,' Mom answered. I simmered in my seat, but Mom touched the back of my hand once lightly, as if to say: *Ignore her, Ledge.*

I didn't care if she was Grandma Dollop's older sister; I glared at Aunt Jules, feeling a vague prickle run beneath my skin. Then I watched, helpless, as the woman's wristwatch fell apart. Gears and pins and cogs flew everywhere. But Aunt Jules didn't seem to notice. Issuing two *tisks* and a *tut* over my sorry lack of talent, she turned back round as the fanfare from the peanut-butter jar wound down.

'Watch it, Ledge!' Fedora leaned across my frozen leg to waggle a finger in my face. 'Don't forget! Safety has no quitting time.' From the corner of my eye, I saw Dad brush a cog off his sleeve, shaking his head at Fedora's puns – or at his defective son.

If Sarah Jane was watching from some hidden spot, I hoped she hadn't witnessed my latest bit of damage –

that she hadn't guessed yet that I was an undeniable danger to metallic, mechanical, man-made things.

Everyone cheered as Fish and Mellie kissed at last. Everyone but me. The cheers set off a frenzied swirl of colour. Hundreds of butterflies rose into the air around the couple in a Technicolor tornado, then scattered and split the scene, all orchestrated by Uncle Autry like some insect rodeo air show. The towering birch trees began to creak and groan, bending and swaying as Fish blasted the glade with a happy, rumbustious storm.

Women clutched their skirts. Men grabbed their neckties. I squinted against the wind but couldn't even raise a hand to shield my eyes.

'Let's hope this is the worst the boy lets his love-struck bluster get,' Great-aunt Jules harrumphed as she lost her flowery hat to the wind. 'I'd hate to see young Fisher damage these fine birches. Trees like these don't grow up overnight, you know. Not since we lost the last Beacham with any talent.'

Another gust of wind carried a cloud of dust and grit in our direction. Great-aunt Jules began to sniff and snort, pressing a round finger beneath her nose to keep herself from sneezing.

'Lands! Don't get me going!' she exclaimed, holding her breath. 'If I start sneezing now, I might send myself back in time to the last wedding on this ranch. It would take me forever to catch back up!' Aunt Jules jumped back in time twenty minutes every time she sneezed, making me wish for a jumbo jar of pepper. I'd happily send her back in time – back to the days of the dinosaurs.

The wind settled as soon as Fish and Mellie swept down the path towards the barn, where the real party was about to start. Looking pleased to see his younger brother hitched and happy, Rocket Beaumont strode with the rest of the family between the rows of chairs, moving electrons in his wake and giving everyone sitting or standing near him a hair-raising moment.

No one could forget that Rocket was electric. When he was seventeen, Rocket triggered serious power cuts and mondo mayhem after a car accident put the Beaumonts' poppa – my uncle Abram – in the hospital.

A year later, Rocket decided he'd be better off at the ranch.

People chatted and laughed as they followed the newlyweds down the hill. Fedora took off at a run, eager to retrieve her helmet; she'd been hopping mad when Mom made her take it off for the ceremony. My parents quickly sidestepped Great-aunt Jules. Mom and Dad must have assumed that I was right behind them as they followed the others down the path. But I was still caught.

Not going anywhere.

And, unlike my cousin Rocket, who'd been here eight years already, the only place I wanted to go was home.

Chapter 5

'SHE PUT A PIN IN YOU, then forgot you were stuck, didn't she?' A man's voice came from somewhere beyond my limited field of vision. I scowled, but the man chuckled softly, moving closer. When Uncle Autry sat down next to me, leaning one arm against the chairs in front of us so I could see him better, I relaxed.

'How did you guess?' I muttered, feeling my face grow hot.

'I didn't have to guess, Ledge,' my uncle continued. 'Dinah's been my sister a lot longer than she's been your mother. And she did the exact same thing to me plenty. I must've spent half the fourth grade stuck like an ant

in tree sap back when your mom first got her savvy.'
Autry O'Connell was younger than both his sisters, my
mom and my aunt, Jenny Beaumont, but his face was
lined from years in the Wyoming wind and weather, and
threads of white salted his yellow hair. Today, instead of
wearing a silk necktie like the other men, Uncle Autry
cut a swell in a western bolo: a thin rope of braided
leather with metal tips and a clasp that looked like a
giant green beetle . . . wiggled its legs like a giant green
beetle . . . and *was*, in fact, a giant green beetle.

If the Flying Cattleheart was unlike other ranches,
Uncle Autry was equally unlike other ranchers. There
wasn't a cow, sheep or horse on Autry's land. Autry
O'Connell was an insect wrangler. Once known east
to west and north to south as the man to call for the
really, really big bug problems – and the really, *really*
big bugs – his savvy gave him sway over all manner of
creepy-crawlies. Though, these days he mostly worked
from home doing small jobs: raising ladybirds to ship to
gardeners, or helping the people in Sundance keep ants
out of their kitchens.

I remembered Mom sighing over a holiday picture postcard sent from the ranch the previous year. For our family's holiday photo we'd all stood smiling in matching red sweaters. The O'Connells' card had a photo of three-legged Bitsy looking up at an enormous pink-toed tarantula sitting on her head. In the picture, the tarantula wore a Santa hat and waved an unusual *ninth* leg at the camera.

'Your brother should've called his place "The Misfit Ranch" instead of naming it after some butterfly,' Dad had said, looking over Mom's shoulder at the picture.

'Tom!' Mom scolded Dad playfully. But she'd sighed again when she looked back at the picture. 'Why didn't Autry send us a picture of the twins?'

'I prefer the spider,' I offered with an unapologetic grin. All my life, complaints about Marisol and Mesquite O'Connell had earned me the same lecture I got then:

'The girls lost their mother when they were born, Ledger. Autry's done his best as a single father, but –'

'But his girls are a pair of wild horses,' Dad finished for her.

50

'Papi? Are you coming?' two teen-girl voices rang through the nearly empty glade. I held my breath, wishing my mom's savvy would wear off as fast as it had in the van. The twins were the last people I wanted witnessing my predicament.

Mesquite and Marisol were like the two knobs of an Etch A Sketch – Marisol in charge of up and down; Mesquite, side to side. Working together they could lift and move objects without having to lift a finger. And, for some reason, maybe because they were twins, they'd been doing it since they were *five*. Now, at fourteen, they'd had a lot of practice. And whenever we met, they'd practise even more – sticking a spoke in my wheels any chance they got, finding gut-busting delight in humiliating me. I was glad the two girls were vegetarians, or they might've eaten me alive long ago. But if Marisol and Mesquite realized I was a sitting soya-bean now, I'd probably be upside down or in a tree in three seconds flat, lucky if they didn't pinch my shoes or try to pants me in the process.

'*Paaaapi!* Let's go join the party!'

'Be right there,' Autry called to his girls, smiling as they began stacking chairs, lifting only a finger – or two. In a voice too low for the twins to hear, Autry asked, 'Do you want me to wait with you, Ledge?'

'No, thanks,' I answered through clenched teeth. The last thing I wanted was a babysitter. 'I'll just sit here and take in the view.'

Autry winked, then looked out across the ranch, his eyes alight with quiet pride.

'It is pretty spectacular, isn't it? This land's been in the family for generations. Your mom and I used to come here when we were kids, long before the deed passed to me.' A sudden frown altered his features and he murmured, 'I never thought I'd be the one to sink it.' Autry held the top of the seat in front of him in a white-knuckled grip. Above us, a cloud of gnats hovered like one of Fish's storm clouds, as if unhappy Uncle-Autry thoughts had summoned the dark swarm. I was about to ask him what he'd meant, but the twins were growing bored of stacking chairs.

52

'Papi!' they groaned together. Autry shook himself, looking up at the cloud of gnats as if he were surprised to see them. He sent the bugs packing with a quick wave, then stood, moving to join his daughters.

'Enjoy the view, Ledge,' he called back. 'Join us in the barn whenever you're . . . er, *ready*.'

I'm ready now, I thought, staring ahead of me at the peeling bark of the birch trees and the slowly wilting flowers, noticing Grandma Dollop's peanut-butter jar on one of the twisted juniper stumps. The jar had been left behind by everyone. Just like me.

Talking with Uncle Autry, I'd briefly forgotten my fear of nosy Sarah Jane and my worry that she might be hiding someplace close, writing down everything. But when a twig cracked behind me, my worries returned.

'Who's there?' I called.

I held my breath and listened. Unable to look at anything but the juniper stumps, the birch trees and Grandma Dollop's jar, I imagined a horror-movie spider the size of a Volkswagen climbing over the chairs behind me – or worse, the twins coming back to the glade to torment me.

'That was a pretty weird wedding.' Sarah Jane's voice was loud in my ear. If I could've jumped, I would have.

'I knew it! I knew you wouldn't leave!' I bellowed. 'I thought we had a deal. You promised!'

'I changed my mind.' She shrugged, moving into my line of sight. 'The candy bars you gave me were all melty.' She clucked her tongue. 'So, I decided I'd come back for something more.' I watched as Sarah Jane dropped her backpack – *my* backpack – and wandered to the front of the clearing.

'So, do you come from a family of circus performers or something?' Sarah Jane looked up, down and all around, as if searching for the lift or wires that had held Mellie off the ground. 'This could be front-page stuff. Front-page!' she murmured, pulling out her battered notebook.

I snorted. From what I'd seen of Sarah Jane's rinky-dink paper, it only *had* one page. Everything she wrote was front-page stuff.

54

'I said it before and I'll say it again,' the girl went on, 'weddings sell papers, Cowboy. A wedding with super-duper special effects and crazy flying stunts will sell even more. The butterflies were a nice touch. I suppose Mr O'Connell had something to do with those?'

'What do you know about my uncle?'

'I know he's good with bugs. People around here ask for his help all the time. He even took a wasp nest down from outside my bedroom window a few years ago. He didn't spray the nest or anything. He just climbed a tall ladder like a knight scaling a tower, stood there for a few minutes like he was having a conversation with the wasps, then pulled the nest down with his bare hands. His *bare hands*,' she repeated, jabbing the air with her pencil for emphasis.

'He didn't get stung. Not even once. He just put the nest on the seat inside his truck – *inside the truck*!' Sarah Jane whistled. 'You come from an interesting family, Cowboy. What other peculiar things will I find if I poke around?'

I didn't answer. I didn't have the chance. With a sudden spasmodic lurch, movement returned in a rush to all my limbs as Mom's savvy hold dissolved. I shot out of my chair faster than I had on the last day of school, knocking over the seats in front of me as I bumbled back into wind-up action.

I shook out both my legs and cracked my neck with a *pop*, suddenly aware of the noise rising from the basin of the ranch, where the wedding reception was in full swing. As the sun began its descent over the west ridge, light spilled from the barn's open doors. The dance was hopping, beams and rafters shaking.

Gazing down at the barn, Sarah Jane looked like she might be composing the newest edition of *The Sundance Scuttlebutt* in her head. Twiddling her pencil in one hand, she brushed her notebook along the papery bark of the birch trees with the other. Then she moved to lean against one of the juniper stumps, accidentally knocking both the flowers and the peanut-butter jar to the ground.

I let out my breath as the jar landed in a safety net

of dry grass and pine needles. Sliding her pencil through the wire spiral of her small notebook, the girl righted the flowers, then bent to pick up Grandma's jar.

'Don't touch that!' I shouted, pushing my way through the sea of plastic chairs. The jar caught the last slanting rays of the sunset, lighting up orange and pink in the girl's hand. Holding my own hand out in front of me, I edged cautiously towards Sarah Jane like she unknowingly wielded a stick of cartoon dynamite.

'You need to put that down.'

Sarah Jane looked at me, then cocked an eyebrow at the jar. Before I could stop her, she dropped her notebook and began to loosen the jar's lid, unleashing the staticky symphonic radio broadcast at full volume. Music flooded the empty glade in a shockwave of sound, startling Sarah Jane. She dropped the jar again, clamping both hands over her ears.

Watching the peanut-butter jar tumble in slow-motion towards a pointed rock, I lunged, knowing if the glass broke or the jar's lid came all the way off, Grandma Dollop's carefully captured radio broadcast would be lost forever. Sliding on my stomach, I made a game-winning circus catch, spinning the lid tight again as I rolled quickly to my knees.

'What the –? The music came from *that*?' Sarah Jane demanded, pointing at the jar.

'Of course it didn't,' I lied badly. 'I-I mean, just forget it. Forget about everything!' Getting up, I shoved Sarah Jane back in the direction of the ranch's exit again, hoping that, this time, she'd leave and stay gone. That the newspaper girl had seen Fish's bride float up the aisle was bad enough; who knew what kinds of savvy talents would be let loose at the reception? I'd heard that the bride's father could charm wild animals. The last thing I needed was Wyoming's preteen queen of paparazzi looking into the barn to see a conga line of cougars, deer dancing beneath a disco ball, or three bears doing the limbo with my mom and dad.

But Sarah Jane wouldn't budge. She squinted from me to the jar, not saying a word, the printing press in her brain clacking away.

Determined to maintain possession, I protected the

jar like a football, securing it in the breadbasket hold
Dad had taught me when he imagined all the things his
super-fast son would do.

'I'll leave, *if...*' Sarah Jane began, a scary-girl gleam
in her eye.

'*If* what?' I asked, not trusting her.

'I'll leave if you give me that jar.'

If I'd got my great-uncle Ferris's savvy, honest to
goodness steam would have shot from my ears.

'Forget it!' I shouted. Changing my grip on the jar,
I waved it in her face with one hand. 'It's just an old
jar. See?' I tried, lamely, to pretend that nothing out of
the ordinary had just happened. But sweat drenched my
palms, making the glass jar hard to hold.

The girl stepped towards me, stabbing her finger
into my chest. 'If it's just an old jar, why can't I
have it? At least tell me how it works.' Sarah Jane
and I stood eye to eye, close enough for me to count
her freckles and smell her watermelon lip balm. She
made a grab for the jar and we began a tug-of-war. But
when a stream of blue sparks shot like Old Faithful

through an opening in the barn's roof below us, I let go. Rocket had started his fingertip fireworks show early.

As Sarah Jane turned towards the crackling stream of electricity, I grabbed her shoulders, turning her one hundred and eighty degrees to face the other way. A second stream of sparks issued from the barn's open doors and Sarah Jane tried again to turn. Not knowing what else to do, or how else to distract her, I held my breath, scrunched up my face and planted my lips on hers, the same way I'd seen people do in the movies.

I'd never kissed a girl before and didn't have Josh the Ladies' Man to offer me pointers. But Josh had never said anything about Misty Archuleta slugging him in the ribs, which is what Sarah Jane did to me without a moment's hesitation.

'Gah! Yuck!' Sarah Jane stuck out her tongue, spitting as she propelled away from me. 'What do you think you're *doing*, Cowboy?' But my diversionary tactic worked, distracting her from the sparks and the barn, making her stomp away after giving me another solid thump – her fist connecting with the point of my chin, knocking me head over heels.

Sitting hand to jaw on the ground, punch-drunk and fuddled, I watched the girl march away until she disappeared into the fading light, still tasting her fruity lip balm. It was only then that I realized that Sarah Jane had taken Grandma Dollop's jar.

Chapter 6

I SUCKED IN AIR, IGNORING THE clang of my pulse as I tried to convince myself that there were worse things than Sarah Jane Cabot having the ancient peanut-butter jar. After all, there were hundreds more jars down in the barn right now. The entire family had brought their souvenirs of Grandma Dollop, and not just for the wedding.

'Why are we taking these?' I'd asked Dad as he loaded our collection of jars into the van. I'd helped him haul the box up from the basement, then watched as Mom dusted and tested each of them, filling the kitchen with music, news reports and old-time radio shows.

Dad and I had listened twice to the goosebump-raising, sauerkraut-scented call of Bobby Thomson's historic home run against the Brooklyn Dodgers. Dad had wanted to keep that one. Mom packed it anyway.

'It was your aunt Jenny's suggestion to bring along the jars.' Dad shrugged as he wedged the box into the van.

'Such a perfect idea too!' Mom sighed as she added extra Gatorade to the cooler. 'Leave it to Jenny to know just the thing to do. Surrounding your grandpa with all of Grandma's jars will give him great comfort in his last days.'

'What d'ya mean, *last days*?' Fedora demanded, yanking off her helmet.

'Grandpa's grown so frail, honey,' Mom explained, using her thumb to wipe jam from the down-turned corners of my sister's mouth. 'Grandpa's been living with Aunt Jenny and her family ever since Grandma died. But he decided long ago that he wants to be at the ranch when he passes on.'

'Passes on?' Fe's eyebrows drew together.

63

'Before he dies, Fedora,' Mom told her gently.

Sitting alone in the glade, I swallowed hard, knowing how dead *I* was going to be when Mom learned I'd lost Grandpa and Grandma's wedding jar. Not just Mom. *Everyone* would be mad. How could I stick to the rule to keep quiet when I'd let slip one of the few savvy objects that made so much noise?

A mosquito buzzed in my ear. Fireflies lit up all around me, despite being rare in Wyoming. Grumpy with the bugs, I pulled myself to my feet, betting Uncle Autry had sent them to check on me.

The evening sky held a lingering glow bright enough for me to see the pages of Sarah Jane's notebook where she'd dropped it. I picked up the notebook and jammed it in my pocket, leaving no trace of our wedding-crasher behind. Stomping my feet, I followed Autry's trail of fireflies, careful to leave a wide berth between me and the Bug House as I passed it. Knocking the door off the conservatory and setting free a hundred thousand bugs would only make my lousy day one hundred thousand times worse. It was bad enough when my zipper blasted into tiny, metal XYZ pieces halfway down the path and I found my good Sunday church trousers down round my ankles.

With dirt staining the front of my shirt and my necktie tied round my middle to keep my trousers up, I stood outside the barn's open doors, staring in. Streamers hung from every rafter in thick, rainbow-coloured webs. There was a dance floor in the centre of the room, and folding chairs and tables filled the rest of the space. The evening air was cool, yet I was drenched in sweat. I was angry, but something else was wrong. My skin itched like mad. There was a jackhammer inside my head. My stomach twisted into nauseating knots.

Gypsy danced near the newlyweds. Her fluff-headed cheer set my teeth on edge. Watching her spin and twirl in a one-person jitterbug made my stomach churn worse. But as she chatted and laughed to the empty space in front of her, I realized that she must be dancing with the ghostly, invisible Samson.

For the first time ever, I envied Samson Beaumont. If

I were invisible, Mom wouldn't know that I'd ruined my clothes skidding to catch the falling jar. I wouldn't have to be Ledge the not-so-supersonic runner, or Ledge the have-to-be perfect kid all the time. I could be anyone I wanted to be, because nobody would be watching.

People talked and laughed over the music rising from the back of the barn, where Grandma Dollop's jars took up two entire tables to themselves. Stacked higher than the three-tiered wedding cake nearby, the jars stood in towering spires. Marisol and Mesquite were already cutting and serving cake, shouting 'Incoming!' as they levitated pieces across the room. Each plate bobbed in front of one of the guests until he or she took it with a laugh and a salute to the twins.

A festive stream of spiralling blue sparks hissed past me like a firecracker, nearly making me jump out of my skin. I spotted Rocket leaning against a beam nearby, smiling awkwardly behind a scruffy beard, looking like a kid pretending to be a grown-up as he set off celebratory sparks. He called out to Fedora as she ran past him in her bobbling helmet.

'Hey, Fe! I like your lid.'

'Safety first!' Fedora called over her shoulder as she dashed away, playing chase with Bitsy and our youngest cousin, Tucker, who followed Rocket, Fish, Mibs, Samson and Gypsy as the last kid in the big Beaumont family. Rocket shook his head with a laugh, his dark, fork-in-socket hair defying physics in the way only spiky-maned cartoon characters ever truly achieved.

'Rocket! Oh, dear!'

Rocket straightened his posture, brushed off his shirt and searched for an exit as my mom approached, looking him up and down. Eyeing his shaggy hair and beard, Mom made a full array of mother-hen noises. With Dinah for a mother, my own hair hadn't touched the tops of my ears once in my life. Seeing the way she fussed over Rocket, I stepped further back into the shadows outside the barn, hoping to delay the lecture I was bound to get when she saw my dusty shirt and ruined trousers.

'You've always been such a good-looking boy, Rocket,' Mom started in. 'Now look at you! It's no wonder you don't have a date for your own brother's wedding. Where's that Meeks girl? Didn't she come? She could've stood in as your date, just like old times.'

Running a hand through his untamed hair, Rocket saw Mom smile and took a step back, looking around for help.

'It's no wonder things didn't work out between you and Bobbi Meeks,' Mom went on. 'A girl wants a cheerful, clean-cut beau, not a moody caveman. What you need to do is go into town tomorrow and get yourself a —'

'Aunt Dinah, stop!' Rocket's blue eyes flashed and he flushed red behind his beard, quickly plugging his ears like a first grader, singing an off-key *la-la-la* to drown out my mom. I'd tried the same move enough times to know it wouldn't work. Earplugs, loud music, headphones . . . drowning out Mom's voice only weakened her control, it rarely stopped it altogether.

'I'm not a kid any more,' Rocket continued loudly, fingers still crammed in his ears.

'If you're so old,' Mom continued her assault, 'why

do you continue to haunt this ranch like a stubborn child refusing to go home at the end of summer camp? You need to –'

'Aunt Dinah! It's so good to see you!' Rocket's sister Mibs broke in, coming to Rocket's aid.

Maybe if I'd had ink on my skin up in the glade, Mibs could've heard my screaming thoughts and saved me from Sarah Jane. A scribble, a note, a tattoo, even a stray jot from a marker on your skin, and Mibs Beaumont could read your mind. Just one more awesome savvy that I could've got, but didn't.

Jags of anger jabbed me. Ten thousand ants in icy football studs raced up and down my arms. My fingers and palms itched with a horrible tingling sensation.

'What happened to you, Ledge?'

I'd been watching the scene between Mom and Rocket so intently, I hadn't noticed Mibs's boyfriend, Will, as he stepped outside the barn.

'Wow, Ledge! Did you butt heads with a buffalo, or what?'

'Something like that,' I muttered. I'd met Will Meeks

before. He was an ordinary guy without a savvy. He'd only been a teenager himself when he and his sister Bobbi first got mixed up with the Beaumonts and learned the family secret.

I looked down at my ragged appearance, comparing it to the put-together buttons and service ribbons on Will's crisp, clean army uniform. I doubted Will had ever made a mistake, been humiliated, or done the wrong thing once in his life. Then again, he had the luxury of being *normal*.

'What are *you* doing out here?' I asked him after a pause.

I was surprised when Will shuffled his feet, getting dust on his spit-and-polish shoes.

'I . . . er, thought it might be safer for me to avoid your mom tonight. When I ask your cousin to marry me, I want her to know I did it without her aunty Dinah making me.'

'You're going to ask Mibs to marry you?' My stomach took a water coaster plunge. The ants still swarming beneath my skin began to bite. I scratched the palms of my hands. Digging my nails in hard. Stopping just short of drawing blood. If Mibs and Will got married, they'd need Grandma's peanut-butter jar, just like Fish and Mellie. Great-aunt Jules had said it earlier: the wedding jar was tradition.

The sick feeling in my stomach rose into my throat.

I should've chased after Sarah Jane, I thought to myself, vibrating with anger. I should have tried harder to get the jar back.

'Yo, Ledge! Incoming!' Marisol and Mesquite called out. I turned to see an enormous piece of frosted cake ducking and weaving full-speed through the crowd. When the cake stopped in front of me, I ignored it. But the twins were persistent. The edge of the plate bumped against my shoulder . . . once . . . twice . . . three times.

'Are you going to eat that?' Will asked, one eyebrow raised as he watched the plate of cake cannon into me. If Will hadn't been standing there, I might've grabbed the plate and thrown it back at the twins like a Frisbee. Not wanting to look like a jerk, I reached for it instead. But my fingers closed on air.

71

Glancing inside at Marisol and Mesquite, I could see them laughing. In seconds, the plate was back. Jabbing me again. Making my blood pressure skyrocket. I made another grab and missed again, only to see the plate coming back fast. *Really* fast. The marble-cake cannonball hit me in the chest, the force of the twins' blow pushing me backwards. Covering the front of my grubby shirt in crumbs and sugar frosting.

The buzz beneath my skin began to multiply. I wiped at the frosting plastered to my shirt, letting a loud barrage of barnyard language rip. After a full minute of noisy cussing, I looked up, realizing that the rest of the world had gone much too quiet. Everyone inside the barn stared out at me through the open doors. Someone had stopped the music. Behind the others, Marisol and Mesquite choked with silent giggles, covering their mouths with their hands and bending over double.

Embarrassed and fuming, I began to pull myself up off the ground. But rising to one knee, I was hit by a sudden wave of dizziness. Unable to stand up without my stomach threatening rebellion, I stayed down.

72

Something was happening.

The tingling feeling that had started in my fingers and palms spread into my back and chest. It surged through all my limbs. My teeth buzzed inside my skull, vibrating like I'd downed six pops and three kilos of sour sugar candy. But the taste in my mouth was metallic, not sweet.

I felt like the boy on that boat in Aunt Jenny's painting, trying to weather a stormy sea. Only, this time when my savvy let loose, it hit the barn with the destructive force of a tidal wave.

Metal folding chairs flew into pieces. Tables wobbled, then collapsed, crashing and spilling plates and glasses everywhere. The jar tables went down in a deafening explosion of shattering glass. Metal lids rolled away like giant coins as polka tunes, country ballads, ball games and love songs jammed the air with the din of a radio factory being hit by a rockslide.

Then the entire barn started coming apart.

When the first heavy beam fell, lurching from its fittings as nails and studs popped free, the party dissolved

73

into chaos. People shouted. Bitsy barked. The twins levitated Grandpa Bomba outside in his overstuffed chair. Grandpa held on tight and let out a thin *whoo-hoo!* whoop as the barn doors fell off their hinges just as he flew through them.

Mom and Dad tried to grab me, to drag me out of the way of the falling debris, while others tugged my sleeves or pulled at my collar. But crouched where I was outside the barn, I couldn't move. I was an anvil: hardened steel and hard to budge. Heavy with the weight of what was happening around me.

The understanding that I had a powerful savvy after all hit me like a hammer blow. It wasn't just watches and windscreen wipers that needed to look out. It was the whole, wide world.

Chapter 7

'NO, NO, NO, NO!' I WHISPERED as my savvy continued to tear the barn apart. Mom and Dad – and even Fedora – stayed by me. I could feel everyone else looking from me to the clanking, clunking, collapsing barn. I could hear people murmuring to each other as the smell of sawdust filled the air.

'Stop, Ledge! Stop!' Mom said the words over and over. But words alone couldn't make me stop, and she couldn't find a way to smile. I kept my head down, trying to stop. Wishing I knew how.

'Ledger, look at me!' Dad kept saying. 'Just take a

breath and look at me.' I couldn't meet Dad's eyes – not while I was destroying everything around me. I knew I was a disappointment to him in every possible way. I'd never get to run the half-marathon now. One false step and I'd topple water tables and dismantle guard rails. I'd deconstruct the marathon clocks into split-second parts and pieces. Or worse, bust the bolts out of a row of port-a-potties in the smelliest cataclysm ever.

Hearing a loud *pop!* I looked up in time to see two thick cables crash down into the garden, sparking and snapping like electric eels caught on dry land.

'Watch the power cables!' someone shouted. 'No one go near them!'

'I suppose y'want me to do something with those?' I heard Rocket say.

'If you'd be so kind,' Autry answered, his voice quick and tight as he shepherded kids and old people further away from the mounting wreckage.

'Happy belated birthday, Ledge,' Rocket growled as he moved past me towards the garden, picking his way carefully towards the fallen electrical lines.

'Rocket!' Fe called out, making him turn. 'Avoid the worst! Put safety first!'

'No worries, little cousin!' he called back with a smile lit by the fitful flashes coming from the downed lines. 'Just don't try this at home!' As Rocket's gaze fell across me, his smile vanished. The look that replaced it was sharp enough to make me suck in my breath.

Rocket moved into the garden, stopping at the place where the cables twitched and seized among the radishes, igniting the air with lethal-looking volts.

My mouth went dry as I watched my cousin pick up the fallen electrical lines like they were as harmless as a pair of green garden hoses. Pulling the two cables together in one hand, he clamped his other hand down over the sparking ends and held on tight. Electric currents shot up his arm and danced around his neck and chest.

After draining the cables, Rocket moved back in my direction. Lit up and crackling, he came to a halt three metres away, at what I hoped was a good, safe distance between an electric man and a demolitions boy. His shoulders rose and fell with every breath. The air around him seethed and shimmered.

I tried to swallow. But couldn't. My heart thumped so hard I thought it might explode. Instead, with a crack like thunder, the last beams of the barn's roof fell in at once. Creaking and groaning, the walls followed, sending shards of wood flying in every direction.

There was a sudden cry and all heads turned.

'You're hurt!' Mellie's voice was soft as she tenderly touched Fish's cheek. In the pale wash of blue light coming from Rocket, everyone could see the drops of blood that marred the front of Mellie's wedding dress. My cousin wasn't badly hurt, but his cheek was bleeding, gouged by something sharp and airborne – a nail or a splintered piece of wood. I knew Fish's injury could have been much worse and was glad I was already on my knees. It made saying a prayer of thanks that much easier.

Bitsy pushed her wet nose under my mom's arm, trying to give me big, sloppy, reassuring dog kisses. The savvy monster inside me had worn itself out. The barn was like a straw hat sat on by an elephant; it couldn't get any flatter. The awful prickling sensation was beginning to ebb. My hands no longer itched.

'Why's it always my face?' Fish asked as Mellie pressed a kerchief to his cheek. A mizzling smatter of raindrops licked the gravel around us, triggered by the pain in Fish's cheek. But he could scumble his savvy, no problem, and the paltry rainfall ended as quick as it began.

As soon as Rocket saw that Fish and Mellie were all right, he charged towards me, stomping so close I could feel every hair on my head and arms stand up.

'You've got to be more careful, Ledger!' Rocket shouted. 'You'd better learn that quick!'

'Back off, son.' My dad was on his feet, stepping between me and Rocket.

I opened my mouth to say something.

Anything.

Sorry, maybe.

But before I could form a single word, a siren chirped in the distance and Rocket turned sharply. There was a collective gasp from the assembled crowd. No one could mistake the sight or sound of the sheriff's vehicle rumbling down the gravel road towards us.

Rocket took off in a blur, headed for the hills. Of all the things that would be difficult to explain to the sheriff, Rocket's bright blue glow just might top the list. But as the truck drew nearer I couldn't help but notice the dark gap where the driver's door should've been, and I knew I might have some explaining of my own to do.

At that moment, if Grandpa Bomba had had the strength to make the earth open wide and swallow me whole, I would have let him do it.

Chapter 8

WE ALL WATCHED THE SHERIFF PARK his truck and climb out of the hole where a door should have been. The last of the dust from the barn settled, revealing the dented silver yowl of the moon, and the basin of the ranch became a patchwork quilt of moonlight and moving shadows.

Built like a pro wrestler long past prime, with muscles gone the way of beer and jelly, the sheriff strode forward, his gait a cautious saunter. As he pulled out a torch and aimed the beam in our direction, Uncle Autry moved to intercept him.

'Sheriff Brown – Jonas – what a surprise.' Autry

offered his hand to the officer, greeting him like an old friend.

'What in blazes happened here, Autry? Your barn, it . . .' The sheriff trailed off, removing his hat and pointing it at the rubble.

'It fell down.' Uncle Autry nodded, appraising the wreckage alongside the sheriff. My uncle crossed his arms and clucked his tongue once with a shake of his head, as if to say: *They sure don't build barns the way they used to.*

'I knew you were having a party tonight,' the sheriff continued. 'But you're supposed to *raise* the roof, not knock it in.' He panned the beam of his torch up the river towards the Bug House. 'At least your spare's still standing. Is everyone okay?' The torch's beam came back around, moving between the wreckage and the scattered family members, some of whom were already leaving, shy of too much unwanted attention.

'Dolly's jars – all gone!' I could hear Great-aunt Jules bemoaning the loss of her sister's savvy life's work as she crept towards her car. 'Her wedding jar too! What a tragedy!'

When the light from the sheriff's torch caught the still-bleeding gash in Fish's face and the drops of red staining Mellie's dress, he let the beam linger and fumbled for his two-way, preparing to call for help.

'Don't tell me we were the only ones who felt that earthquake, young man!' Grandpa Bomba's voice surprised everyone as it rose, quavering, from the overstuffed armchair that now sat in the middle of the drive.

Sheriff Brown smiled at Grandpa, raising one eyebrow.

'Earthquake? No need to worry about one of those, sir. There haven't been more than two earthquakes worth paying any mind to in Crook County in the last hundred years.'

'You're probably right about that, Officer. You're probably right.' Grandpa nodded and wobbled his head, but there was mischief in the old man's eye. Grandpa sat straighter now, as if he suddenly remembered what it felt like to be twenty years younger and ten times stronger, and the ground under Jonas Brown poppled and surged, nearly knocking the officer off his feet. And whether it was the moonlight playing tricks on me, or something real, I thought I caught a glimpse of Samson Beaumont, now tall at sixteen, standing with his hand on Grandpa Bomba's shoulder, as thin as a slip of shadow and just as transparent. But the moment I blinked, the vision was gone.

'You've got to watch out for them aftershocks,' Grandpa said, giving me a wink that made me wonder if he was talking to me or Sheriff Brown.

'That's enough, Dad,' Mom told Grandpa, getting up from where she'd been crouched over me. Everyone sucked in their breath as Mom turned towards the unsuspecting sheriff. Slowly, Mom advanced on the officer, savvy smile drawn and ready.

Dad pulled me up off the ground by my collar. 'Here she goes,' he said under his breath.

'Sheriff,' Mom said, 'why don't you tell us what brought you here tonight so that you can continue on your way. You can see that there's nothing here for you to be concerned about.' Her smile grew wider. 'You can forget about the barn now.'

'Yes, yes . . .' Brown's speech grew muddled. 'Nothing here to worry about, nothing at all. I just came looking for a lost girl.' Forgetting about the fallen barn as Mom instructed, the sheriff turned back to my uncle. 'Cabot's girl has run off again, Autry. I'm sure she'll turn up when she's done chasing stories. But I've been making the rounds, in case anyone's seen her.'

'Sarah Jane?' A deep frown creased Autry's brow. 'Sorry, Jonas. I haven't seen her. How long has she been gone?'

Brown snorted his reply. 'Just since this morning, but you know Noble Cabot. He's got me out combing the hills. Sarah Jane slipped past the housekeeper before breakfast.'

'What makes you think she might have come this way?'

Brown scratched head. 'Willie said she was in his shop earlier today making copies of those tomfool papers of hers.' He smiled. 'That one about Bigfoot staying at the bed-and-breakfast really had me going – I almost dropped by to take a look. That girl writes whoppers and steel traps where other folks write words and sentences.' Finding himself chuckling, Brown stopped and straightened his belt.

'Apparently, Sarah Jane took off at the same time as a couple of other kids who were in his shop today: a young girl wearing a football helmet and an older boy – brother and sister maybe. Willie said the girl mentioned your ranch and the wedding here tonight. So I thought I'd give it a shot.

'I was also hoping the kids might've seen what happened here,' he added, pointing his torch towards the large hole in his vehicle. 'My truck got busted up about the same time the kids were in Willie's shop – my truck and one of Gus Neary's motorcycles, which fared a heap worse. The entire thing's in pieces. Looks like someone took the whole bike apart quicker than grass through a goose.'

I held my breath as everyone but the sheriff looked from the truck . . . to the barn . . . to me.

Sheriff Brown, and maybe seven-year-old Tucker Beaumont, who stood picking his nose by his poppa, were the only ones who didn't understand immediately that I was responsible for the destruction. *All* the destruction. Both here and in town.

Autry raised his eyebrows. Dad cleared his throat and pulled me behind him quickly. Mom, Mibs and Aunt Jenny all moved to block the sheriff's view of Fedora where she knelt, picking up scattered jar lids the same way she'd scrabbled for her fallen change inside the five-and-dime. Having removed her helmet, she now filled it with as many loose lids as she could, like it was the pot of gold at the end of the disaster.

The sheriff didn't notice. He had other concerns.

'I thought Willie was going to have a stroke worrying that he'll be sent to the top of Cabot's list just for letting Sarah Jane set foot inside his store,' Brown went on. 'Like everyone else in these parts, Willie owes Cabot his pound of flesh – and more than a few mortgage payments. Listen, Autry . . .' The sheriff stepped closer to my uncle, lowering his voice. 'The last thing you need right now is Noble Cabot thinking

87

Sarah Jane's been hanging round up here. It doesn't take much for any of us to become a spindle in Cabot's fire, and there's enough trouble between you and him already.'

'Nothing I can't handle, Jonas.' Autry brushed aside the sheriff's warning, but his hands clenched into fists. Marisol and Mesquite moved forward to stand closer to their dad.

'Look, Autry,' the sheriff continued, 'every time that girl takes off, old Noble gets cranky. And a cranky Noble Cabot is bad for Sundance. A cranky Cabot is bad for us all.'

'Sarah Jane hasn't been here, Jonas,' Autry assured the other man. I closed my eyes, feeling the low-down shame of knowing different.

'What about the kids from Willie's shop? Do you know anything about –'

'It's time for you to go now, Sheriff,' Mom cut in, smiling.

Brown paused, checking his watch in the glow from his torch.

'Time for me to go,' he echoed mechanically, moving back in the direction of his truck. 'Let me know if you see hide or hair of Sarah Jane.'

Watching the sheriff go, I began to shake.

'You all right, Ledge?' Autry asked, coming to stand next to me. I nodded, saying nothing, trying not to flinch as the studs on my uncle's shirt began to pop off one by one and ping into the gravel.

Autry looked down at his missing studs and shook his head. I wondered if this would be the final straw. The thing that tipped the scales and triggered a total meltdown tongue-lashing from my uncle. But to a guy who'd give you the shirt off his back, apparently a couple of studs – and an entire barn – were nothing.

When Autry looked up, he was grinning.

'Dude, you are a *bulldozer*.' He shook his head again. 'What a powerhouse. Imagine what you'll be able to do once you finesse that a little.'

I couldn't imagine. I'd wrecked everything. The barn. The wedding. Dad's dreams. Not to mention my hopes of ever having any kind of normal life. Where was the *finesse* in that? I'd even robbed Grandpa of the perfect comfort in his final days; all of Grandma's jars were smashed to smithereens.

All but one.

And I'd let that one get away.

While Sarah Jane Cabot may not have known what it meant to have a savvy, she'd seen enough to start asking all the wrong questions. Now, with Grandma's last surviving jar, she had what every good reporter wants most: proof.

As the lights of Jonas Brown's truck disappeared over the south ridge, I prayed again. Prayed that this would be the last time I'd ever see the Crook County sheriff. Prayed that Mom and Dad wouldn't go back to Indiana without me. Prayed that they wouldn't leave me on the misfit ranch with the twins – with *Rocket* – just another three-legged dog, like Bitsy.

But even as I prayed, I knew my prospects didn't look too good.

Chapter 9

'YOUR MOM AND DAD SURE LEFT in a hurry yesterday.' Mesquite jostled my elbow at breakfast on Monday morning, making the muffin on its way to my mouth bounce and roll to the end of the picnic table, where we sat at a safe distance from the O'Connells' house. While the sun worked hard to warm the day, I worked harder to keep my cool. Gypsy's puff of curly hair bobbed as she grabbed too late for the runaway muffin. Between Gypsy and Fedora there was a gap just big enough for Samson. Though, if he was sitting between the two girls, I couldn't tell. Rumour was, Gypsy could see her spectral brother all the time. But she was the only one.

I just did my best not to stick my hand through him accidentally.

'Yeah, *Sledgehammer*,' Marisol chortled as she branded me with a new nickname. 'Your folks ditched you and Fe pretty fast.' Marisol stopped my muffin before it hit the ground, levitating it back up to hover over the table.

'They both have jobs.' I bit off my words, trying to keep my temper in check. Snatching my muffin out of the air, I stuffed half of it into my mouth, unable to say anything more. Mom had told me to try to get along.

Rocket was working in the garden and Autry was in the drive, signing for a package that had come overnight-delivery.

It had been Autry who suggested that Fedora and I both stay. Mom had worried about leaving us. From the start she and Dad had planned a quick trip. Dad's company was making cuts and he couldn't risk losing his job by asking for time off. Mom would've quit her job in an instant, risking the mortgage and the car payment, if Autry and Dad hadn't convinced her that a summer in Wyoming might be good for me – and for Fedora too.

'Relax, Dinah. The kids will be fine,' Autry had assured Mom as she and Dad prepared to leave. 'How many summers did we spend here as kids? Remember when the Beachams were here with us? We all ran wild – including you.' Autry grinned. 'This place never did us any harm.'

'You broke your leg here, Autry,' Mom stated flatly. 'Your collarbone too. You also fell in the river and nearly drowned before Cam Beacham fished you out. The two of you weren't even dry before you wrestled him into a cactus patch and got nearly a thousand stickers in your –'

'What?' Autry quickly cut Mom off. Then he'd winked at me and Fedora. 'I don't remember any of that. Besides, we'll have Fe here to keep us safe.' My uncle gave Fedora's new brain bucket a thump. Marisol and Mesquite had found an old motorcycle helmet in the attic for my sister after she gave her football helmet to Grandpa Bomba. Red and orange flames blazed across its scuffed white dome, making Fe as happy as a clam with a showy new shell. She'd been more proud yet when she learned that she, at eight years old, was old enough to stay at the ranch, while Tucker, at seven, was not.

Mom sighed and Dad grabbed her hand, stopping her before she could reach out to comb my hair flat with her fingers.

'Ledge will never learn to control this thing if you're always doing it for him, Dinah.' He punched my arm with his free hand as if to say: *Right, Ledge*? I mustered a reluctant shrug, wishing I could crawl under a rock.

'A boy's got to fall a few times so he can learn to pick himself up and put himself back together,' Grandpa Bomba wheezed from his armchair on the porch. Stretched at his feet, Bitsy snuffled at Dad's old football helmet. The helmet wobbled next to Grandpa's chair, still packed full of jar lids, reminding me of all the memories of Grandma Dollop I'd destroyed the night before. Seeing Grandpa fumble through a football helmet full of useless lids was like watching someone eat crackers and call it cake.

'When I turned thirteen,' Grandpa carried on, 'my

savvy opened a crack in the earth so deep, I fell in and conked my noodle on the earth's very core. I was nearly a grown man before I found my way back up from the depths and the darkness. And the headache I got lasted years.'

'You should've been wearing a helmet,' Fe said, nodding gravely. She was too young to know that Grandpa Bomba had a dozen different tall tales about his savvy birthday. No one knew which were true and which were super-sized servings of deep-fried baloney.

Mom sighed again. Autry wrapped an arm round her shoulders. 'Don't worry, Dinah. Gypsy and Samson are staying too.

'You'll see,' Autry went on. 'A few weeks with us and Ledge will get his feet under him.'

'Yes, because we can all see how well that plan worked for Rocket.' Mom served her words with a hefty side order of sarcasm.

Autry looked towards the garden, where Rocket was picking pieces of the barn out of the lettuce beds. No longer glowing blue, Rocket had got up before dawn with Autry, Dad and anyone else who'd been able to stay to lend a hand. He'd repaired the downed cables and re-juiced the generator, while the others assessed the damage and tried to clean up what they could of my mess. Nobody let me help.

My uncle rubbed his jaw thoughtfully as he considered his oldest nephew. 'Rocket's got one last thing to learn about scumbling,' he said. 'And he's got to figure it out himself. I'm confident he'll find his way off this ranch someday.'

The thought of *someday* hadn't made me feel any better.

Yet, as I sat at the picnic table with the other kids the next day, I realized that there was a bright side to my forced stay at the Flying Cattleheart. I'd tossed and turned the night of the barn disaster, wondering how I'd ever make amends. If I went straight home, Autry might never know how sorry I was about the ruined barn. And I still needed to get Grandma's peanut-butter jar back from Sarah Jane. Now, at least, I might have a chance to try to fix some of the things I'd broken.

'Hey, Ledge! What if your parents never come back for you?' Mesquite jabbed my elbow again, clipping the wing of my positive attitude.

Marisol forged her features into a mask of concern. 'If your parents leave you here for good, you'll have to live with Rocket *permanently*. I hope the two of you can get along. If not . . . *zzzzttt!*' She playacted giving her sister an electric shock, then laughed as Mesquite collapsed against the picnic table with her eyes crossed and her tongue sticking out.

'You'll be toast, Ledger.' Overflowing with mock melodrama, Marisol sniffed, then dabbed her eyes with a paper napkin.

I spewed muffin crumbs as a wave of panic hit me. If I ever managed to get home again, I didn't want to show up on the steps of Theodore Roosevelt Middle School roasted, charred or extra-crispy. The feeling of ants swarming beneath my skin returned and both of my knees hammered up and down beneath the table.

I knew I shouldn't listen to the twins, but that didn't stop unwanted savvy energy from building as I watched their skit depicting my demise, every crackerjack retort dying on my tongue.

I looked from the house to the conservatory to the windmill to the trucks in the drive. With a flash forward, I saw everything in ruins. My savvy may not have made me supersonic fast, but it did give me plenty of steam to vent. And, until I learned to scumble, there was only one way I could think to do it.

'I'm going for a run.'

Chapter 10

SEEING ME TAKE OFF, BITSY LEAPED down from her place on the porch, hobble-bobbling next to me like she intended to come along.

'Go back!' I said, shooing her away. 'You're not fast enough, girl. Go back to Grandpa!'

When I reached the ranch's entrance sign by the highway, I stopped to catch my breath, struggling to adjust to the thinner, dryer Wyoming air after sprinting up and over the south ridge full throttle. The sign over my head was a towering ten-gauge steel construction with the name of the ranch and the hand-cut figure of a butterfly with upside-down, heart-shaped spots: the

Montezuma's Cattleheart – the butterfly Autry had been following in Mexico when he met the twins' mom.

The heavy sign shivered over my head. Moving away from it, I turned east, following the road, telling myself I'd turn round before I reached Sundance.

I settled into a lung-pushing, blood-pulsing rhythm. The soles of my trainers slapped the pavement. My arms pumped at my sides. Not wanting to cause a car crash or blow apart another bike, I stepped off the road whenever someone passed me.

I tried to forget about the twins' playacting. To forget what they'd said about my parents leaving me at the ranch for good. I didn't know how long I could live with Rocket and survive. The last two nights, I'd been forced to hit the hay up at his small, rammed-earth house at the top of the east ridge. With its thick, cement-like walls, sparse furnishings and lack of electronic equipment or gadgets, everyone agreed it was the safest place for me.

Rocket and I had barely spoken as he set up a place for me to sleep after I wrecked the barn.

'Got what ya need?' he'd asked, tossing me a sleeping bag.

'Y – *oof!*' I answered, getting the breath knocked out of me as I caught it.

'Toothbrush?'

I nodded.

'Need a pillow?'

I paused before nodding again, not wanting to seem too demanding.

Rocket's final question came with a baleful look:

'Do you snore?'

All I could do was shrug and repeat over and over inside my head: *Don't snore, Ledge . . . Don't snore . . .*

As Rocket disappeared to grab a pillow, I glanced carefully around the room. He'd taped maps and pictures of motorcycles to every wall and stacked travel magazines and books about adventure on every surface. There were photographs too, pictures of family and people I didn't recognize. Rocket may not have left the ranch in years, but he obviously dreamed about it.

Shaking out the sleeping bag, I accidentally knocked

down a bunch of his photos. I'd rushed to pick them up and stick them back on the wall. But one kept slipping down – a photo of a much younger Rocket holding hands with some girl. The girl was tall, with blonde hair, a long fringe and a pink gum bubble the size of a grapefruit hiding half her face.

If I hadn't been afraid Rocket would light me up like an X-ray skeleton, I might've asked for tape to re-hang the picture. But I'd been pretty sure it would've been safer to ask an angry grizzly bear to dance.

Autry might not have stopped me from running from the Flying Cattleheart, but I soon realized he hadn't let me go alone. A tight group of cobalt dragonflies zipped beside me like a squadron of Blue Angels. Executing coordinated loops and rolls, the insects jetted so close, I could feel the vibration of their wings against my skin.

Halfway between my uncle's ranch and town, I stopped. On the south side of the road, a salvage yard sprawled beyond a low hill, nearly hidden by a stand of dark pines. The sign for *Neary's Auto Salvage Acres* was overshadowed by a foreclosure notice, just like the ones I'd seen in town. It seemed as though the people in these parts were having trouble making the payments on their loans. But I knew times were tough all over.

Looking between the trees at the sea of crumpled cars and trucks, I wondered if a junkyard would be the best spot in the world for me . . . or the worst. Was I looking at my life to come? I shook my head and picked up my pace.

Sweat-soaked and parched, I reached the town of Sundance twenty minutes after I left the ranch. Ignoring the inner voice hollering at me to turn round, I made one last push past the heavy equipment yard of a building whose sign read: *CAD Co. – Cabot Acquisitions & Demolitions*. The name on the sign made me think of Sarah Jane. In a town the size of Sundance, there couldn't be too many Cabots.

When I reached the *Welcome to Sundance* sign, I stopped, my mind still full of Sarah Jane Cabot. Cars moved along I-90 in the distance, and a low mountain rose up above the rolling hills. Autry's dragonflies landed near my feet, taking up resting positions along the white line on the pavement, tiny aircraft queued up on a ten-centimetre-wide runway.

Pacing beneath the sign, I pulled the *Sundance Scuttlebutt* notebook from my pocket. Unable to sleep, I'd glanced at some of Sarah Jane's crazy notes the night before. The girl had a way with words that was solid. In the dead of night, I believed every one of them, until the light of morning came and common sense returned. It was hard to stay convinced for long that Sundance was being overrun by Axehandle Hounds – small dogs that ate the handles off unattended axes – or that there was a race of tiny people who lived in the stacks at Crook County Public Library, coming out at night to shelve books for the librarians.

I slapped the notebook against my palm, still pacing beneath the *Welcome to Sundance* sign. She'd written her name and address on the paperboard cover. The longer I paced, the looser the bolts holding the sign to its post became, until the sign lurched, swinging like a pendulum from a single remaining bolt. I stopped and stared again at Sarah Jane's address, realizing that I might be able to use the notebook as leverage. Maybe Sarah Jane would want her notebook back badly enough to make a trade. I knew if I could just get Grandma Dollop's jar, I'd feel a whole lot better. It would be easier to learn to scumble my savvy if I didn't have that shanghaied jar lingering cruelly on my conscience.

Fifteen minutes later, I found myself on the front porch of the Cabot residence, after getting directions from someone on the street. It had taken a while. The town was as quiet as it had been two days before, and the few people I ran into hadn't been eager to tell me how to find the Cabots.

The house was a hulking Victorian structure that sat alone above the town, surrounded by dozens of stumps and one tall birch tree. It looked like a maniac logger had hit the place overnight and been chased away by Axe-handle Hounds before he could cut down the last tree. The remaining paper-white birch bent over the house, its branches hugging the place like pale arms. A spiked, wrought-iron fence encircled the entire property.

Cautiously, I moved through the gate, climbed the stairs to the porch and reached for the door knocker, hoping that nothing would fall apart.

Sweat dripped from my hair, stinging my eyes. Autry's dragonflies pestered me. When the Cabots' housekeeper opened the door, I took a step back. Standing in the doorway, the frizzy-haired, bug-eyed woman clutched the handle of a carpet sweeper in one hand, and a glossy, rolled-up supermarket tabloid in the other, a headline about UFOs barely visible between her fingers. Whether it was the rolled-up paper that motivated them, or something else, Autry's dragonflies gave up their bullyragging and struck off in a blue streak.

Without blinking, the housekeeper raised her eyebrows a fraction of a centimetre, indicating quite clearly, and with the smallest possible effort, that I should speak quickly or get my little dogies *yippee-ti-yi-yo* gone.

'Um, did Sarah Jane get back okay the other night?' I asked, my words tripping over themselves, as if Mom were standing over my shoulder telling me to be quick. 'I mean, is Sarah Jane here? Can I see her?' I held my breath, watching out of the corner of my eye as the screws that held the doorknocker in place began to work their way loose.

A full ten seconds passed while the housekeeper stared at me blankly. My request to see Sarah Jane appeared to have left her baffled.

'Are you a . . . *friend* . . . of Miss Cabot's?' she asked, and the way she said the word *friend* made me guess I was the first kid to come round knocking in quite some time. Maybe Sarah Jane had been telling the truth when she'd told me she had no friends.

'Sure. Yeah. Okay,' I answered, rubbing the faint bruise that shaded my chin like a smudge of newsprint, a souvenir from my last encounter with the intrepid Sarah Jane and her friendly, friendly fist. I held up Sarah Jane's notebook. 'See? I've got her notebook right here. Trust me, SJ and I go way back.' All the way back to Saturday.

The housekeeper stepped back, nodding me into the house with the point of her chin. 'I'm cleaning,' she said gruffly, rattling the carpet sweeper in my face. 'You can wait in Mr Cabot's study while I call Miss Cabot down. Mr Cabot's not here and I always save his room for last.' She turned a sharp eye on me, rimpling her nose like she smelled something bad. Then added, 'If you value your skin, don't touch anything. Or Mr Cabot might make you part of his collection.'

'His collection?'

The woman didn't elaborate. She didn't have to. Cabot's study spoke volumes for itself – and I didn't think I liked what it had to say.

Chapter 11

LOOKING UP, I GAZED INTO THE glassy, staring eyes of a zoo's worth of stuffed and mounted trophies: antelope, elk, deer – even a jackalope or two. Opposite me, a one-eyed buffalo jutted into the room like it had been stopped dead in its tracks while breaking through the wall. Stepping into the dimly lit study, I knew I never wanted to be part of Noble Cabot's collection. Not if I wanted to keep my head.

But Cabot had other things in his trove: a coin shot through the middle by Annie Oakley and a set of dried gourds that resembled the founding fathers all sat together on one shelf, and a clock made out of the jawbone of a crocodile hung on the wall, *tick-tick-ticking*.

The housekeeper pushed past me to open a curtain, allowing a rectangle of sunshine to light the wings of Cabot's assortment of butterflies. There were dozens of them. I even thought I saw a Montezuma's Cattleheart – black with red, upside-down heart-shaped spots. But instead of flying around the place the way the butterflies did at my uncle's ranch, here every one was pinned down dead, stuck in place between thin layers of glass and mounted on the wall with the rest of Cabot's treasures.

If I wasn't careful, I knew I could end up under glass myself. I was certain Mr Cabot would consider an unusual kid like me a unique addition to his collection . . . a real conversation piece . . . or maybe just a brand-new tool over at the *CAD Co.* acquisitions and demolitions place. With a good Ledger Kale around, who needed a digger or a wrecker?

No wonder Sarah Jane had wanted Grandma Dollop's jar! She'd probably swiped it for her dad. I looked around Cabot's study for the peanut-butter jar, but found no sign of it. I tapped my finger against the pocket that held Sarah Jane's notebook. With her passion for peculiar stories, Sarah Jane was clearly following in her father's footsteps. It made me wonder what her mom was like. Mrs Cabot looked normal enough in the portrait hanging behind Cabot's desk. Tall, thin and graceful, Mrs Cabot reminded me of the one tree that still stood outside the house.

A fly buzzed in the window, breaking the stillness that choked the room. The housekeeper dispatched the bug with three swift smacks of her alien-invasion tabloid – *Ka-thwap! Ka-thwap! Ka-thwap!* – busting the silence into smaller and smaller fragments. Then she pointed the tabloid my way, making it clear that I would share the fly's fate if I stepped out of line.

As soon as the woman left to call up the stairs to Sarah Jane, I moved to check out the rest of the room. Backing into a rack of rusted barbed-wire snippets, I let out a yelp and leaped forward, colliding with a display of rocks and minerals, and knocking over a trash can filled with wadded-up paper. Righting the trash can,

III

I grabbed the scattered scraps. It was only when I was stuffing them all back into the trash that I realized they had been copies of *The Sundance Scuttlebutt*.

Sarah Jane's father must not have been a fan.

Trash picked up, I did my best to straighten Cabot's rock collection, admiring a cluster of pyrites – fool's gold – as heavy as a can of baked beans. I remembered seeing a ton of the stuff at Willie's Five & Dime, so I knew it couldn't be worth too much, even if it did look a lot like gold.

I carried the rock with me as I continued to poke around, trying to ignore the image of my own head, and the heads of everyone in my family, mounted on the walls with all the wildlife. Disregarding the house-keeper's orders, I touched everything. The frizzy-haired woman was not my mother. Just because she said something, that didn't mean I *had* to do it. Here, I had a choice.

Juggling the pyrites from hand to hand, I stopped to investigate a pair of antique wrist shackles hanging from a hook near the one-eyed buffalo, trying not to think about the sheriff who'd come asking questions at the ranch.

'Hands in the air!' I jumped as I felt something jab me in the back. Sarah Jane's watermelon-scented lips were by my ear – so close, I could feel her warm breath on my cheek. The girl was as silent and sneaky as a bushwhacking, story-slinging ninja.

'Those cuffs once held the Sundance Kid, you know.' She giggled. 'Maybe you're his reincarnation. That would make a really great headline!'

As soon as she dropped her finger from my back, I turned, whacking my head against the buffalo's shaggy chin. Two of the heavy-duty bolts that held the trophy to the wall came loose and the buffalo head lurched sideways as if cocking its head to get a better look at us. At the same time, the hands fell off the crocodile clock, even as it kept on ticking.

Sarah Jane shook her braids. 'You are the King of Damage, you do know that, don't you? What are you doing here, Cowboy? Did you come for another right hook in the kisser?' She bent towards me again, cracking her knuckles with a teasing smile. Then she stopped and wrinkled her nose the same way the housekeeper had done when she'd let me in.

'Wow! You smell worse than that bison once did, Cowboy. What did you do, *run* here?'

'Um, yeah actually. I did,' I answered, trying not to flinch as the buffalo took another lurch down the wall. 'And the name's Ledge, remember?'

'Yeah, yeah. *Ledge* – got it.' Sarah Jane eyed the buffalo, then looked back at me. 'I see you're getting acquainted with all my father's favourites.'

'Favourites?'

Moving away from me, Sarah Jane idly brushed her fingers over other things in the room, stopping in front of a murky glass case next to her father's desk. She sighed as she stared through the glass.

Squinting, I moved closer.

'What's in there?' I asked.

'Look for yourself.'

'What the – whoa!' The sight of a two-headed rattle-snake caught me by surprise. I stepped back, dropping the heavy pyrites cluster on my toe, then hopped quickly to the other side of the room, trying not to react as a rocking chair in the corner fell off both its rockers. It had been stupid of me to come here. Stupid, stupid, stupid. I needed to get Grandma Dollop's jar and go before I revealed how completely I belonged in Cabot's exhibition.

Sarah Jane looked from me to the chair and rolled her eyes to heaven, repeating, '*King of Damage*,' under her breath.

'Relax, Ledge. It's not alive,' she explained, sounding like a bored tour guide as she dissed me, the clumsy tourist. 'I don't think it's even real. Even so, it's my father's favouritest favourite.'

As I did what I could to right the rocker, Sarah Jane bent to retrieve the glinting chunk of pyrites.

'Maybe if I were this shiny, I could get some attention too,' she murmured. 'I can't even get Daddy to read my newspapers – no matter how wild I make the stories.'

I looked away, unsure what to say. The soft tick of the crocodile-jaw clock filled the room – the only sound until Sarah Jane sighed a second time and returned the fool's gold to its proper place.

'So, what's up, Ledge? Why are you here?' She turned back to me.

'I . . . er, have your notebook. I thought you might want to make a trade.'

'A trade?'

'You took something that doesn't belong to you on Saturday,' I answered. 'I came to get it back.'

Sarah Jane pulled a face, but before she could reply, a man's voice made us both turn.

'What, precisely, did my daughter take, young man? And who in Sam Hill's kitchen are *you*?'

Chapter 12

SARAH JANE'S FATHER STOOD IN THE doorway, a silver-tipped cane in one hand, a heavy red-and-white foreclosure sign gripped in the other. Mr Cabot's yellow hard hat, with its CAD Co. logo, was paired with a dark western-cut suit. His scowl looked unbreakable as he blocked the only exit from the room.

A cranky Cabot is bad for Sundance, the sheriff had said to Uncle Autry. *A cranky Cabot is bad for us all.* A creep of crimson, as red as the foreclosure sign, coloured Mr Cabot's face as his stare drilled through me. He didn't look once at Sarah Jane. I guessed finding a strange boy talking to his daughter in the middle of his private room didn't make the man too happy. In fact, judging by the way the red in his cheeks was morphing into a deep and dangerous-looking purple, I guessed that I had, in one fell swoop, just made Noble Cabot cranky.

He dropped the sign with a heavy thud, letting it lean against the doorjamb.

'Sarah Jane, go to your room,' he ordered. 'I've told you before that you don't belong in here.' Mr Cabot's words were aimed at his daughter, but his eyes never left me once. Sarah Jane flushed.

'But, Daddy –!'

'Sarah Jane, do as I say!' Even without a remarkable talent backing him up, Mr Cabot's voice had the same kind of power over Sarah Jane as Mom's had over me. Before her father could tell her again, Sarah Jane fled past him in a blur, knocking over the sign and stomping up the stairs. She slammed a door above us, rattling the entire house as powerfully as my savvy might've done. Mr Cabot didn't even blink. He continued to stare at me.

'Er . . . I was just leaving.' Jar or no jar, it was time

for me to go. Tripping over the foreclosure sign, I tried to slip past Mr Cabot. But he raised his cane – *swish* – to stop me.

'Not so fast, young man.'

A telltale tingling itch crawled into my palms. I had to get out soon. Supersonic soon. I clenched my fists and focused on a spot on the floor between me and Mr Cabot.

Above us, Sarah Jane opened and closed her bedroom door again – *SLAM!* – and again – *SLAM! SLAM! SLAM!* Reminding everyone that, just because she was upstairs in her room, she hadn't disappeared.

'You! What is your name?' Mr Cabot demanded. 'Who do you belong to?'

I bit my tongue. Filled with freaked-out savvy fuel, my hands began to shake and my skull buzzed like a big, round beehive on my shoulders. After what happened to my uncle's barn, I knew I could huff and puff and blow the Cabots' house down at any second. I knew it with terrible, horrible, nauseating certainty.

I was three crocodile-clock ticks away from breaking

119

family rules, ready to spill my guts and yell, *'If I don't leave now, I'm going to destroy your house!'* when the doorbell rang and saved me from Mr Cabot – saving Mr Cabot's house from me at the same time.

I drew a deep breath and listened as the housekeeper opened the front door. A moment later, she was standing behind Sarah Jane's dad, her brow creased at the sight of the buffalo head tilting precariously from the opposite wall.

'What is it, Hedda?' Mr Cabot demanded without turning.

'Mr O'Connell's at the door, sir,' Hedda said, eyeing me with distaste. 'He says he's looking for his nephew.'

The dragonflies, I thought. Autry's squadron of insects had taken off as soon as I'd reached the Cabot house. While the bugs had seemed like a nuisance before, now I was grateful to them for getting my uncle here so fast.

'O'Connell?' Mr Cabot spat, turning on the housekeeper as if she'd picked up a dirty word off the floor and jammed it in his ear. *'O'Connell?'* Mr Cabot left the room without another glance my way, smacking his cane against the fancy moulding of the door frame with a *CRACK!* as he headed for the front door like a bolt of lightning with a hitch in its jag. I followed quickly, ignoring the way every spindle in the stair rail jogged up and down in its setting, making the sound of a giant millipede running a marathon in wooden shoes as I passed by.

Uncle Autry stood on the other side of the screen door. Beyond him, half a dozen gumball-sized spiders worked busily between the porch's ornate columns. The presence of the spiders was the only sign that my uncle wasn't as relaxed as he appeared. Autry's features were calm and composed. His posture easy. Yet all six spiders looked like they'd sucked down seven pots of super-sweetened coffee. Beneath the eaves, chaotic, disorderly webs were going up faster than shake-and-bake dinners, each one big enough to nab an entire thirteen-year-old boy.

I shot past Cabot as he reached the entryway. Flying out of the screen door, I pushed past Autry too, not even daring to pause. I felt just like I had at school when I'd had to rush out of art class after looking too long at a weird painting of melting clocks. Only, on that day – a month before my birthday – Josh and Ryan had been there to drag me to the nurse's office, even while Big Mouth Brody announced to everyone that I'd barfed after getting freaked out by a painting. Though, now I wondered if it hadn't been some sort of savvy premonition.

Ducking under the drooping webs draping Cabot's porch, I leaped the stairs and cleared the perimeter of the pointed iron fence, hustling past my uncle's white pick-up. All without wrecking a single thing more.

I leaned against a row of mailboxes across the street, not realizing my error until too late, when I toppled them all – seven in one blow. I fell with them, making a raucous racket.

The din brought Sarah Jane to her window. She opened the circular pane set into the small tower at the very top of the old house and leaned out, shaking her head.

Hobbled and kicking, I picked myself up, trying to

122

be cool even though my left foot was trapped inside one of the curved aluminum mailboxes. I may have got free of Cabot's side-show study, but I still looked like a clown in a three-ring circus. All I needed was a banana peel, an exploding cigar and a human cannon launcher. Then my life would be complete.

Chapter 13

THE MOMENT HE STEPPED AROUND THE side of his truck, Autry found me stuck up to my knee in the Cabots' reinforced mailbox. My uncle stopped and stared, scrubbing his face with one hand. I guessed he might've been rethinking my potential for any future savvy *finesse*.

'If that's the worst damage done here today –' Autry nodded towards the mailboxes – 'I think we can count ourselves lucky. Do you think you can make it back to the ranch in the truck?' Autry's voice was rigid, but a corner of his mouth had begun to twitch.

I looked down and shook my leg again. A stifled snort erupted from my uncle. It took a moment before I

124

realized that Autry was doing his darndest not to bust a gut and guffaw out loud.

'Can you make it a few miles without, you know –' He waved a hand towards the scattered rubble around me, still trying not to howl with laughter. 'Without *recycling* my truck?' Autry did what he could to compose himself as I stared at him without a lick of humour. One look back at the Cabot house did the trick, sobering him fast. I hadn't made out the words that passed between him and Mr Cabot, but I'd heard enough of the tone to know there'd been an argument.

'Any idea how I might go about doing that?' I asked, sitting down on the pavement to prise the mailbox from my leg. If I was going to learn to control my new anti-talent in time to get back home before school and the father-son half-marathon in the autumn, I was going to require some concrete advice. I was willing to give anything a try. If my uncle told me to sit on my hands, cross my eyes, and sing 'Yankee Doodle' with a peanut shell up my nose, I would've given it a shot. But Autry's reply was even less helpful than a nostril full of salted nuts.

125

'You'll put it together, Ledge. At some point you'll figure out what you need to learn from this savvy of yours and then everything will get a little easier. I promise.' Holding out a hand, he hooked his thumb round mine and pulled me up from the ground. Then he kicked the rest of the mailboxes out of the street before climbing into the truck.

I followed my uncle, crossing fingers and toes, hoping that God or luck or sheer force of will might keep the automobile intact.

Turning the key in the ignition, Autry spared one last look at the hulking Cabot house and the collection of stumps surrounding it, letting his gaze linger on the highest branches of the tall white birch. Sarah Jane was still at her window, pencil in hand, scribbling rapid notes. Then she leaned forward, long braids dangling over the window sill, and called out:

'Hey, Ledge! I'm signing you up for a free issue of *The Sundance Scuttlebutt*! But the next edition might take a while. It's going to be a super-duper humdinger!'

Free issue. I snuffed out a breath. Meeting Sarah

126

Jane had already cost me plenty. Money, candy, comics, Grandma's jar and *my entire future* should've been enough to foot the bill for a lifetime subscription if I'd wanted one – which I *didn't*.

Autry shook his head, giving me a look of warning. 'I don't know what drove you to run all the way to town today, Ledge,' he said. 'But it's best you stay away from Sarah Jane from here on out, got it? Noble doesn't want you, me or anyone else like –' He stopped before finishing his sentence, roughly jamming the truck into gear before turning it round, tyres kicking gravel – *ping, clang, ping* – against Mr Cabot's prison-like fence. 'Well, he just doesn't want anyone around his daughter, that's all.'

'What about *Mrs* Cabot?' I asked, remembering the portrait above Mr Cabot's desk. 'Doesn't she want SJ to have any friends?'

'Is that why you ran all the way to Sundance?' My uncle sounded surprised. 'To make friends with Sarah Jane?' Suddenly, his expression changed. His eyebrows shot up and his mouth formed a silent *oh*.

'I think I understand now,' he said. 'The sheriff said

something about both of you being at Willie's Saturday when things . . . er . . . fell apart?' Autry coughed once meaningfully, glancing sidelong at me as he drove us out of town. 'Did all that five-and-dime damage happen when you met Sarah Jane?' He flashed me a quick grin. 'You know, Ledge, I used to get nervous around the ladies too. Sarah Jane is a pretty gir–'

'Aaagh! No! It's not like that.' I cut my uncle off before I had to find the nearest mineshaft and dive in head first. Heat rose up my neck, flooding my face, and the *Welcome to Sundance* sign spun like a pinwheel on its remaining bolt as we passed it.

'Y-you've got it all wrong,' I spluttered. My stomach flip-flopped like a fish caught in the jaws of a bear. I didn't want to talk about what happened at the five-and-dime. I didn't want my uncle thinking I was sweet on Sarah Jane either. But when the unbidden memory of kissing Sarah Jane popped into my head like a horror-movie monster trying to eat my brain, the connection between my grey matter and my vocal cords was temporarily severed. The dashboard panels inside the truck began to rattle. And when a radio knob flew off and hit me in the nose, Autry was at least kind enough to flinch instead of laugh.

Embarrassment, anger, pain, fear, frustration – I had my very own trigger-happy Wild Bunch gang of emotions. Pinching my nose where the knob had hit it, I took a deep breath through my mouth and let it out slowly, determined to pull myself together.

'I found Sarah Jane's notebook,' I explained, trying to keep my voice steady as I spoke the partial truth. I pulled the small notebook from the pocket of my cargo shorts and held it up. 'It has her address in it. See?' I showed my uncle the cover, then flipped through some of the pages.

'I just thought I'd return it to her . . . and make sure the sheriff found her Saturday night.'

Autry raised an eyebrow. Stopping to let a rafter of wild turkeys cross the road, he took Sarah Jane's notebook from me to read what she'd written above a wacky sketch of a horse wearing shorts, braces and a jaunty feathered hat.

'How in the world is Hal Gunderson training his mare to yodel in time for the county fair?' Autry murmured. We were quiet for several minutes as he appeared to consider the idea of Mr Gunderson's horse performing a whinnying *yodel-eedle-idle* in front of a fairground crowd. Shaking himself as the last gobbler cleared the highway, Autry laughed abruptly, like he'd just thought of the answer to a riddle that had been bugging him for months.

'Maybe Sarah Jane takes after her mom after all,' he said as he handed the notebook back to me.

'Takes after her *dad*, you mean,' I corrected him, sticking the notebook full of bunk back into my pocket. 'Have you *seen* her dad's collection?'

Autry's face fell into a scowl, his foot heavy on the accelerator as we passed the foreclosure sign in front of Neary's Auto Salvage Acres.

'I've been watching Cabot's "collection" get bigger every day,' he muttered.

Then, in a louder voice: 'Well, Ledge, I'm sure Summer Cabot looked down from above, glad to know that you were watching out for her daughter. But since *Noble* Cabot's the one we all have to worry about –'

'Down from above?' I echoed. 'Sarah Jane's mom is dead?'

Keeping his eyes on the road, my uncle shifted in his seat. His answer came slow and his words were measured: 'Summer's been in the earth for some time,' he said. 'She got sick when Sarah Jane was just knee-high, and . . . well . . .' He trailed off. It was only then that I remembered that Autry's own wife was buried in the town cemetery too.

'. . . And people don't always get better,' I finished for him, feeling like a bonehead for bringing up the subject. 'Sorry,' I added as an afterthought. Autry dipped his head to the side, but said nothing more. I wondered if he was thinking of Summer Cabot's passing or his own wife's. From what I could tell from my brief run-in with Noble Cabot, it was the only thing he and my uncle had in common.

'Look, I don't have many rules for the summer, Ledge,' he said at last. 'But this is one: stay away from the Cabots. I'm sure Sarah Jane can find herself a new notebook. Promise me you'll steer clear of her after today.'

'I promise I'll never put a shoe inside the Cabots' house again.' I raised my hand and vowed. It wasn't the exact promise Autry had been looking for, but seeing the remaining radio knob begin to spin, he let the subject drop.

Chapter 14

I SPENT THE NEXT FEW DAYS ignoring Fedora and the nut-mix of cousins I was stuck with for the summer. I woke at dawn every morning, just like Rocket. While my cousin did his best to move quietly around his small house, I did my best to stay on his good side by pretending to be asleep until he was gone.

When I wasn't running, restlessness chewed on me the way Bitsy chewed on rawhide. Not wanting to risk my uncle's phone or computer, I didn't talk to my parents when they called, or ask to email my friends. Josh, Ryan and Brody were probably too busy riding bikes and water coasters to even notice I was gone.

Alone, I moped around the ranch, pitching pinecones into the river or climbing the birch trees in the glade. I constructed stone towers and knocked them over. I even built a fort. But when a squirrel leaped on to my lean-to of fallen branches, the whole thing fell in on my head. Rounding out its imitation of me, the shaken squirrel took off running.

Wanting to avoid another disaster of my own, I kept my distance from the main house, Rocket's potting shed and the orchard of bee boxes in the meadow. Once, I got too close to the conservatory and Marisol levitated me fifteen centimetres off the ground, while Mesquite propelled me in the opposite direction.

Even as I did everything I could to avoid the Bug House, Gypsy was drawn to it like it was built for her. She spent hours watching the butterflies inside, or picking flowers in the meadows around it. With her thirteenth birthday still a few months off, I could only guess what sort of savvy Gypsy might get. I pictured my cousin blowing out her birthday candles and sprouting pixie wings, shrinking down to the size of Thumbelina

to spend the rest of her life living on a toadstool surrounded by dandelions and daisies, farting glitter and
singing *kumbaya*.

Autry lit the evenings with enormous, crackling
campfires, staving off the rapid cool-down of the Wyoming summer nights, while keeping me away from the
main house at the same time. By our third night at the
ranch, Fedora was in full fire-safety mode:

'Always build campfires away from dry grass and
leaves, Uncle Autry!'

'Do we have enough water handy?'

'What about a shovel?'

'It's all good, Fe,' Autry laughed. My uncle was in
a good mood. That morning, he'd received another
overnight delivery box, this one filled with butterfly chrysalides. He'd spent all day inside the Bug House, as happy
as me when I got my first Transforminator toy on my
sixth birthday.

Grandpa Bomba dozed in his armchair, holding his
helmet full of golden jar lids. According to Gypsy, Samson was never far from Grandpa, even when Marisol

and Mesquite lifted him in that chair and gently sent him wherever he wanted to go. Already, I'd seen Grandpa sitting in the shade of the big cottonwood by the river, out in the meadow, and in a clearing high on the north ridge, where he swore he could see all the way to the massive stone columns of Devil's Tower.

'I always dreamed of moving that monument closer to the ranch,' Grandpa had chuckled when I found him there. 'But now I couldn't budge that rock more than an inch or two – not even with help.'

While Grandpa napped comfortably in his soft chair by the fire, the rest of us sat on sawn-off stumps, spearing tofu hotdogs on the ends of sticks and roasting them black over the fire. Fingers licked clean, Marisol and Mesquite cleared everyone's dishes without getting up, floating plates and cups up and over the fire, stacking the dirty dishes on the picnic table. It killed me to watch the twins control their talents so easily. I had to remind myself that they'd started levitating things before they'd learned to read. But their skills still made me stew. Not only was their control perfect, their talents were *useful*.

To distract myself from the twins' excess of awesome and my total lack of it, I concentrated on the pages of Sarah Jane's notebook, straining to read by the light of the fire.

'What's that you got, Ledge?' asked Marisol. I lifted my head. Everyone was looking at me. I closed Sarah Jane's notebook fast.

'Are you keeping a diary these days?' asked Mesquite. 'Or writing love letters to some unfortunate girl in Indiana?'

My face burned as I tried to cram the notebook back into my pocket, but the thing jerked and tugged in my hand as the twins tried to levitate it away from me. The girls managed to free the cover, tearing it from the spiral binding.

'*The Sundance Scuttlebutt*?' Marisol howled as she read what was written there, the name of Sarah Jane's newspaper acid in her eye. 'How did you get this?'

'Traitor!' Mesquite shot a pinecone at me, bristling. 'Sarah Jane Cabot's the enemy, you big dolt!'

'Sarah Jane's nosy!' said Marisol. 'And her dad is

wrecking everything! He's already threatening to –'

'Girls, that's enough,' Autry cut in. 'Sarah Jane's not our *enemy*. But Ledger knows to steer clear of the Cabots now. He'll be careful. Right, Ledge?'

Everyone was still staring at me – everyone but Rocket. Rocket sat prodding the embers of the fire with a stick, pulling on his beard as he scared orange sparks into the night and watched them disappear.

'Yeah, yeah. I know the rule,' I answered with a shrug, batting away a white moth before it could land on me. More moths began to flit around the fire. Gypsy watched them with a contented sigh.

'Your thirteenth birthday must have been a doozy, Uncle Autry,' she said, mercifully shifting the group's attention away from me as she got up and twirled among the insects like a dancer inside a snow globe. 'What was it like to find out that your savvy was all *buggy*?'

'Oh, Papi had no clue what he was in for that day!' Mesquite announced before Autry's mouth was half-way open. Eager to tell the story, Mesquite tossed the cover of Sarah Jane's notebook into the fire, not even pausing to watch it burn.

'When Papi awoke on his thirteenth birthday, he felt one hundred tiny legs crawling across his wrist.'

Autry chuckled, but he scratched his wrist like he could still remember the feeling of all those legs.

'It was a centipede!' Marisol took up the story, stretching her arms wide enough to measure something closer to the size of a Bassett hound than a bug. 'A big one,' she added. 'And it wiggled right up Papi's arm like a chain of hula dancers.'

I shuddered and scratched my own arm. Rocket tossed his stick into the fire, shaking his head at the twins; he'd obviously heard this story before.

'By lunchtime,' Mesquite continued, 'spiders were plucking the "Happy Birthday" song on webs in every corner of Grandpa and Grandma's house.' Gypsy and Fedora both laughed. The sound woke Grandpa Bomba with a start.

'After that,' Marisol pressed on, 'termites ate the

back door clean gone and an army of ants carried the refrigerator out of the house on their backs!'

Grandpa looked as though he'd been pulled from the wool of a yarn-spinning dream, but his eyes were bright in the firelight as he caught up with the story.

'That's right!' he wheezed. 'By noon that day, your pop had his first flea circus up and running. By suppertime, he was racing horseflies in the backyard, taking bets from all the neighbour kids.'

While the others laughed louder, I slumped on my stump, turning thirteen-shades-of-envy green. Sure, Uncle Autry's birthday had started out a house of horrors, but it had ended like a day at Coney Island. Why couldn't my birthday have ended so well?

'Is that what really happened?' I asked as the girls went on giggling.

Still chuckling, Autry looked at me. Then his gaze grew serious.

'Not exactly, Ledge,' he offered, scratching his wrist again. 'But, these days, it's close enough. It's not like I was the first person to have a savvy birthday.'

140

Abruptly, Fe stopped laughing, her eyes as round as the rising moon. 'Who *was* the first person, Uncle Autry?'

'Yeah,' Mesquite and Marisol said together. 'Who was it?'

'Was it you, Grandpa?' Gypsy swivelled her face towards Grandpa Bomba.

'The first person with a savvy?' Grandpa's voice rumbled, an old engine sputtering to life, revving up for a journey down a well-worn road. 'Have you children never heard the story of Eva Mae El Dorado Two-Birds Ransom?'

'Eva Mae *who*?' Fe's face shone with excitement. Marisol and Mesquite looked at each other, then turned accusing eyes on their dad as if he'd neglected their home-school education by withholding important stories.

Autry lifted his coffee mug and grinned at Grandpa. 'Go ahead, Dad. Share a tale if you're feeling up to it.'

The chance to tell a story gave Grandpa a bit of strength. He sat up straighter in his chair as he began . . .

'Very few people know the story of Eva Mae, children.

She was the great-great-great- and even-greater-than-that-grandmother to half our kin and the very first person under these spacious skies to call her talent a *savvy*.' Grandpa tipped his head back and looked at the starlit sky.

'When Eva Mae was just a young girl travelling west across this land with three older, burlier brothers, in the hopes of finding an all-new way in an all-new place, she fell into the Missouri River on the morning of her thirteenth birthday and never saw her brothers again.'

A shadow shifted next to Grandpa and, for the second time since coming to the ranch, I thought I saw Samson. But as soon as I blinked he was gone. I thought about asking the others if they'd seen him, but I didn't want anyone to think I was going crazier. Still, I wondered if turning invisible for the first time had felt anything like falling into a river and getting washed away.

'Young Eva Mae bumped and tumbled down the Big Muddy for a good long time,' Grandpa went on. 'Back then, that river was still free-flowing and flooded, and

142

full of the magic of a flawless, untamed land. As Eva Mae trundled through the currents, gold dust covered her, bonnet to boots. When she stepped out of those waters, she was a vision to behold. And forever after, that girl could charm gold from wherever it lay hidden.'

Now, that *was a savvy*, I thought to myself. If I'd got a savvy like Eva Mae's, no way would Mom and Dad have left me at the ranch. We'd be rich! So rich, my parents wouldn't have to work. I could make my dad his own gold medals. I could buy Big Mouth Brody's house back for him and his family – maybe even put in a pool.

'Eva Mae knew she had a power like no other,' Grandpa continued. 'And it wasn't long before others knew it too. Men-folk flocked to her like crows to a shimmering thing. And as Eva Mae married one after the next – a trapper, a trader, an explorer, a baker, a mighty Sioux warrior, a farmer, a painter – each one found his own early death. After a time, Eva Mae began to fear that she was ill-fated.'

'Hmph. I know all about *ill-fated*,' I muttered.

'Tell me about it.' Rocket's voice was sharp enough

to tear a hole in the night sky. I shrank down on my seat as blue sparks crackled at his fingertips.

'Shh!' All four girls shushed us loudly as Grandpa sucked in a breath and barrelled forward, his voice beginning to shake from the effort.

'As Eva Mae's family grew, she found herself on the run from every outlaw, banker and ne'er-do-well who caught wind of her savvy and wanted to use her gift for gain. So she fled west into the wilds with her young'uns in tow, determined to make her talents secret and let the gold sleep where it lay. But folks say she left a treasure behind –'

'Treasure?' Marisol and Mesquite blurted together, interrupting Grandpa Bomba. 'Eva Mae left behind a treasure?'

'Was it gold?' Fe asked.

'Of course it was *gold*, Fedora,' Marisol snapped.

'What else would it be? Barbecue sauce?' Mesquite snickered.

'But where did Eva Mae leave her treasure?' Fe wanted to know.

144

Grandpa looked around, letting his gaze linger on each of us in turn. 'Why, right here, Fedora.'

'Here in Wyoming?' I asked, surprised. The girls exchanged excited, wide-eyed looks. I looked to Autry for confirmation, but my uncle only shrugged.

'You don't mean . . . here on the *ranch*?' I asked, not sure what to believe.

'This land *has* been in our family for a really long time,' whispered Marisol.

'That's right! It has!' Mesquite grabbed her sister's hand. 'Is it possible Eva Mae lived right here?'

'You should know by now that anything is possible, children.' Grandpa nodded in his chair. 'Anything.'

'Hold up, Ledge.' Before I could trudge up the east ridge in the dark, Autry stopped me, letting the others go on to bed. Watching a small spider construct a midnight web between us, I sat back down next to my uncle.

'I have to say something, Ledger,' Autry began.

I held my breath, wondering if I was finally going to

145

be punished for all the trouble I'd caused since coming to Wyoming.

'The others made the story of my thirteenth birthday sound pretty funny,' he said, adding a quick, wry smile that was more grimace than grin. 'And, like any good story, that one's grown a pinch over the years. But there's something about that day I've never told anyone. Not even the girls.'

I waited for Autry to continue, steeling myself for some fantastical epilogue to his birthday story that would make me feel even worse. But when Autry continued, his words threw me a curveball.

'I think you should know, Ledge, that when I was a kid, I hated bugs. *Haaated* them!' Autry pulled a face as he drew out the word. 'It's true!' he laughed, seeing my surprise. 'Insects raised my hackles, and spiders made me all colours and flavours of fearful. That centipede that woke me on my birthday nearly sent me over a cliff in my pyjamas.'

'So, what changed?' I asked, remembering the flea

circuses and horsefly races Grandpa had told about. 'When did you stop being scared?'

Autry reached down, allowing the small spider between us to crawl on to his hand. 'Who says I ever stopped?'

'What?' Now I was really confused. 'You *can't* be scared of spiders any more. Don't you have one the size of a bulldog living in the Bug House?'

'No, no. Not a bulldog . . .' Autry chuckled. 'A *Chihuahua*, maybe.'

I couldn't tell if he was being serious.

'Some fears can be conquered, Ledge,' he went on after a lengthy silence. 'Others have a way of coming back around. Sometimes at the moment you least expect. Often with the very worst possible timing. Fear makes it hard to think. And when you can't think, it's hard to figure out your choices. When you can't see all your options, all you can do is react.' Autry whispered something to the spider and it leaped away, disappearing into the night to find some other place to build a web.

'*I* don't react,' I grumbled. 'My savvy does. I can't control it.'

'Pay attention to what scares you, Ledge,' my uncle concluded, brushing his hands together. 'Then you'll be able to start controlling your savvy instead of letting your savvy control you. That's when you'll *really* learn to scumble.'

I filed Autry's advice in the dusty tumbleweed corners of my brain. It wasn't helpful. I wanted paint-by-numbers. Step-by-step. I needed *The Clueless Boy's Guide to Scumbling a Savvy Fast.* Or a brochure detailing The Ten Things to Know About Being Dangerously Different, not all this clear-as-mud talk about choices and fear.

I already knew what scared me. But I wasn't about to tell my uncle.

Chapter 15

'WE'VE DECIDED TO TEACH LEDGER HOW to scumble,' Marisol and Mesquite announced at the picnic table the following morning.

This was news to me. News that made me choke on my porridge.

'Oh?' Autry answered, not looking up from the Lepidoptera journal – the scientific butterfly magazine – open on the table in front of him.

'We need to do a good deed,' Mesquite explained.

'To improve our karma,' Marisol added. 'You know – make our luck better.' Autry raised an eyebrow, still studying the journal.

'Your karma's fine, I'm sure,' he replied. 'But it might be more difficult than you think to –'

'Oh, Papi! Helping Ledge learn to scumble will be simple!' Marisol waved away her dad's concern. 'No one else here's been scumbling since they were five.'

'Yeah! It's not like we're amateurs, Papi. Teaching Ledge will be easy-breezy!' added Mesquite.

'Or it'll be like trying to nail jelly to a tree,' Rocket muttered into his orange juice as he flipped through his own magazine – one with pictures of custom choppers that looked more like Uncle Autry's insects than motorcycles. Rocket would've loved the Knucklehead I'd wrecked.

I pushed my half-finished porridge away. I couldn't eat another bite – I didn't have time. I was too busy playing a pick-up game of Whac-A-Mole with the table, using my thumb to push nails back into the wood as fast as they popped up.

'I don't suppose it would hurt for you girls to give Ledge a few pointers.' Autry okayed his daughters'

plans, still too immersed in his magazine to notice my mute indignation.

Gypsy leaned forward to look closer at the title of the article that had Uncle Autry so engrossed.

'"The Flight and Plight of the Queen Alexandra's Birdwing"?' Gypsy's eyes grew round and bright, absorbing the iridescent blues and greens that lit the brown wings of the butterflies in the pictures. Her lips formed a small O, and when she spoke again, her voice was a wonder-filled whisper.

'Is that what came in the box you got yesterday, Uncle Autry? Queen Alexandra's Birdwings?'

'Yes! I think so.' Autry looked up at last, his face alight. 'Can you believe it? The world's largest butterflies.' He stabbed a photograph with his finger. 'As big as dinner plates – and we have twelve of them! Twelve! Or we will, as soon as they emerge from their chrysalides.'

'Why do you have to read about them?' I asked, glancing at the journal before attacking three more protruding nails. 'Shouldn't you just, you know . . . *know*?'

Autry smiled. 'Just because someone's got a knack for something, doesn't mean he can't learn more, right? And if I'm correct about these chrysalides and they are the Alexandras, then I need to learn everything I can. They're endangered, you know, and not from around here – not by a long shot.'

I know what you mean, I thought, feeling far from home and – thinking of the twins and their lessons – fearing I might be endangered soon too.

'What're *crystal lids*?' Fedora asked, smacking a protruding nail down with her spoon.

'*Cris-uh-lids,* Fe.' Autry sounded out the word. 'Some people call them *cocoons*,' he explained. 'But that's not quite right. Moths make cocoons, not butterflies. Wildlife agents took these chrysalides off some crooks – butterfly smugglers – who were trying to sell them illegally for big bucks. No one could identify them, so they sent them here to me. If all goes well, I may be able to get more work. Work that pays me in real money, not just in snickerdoodle cookies and canned peaches.'

The twins both nodded.

'Yeah, Papi. Mrs Witzel's pies are delicious . . .' Marisol began.

'But they don't pay the mortgage,' Mesquite finished, frowning. 'You need to charge people *cash* to get rid of their ants.'

'And their termites.'

'And their wasps.'

Sarah Jane's account of Autry climbing a ladder to remove a wasp nest from her window came back to me. I imagined Mr Cabot paying my uncle with a gourd shaped like George Washington. It had to cost a lot of money to keep a place like the Flying Cattleheart up and running. I doubted that the ladybird business was making my uncle all that rich. Maybe that was what Autry had meant when he'd talked about sinking the ranch.

As soon as Autry closed the glossy journal in front of him, Gypsy swept it towards her. Enthralled with the newest inhabitants of the Bug House, she began whispering excitedly to the empty space where Samson sat next to her. But whatever Samson thought about the butterflies, he didn't share it with the group.

153

The next morning, I got my run in early. Running cleared my head. And with a savvy like mine and scumbling teachers like the twins, my brain cells needed to be crystal. As I ran, I tried to convince myself that Marisol and Mesquite might be able to teach me something. Their control was flawless. But as soon as my first lesson began, all my doubts returned.

'Does a drop of water know it's part of a river, Ledge?'

I rolled my eyes as Marisol shouted philosophical-sounding flapdoodle at me from the riverbank. The sun burned one side of my face as I sat, stripped to my shorts on a large boulder in the middle of the rushing current, watching the twins surround me with the small kitchen appliances from inside their house.

'Does a crank spring know it's part of a toaster?' Mesquite made her expression serene as she floated a gleaming, stainless steel four-slice toaster my way.

'Meditate on the heating mechanism, Ledge.'

'Concentrate on the crumb tray.'

I tried to do as the twins instructed, focusing on the toaster. But for all their talk, the two girls got bored fast watching me stare uselessly at the appliance.

'Just break it already, Sledgehammer!'

'Smash it!'

'Crash it!'

'Bash it!'

'*Shut it!*' I yelled back at them. 'I'm *trying*!'

Marisol and Mesquite tisked their tongues in a perfect imitation of Great-aunt Jules, then flipped me backwards off the boulder. I came up spewing brisk water and bad words, immediately sending pieces of the four-slice toaster floating down the river – along with the blender, the food processor and the blades of a rotary eggbeater.

My lesson the next day wasn't much better. Fedora chanted her animated '*Bricka bracka firecracker, sis boom bah!*' as Marisol and Mesquite blindfolded me before levitating washers and bolts my way. Their goal? To see if I could sense the approaching shrapnel and dodge it before it hit me.

I couldn't.

The girls beaned me three times in the head, twice in the chest, and once below the belt – or, in my case, below the drawstring – before I was ready to throw in the towel. Or to use it to strangle my cousins in their sleep.

The twins had been scumbling so long it was second nature. I began to realize that they didn't actually *know* how to scumble. They simply did it because they always had.

Occasionally, during 'lessons', I'd hear a crackling sound and look up to find Rocket watching my failures from a distance.

'Focus, Ledge!' Mesquite would say, snapping her fingers in my face. And Marisol would flick my nose. 'Ledger! Pay attention!'

But it was hard to concentrate when Rocket stopped weeding and leaned against the garden fence to watch, his expression grim as he observed my humiliation.

On my third day of lessons, the twins chained and padlocked me and Fedora to the sticky trunk of a pine tree halfway up the east ridge, then left us there until I managed to break us free. That was when I decided I'd had enough of the girls' cut-throat coaching. Stomping back down the hill, I found the twins leaning their identical mountain bikes against the potting shed behind the garden after a nice long ride. If only I could've been back home riding bikes with Josh and Ryan and Brody instead of letting Marisol and Mesquite entertain themselves at my expense.

Wishing the girls' bikes were in as many pieces as my pride, I shot the two bicycles an enraged, unblinking glare. In moments, alloy rims flew like Frisbees, chains slithered to the ground and pedals sailed like hockey pucks. The side of the shed looked like it was under attack from a rabid, robotic porcupine as one hundred and forty-four wheel spokes thudded into it.

I was getting good at wrecking bikes.

'That was awesome, Ledge!' Marisol commended me with a hearty jostle, not even giving me the satisfaction of making her mad as pieces of her bike continued to rain from the sky, taking out two of Rocket's tomato plants and riddling courgette leaves with bolt-sized holes.

'You aimed that time, right?' Marisol asked in an excited voice. 'You busted the bikes on purpose!'

'See?' said Mesquite. 'Practice makes perfect. Or, in your case, practice makes *pieces*.'

I scowled. Had I aimed? I hadn't even been aware of feeling the familiar icy itch of my savvy hitting my system. Even if I'd shown a hint of control, could breaking something on purpose rather than by accident really be considered progress? Somehow, I didn't think so.

I was lucky none of the sailing pieces hit the glass roof of the Bug House. I could picture a bicycle wheel crashing through the roof to hit Gypsy on the head; she spent every day in there now with Uncle Autry, watching over the Alexandras. But knowing Gypsy, she'd probably just smile and think it was *peachy keen* that the sky was raining bicycle wheels.

The twins may have been happy to celebrate my bicycle butchery, but I knew that when Rocket saw the damage to his garden, I'd be mincemeat.

It was time for me to make myself scarce.

Chapter 16

IT WAS ONLY A FIFTEEN-MINUTE run to get to the salvage yard, though I hadn't known when I set out that I'd end up at Neary's Auto Salvage Acres. I'd been heading for Sundance, thinking Rocket might not kill me quite as dead if I had Grandma's last surviving jar in my hands. But reaching the sign for the salvage yard, I'd stopped, drawn to the sea of scrap. Ruined vehicles covered the open, rolling landscape: trucks, cars, tractors, even a motorhome and an old boat or two.

I followed the access road into Neary's, looking out at the bone orchard of broken-down bolt buckets.

Maze-like lines of metal radiated from a single large, steel structure, a building that appeared to double as a repair shop and a house.

I didn't know what I was doing. Or why my knees knocked so badly. Here, everything was already broken; I shouldn't have been scared. But walking into the salvage yard, the metallic taste in my mouth grew so strong it made me want to spit.

A slim figure emerged from the steel building and I stopped. It took me a minute to realize that the person approaching was a lady. No older than Rocket, the woman had an ink spill of straight black hair working its way out of a hair band to frame a perfectly oval, copper-coloured face. Her eyes were as sharp and black as chiselled obsidian as they surveyed me.

'If you're looking for Gus, he isn't here,' the lady called out. But *lady* might not have been the right word for this woman – not with her grey-green overalls coated collar to cuffs in axle grease.

Striding towards me in rubber-soled work boots, she

clutched a set of ape-hanger handlebars in her hand. As she drew closer, I could see the name *Winona* stitched on her overalls.

'And the policy at Neary's is: *You fix it, you buy it!* So watch your step, kid!' Winona winked at me and smiled.

'Gus?' I choked, remembering what Sheriff Brown had said when he came to the Flying Cattleheart almost a week before: *My truck got busted up about the same time the kids were in Willie's shop – my truck and one of Gus Neary's bikes, which fared a heap worse.*

Crud, I thought, knees knocking worse than ever.

I looked past Winona into the fabrication shop behind her. Sure enough, a pile of scrap metal powder-coated in shimmering gold paint glinted just inside the door like a haul of treasure ready to be buried.

Crud, crud and super crud.

'Gus isn't here?'

'Nope,' Winona replied. 'Pops took off for Vegas like the old fool that he is, thinking he might win himself enough money to save this dump.' She pulled the rag from her pocket and wiped at a smudge of motor oil on her cheek.

Glancing again at the rubble of the Knucklehead inside the shop, I asked, 'Is Gus coming back anytime soon?'

'I haven't heard from Pops since the day he left,' she answered. 'And after I came to help him out too! I even brought the Harley he restored for me so we could enter it in a bike show in Spearfish to try to win some cash. It was worth a try, right?'

'Er . . . what kind of Harley?' I asked, flinching, pretty sure I already knew the answer.

'I *had* a '47 Knucklehead. Now I've got a kit.' She pointed over her shoulder towards the pile of dismantled pieces. My stomach felt like lead. Inside my chest, my heart hammered against my ribs: *My fault. My fault. My fault.*

'The bike will go back together, of course,' Winona added. 'But not in time for the show.' She shook her head. 'If running away from problems were an Olympic sport, ol' Gus would have a wall of medals.' I frowned, thinking maybe Gus Neary and I should start our own

162

pro team. Winona cast another long look behind her at the ruined Knucklehead.

'I thought we might be able to rebuild the bike together – you know, make it one of those father-daughter things – but I guess it wasn't meant to be.'

Thinking of the half-marathon, I knew exactly how she felt.

'I could help you.' The words were out before I could stop them.

Winona rested the chrome handlebars over the back of her neck, gripping the ends on either side of her shoulders like a milkmaid with a yoke – only tougher.

'I don't even know who you are, kid. Or why you came here in the first place.' She raised a quizzical eyebrow, signalling that it was my turn to start spilling.

'I'm Ledge. Ledger Kale,' I said, starting with the easy part. I held out a hand to introduce myself, the same way Sarah Jane had when she climbed out of my family's minivan. Only, instead of batting my hand away the way I'd done to Sarah Jane, Winona smiled . . . and shook it.

Chapter 17

'AH, LEDGER! DID YOU HAVE A good ramble?' Grandpa asked as I jogged up.

I nodded and smiled, water dripping from my hair after a dip into the river.

I'd stayed at the salvage yard until the afternoon shadows had grown long, listening to Winona talk bikes and reading through a dusty Knucklehead manual as she started sorting pieces. By the time I returned to the ranch, I was happier than I'd been in weeks.

Forgetting that the Knucklehead wouldn't even need rebuilding if it weren't for me, I hummed a contented, tuneless hum. I liked the idea that I was *fixing* something for a change. It gave me the confidence to climb the stairs of the log house when I thought I saw Samson sitting solid next to Grandpa Bomba. Maybe I could tell *him* about Winona and the salvage yard.

But when I got to the top of the stairs, the chair next to Grandpa was empty and the screen door was swinging shut. A corner of my good mood got chipped; I wished that Samson would show up and stick around for a change. If he could appear for Grandpa, why didn't he trust me enough to let me see him? Was there something about him he didn't want anyone else to see?

'Where is everybody, Grandpa?' I asked, surprised when Grandpa Bomba stood from his chair without help. His bones made cracking, popping noises that woke Bitsy where she slept at the foot of his chair. She lifted her head and wagged her tail.

'Your uncle's checking the bee boxes,' Grandpa answered, his voice shaking only a little. 'And the rest of the herd? Who can tell where they've got to. The twins disappeared with Fedora after lunch – out hunting again, I s'pose. Said they were hoping for better luck

165

today.' Lately, Fedora had been tagging along behind Marisol and Mesquite non-stop, but the twins seemed happy to have a plucky new sidekick.

'Hunting?' I asked, realizing that I'd never paid attention to what Marisol and Mesquite did once they were done with me, their token karma booster. Now I wondered what Marisol and Mesquite might be wrangling my sister into. Hunting? I could picture Fedora in her helmet, crouched low in the grass, lecturing the twins about the dangers of bows and arrows or the right and wrong ways to safely set a snare.

'What are the vegetarians hunting?' I asked. 'Wild tofu?'

Grandpa chuckled. 'Your cousins have got other prospects in mind, I reckon.'

'Prospects?'

Grandpa just smiled and stretched again. 'Rocket's rustling up some wire to put round his garden to keep the rabbits and the crank springs out,' he continued. 'And Gypsy's giving your friend from town a butterfly tour.'

'Friend from town?' I echoed, confused. '*What* friend from town?'

Grandpa waved in the direction of the Bug House, trying his best to wink. 'A pretty girl came looking for you earlier, Ledge. Can't remember her name now.' He scratched his head. 'But I do remember she had two.'

'Two?' I repeated, even as the chair next to Grandpa's shuddered.

'Two first names,' Grandpa clarified, not even glancing at the chair. 'Betty Jo? . . . No, that's not right. Mary Ann?'

I shut my eyes and whispered, 'Sarah Jane?'

'That's it!' Grandpa slapped his leg and snapped his fingers. 'But since you weren't here, Gypsy took it on herself to entertain your girlfriend till you got back. You know how she is about them butterflies. Loves 'em more than a box full of mittened kittens.'

'No.' I shook my head in disbelief. 'No . . . no . . . no!'

'Ledger?'

'I've got to go, Grandpa!' I had to rescue Gypsy from the grip of Sarah Jane. Gypsy was too nice. Too sugar-gumdrops, stick-to-your-teeth sweet. Sarah Jane Cabot would run over her as easily as if she were driving one of her dad's CAD Co. demolition wreckers into the side of Candy Mountain.

'And she's *not* my girlfriend!' I hollered as I leaped from the porch, vaulting up and over the railing, not bothering with the stairs. But the ground on the other side was further down than I'd expected, and my leap was going to land me on my face for sure.

I should've wiped out. I should have busted bones. Only, before I could, the earth jumped up to meet me with a rumble, accounting for my error in judgement by catching me halfway.

'Thanks, Grandpa!' I shouted over my shoulder, wondering where in the world Grandpa had found the strength to raise a column of earth and gently level it flat again.

'Don't thank me, thank Samson!' I heard him call back. I couldn't guess what he might mean. But with bigger worries elbowing to the front of my crowded mind, I knew I'd have to mull Grandpa's comment over later.

Still looking back at Grandpa, I bumped into Rocket as he came round the corner of the house carrying a heavy roll of chicken wire.

'Gah! Sorry!' I backpedalled as I squawked a skittish apology.

'Ledge!' Rocket dropped the wire. 'Hey, Ledge! Stop! I need to talk to you.'

'Later!' I took off towards the Bug House before Rocket could yell at me for sending a hailstorm of bi-cycle parts down on his garden. Before he could give me another lecture about being careful.

'Ledger, just stop for a minute! There's something I need to clear up.'

I didn't stop. I valued my life too much. And I needed to put myself between Sarah Jane and Gypsy fast. I could just picture Gypsy telling secrets – giving Sarah Jane a handful of seeds that she could water to grow a giant, wordy beanstalk, a story so big, so fantastic, that people would come flocking to the ranch just to see if it was true.

'Later!' I repeated, heading for the conservatory,

relieved when Rocket picked up his roll of wire and shouldered it towards the garden, head down, work boots stomping.

But when I reached the door to the Bug House, I didn't know what to do. It was still too dangerous for me to go inside – I pictured swarms issuing from the busted roof to descend on the town of Sundance in legions of wings and legs and pincers and stingers. I circled the building twice, trying to figure out what my next move should be. Then stopped to pace outside the door.

Ten minutes passed, as slowly as ten hours, and I thought I could hear voices on the other side of the door at last – girls' voices – laughing and chatting, though I couldn't hear what they were saying.

I had my hand on the door handle when I saw Marisol and Mesquite coming over the ridge, Fedora walking between them carrying a shovel over one shoulder and a small pickaxe over the other. At the same moment, Uncle Autry appeared at the top of the path that led from the bee boxes to the Bug House.

Autry and the twins couldn't find out that Sarah Jane

was at the Flying Cattleheart. They'd blame me for sure. If they kicked me off the ranch, where else could I go?

I had to distract the others – to keep them from seeing SJ. I remembered the night of Fish's wedding and the way I'd puckered up to Sarah Jane to keep her from seeing Rocket's sparks. I needed another distraction. Kissing everyone on the ranch was definitely not an option . . . but the windmill on the other side of the log house just might be.

I was at the base of the windmill in a flash. The late-afternoon breeze toyed lazily with the faded wedding streamers that still clung to the cross braces of the six-metre steel tower. Above me, the blades of the wheel turned slowly.

I didn't want to wreck the windmill. I just needed a commotion big enough to keep all eyes away from the Bug House for a short while. Gypsy and Sarah Jane had been standing at the door. Sarah Jane would step out at any moment.

Gripping the cross brace closest to me, I ignored the

171

sharp, metallic taste now becoming so familiar. Grinding, scraping noises rent the air as I began to bend the four towering supports of the windmill, making them totter. The windmill wobbled, a drunken mechanical spider that had lost half of its legs. Rocket and Grandpa looked up. Bitsy barked. I could see the others changing direction: Autry racing towards the windmill, the twins and Fedora moving at breakneck speed down the slope of the basin.

As the beams of the windmill swayed and groaned, I tried to strike a balance – to hold the thing together while allowing it to twist like crazy. I did my best to tame the chaos, inside and out, breathing through my panic the way Dad taught me to breathe through a stitch. But I continued to let the itch and prickle of my savvy flow. I knew I couldn't maintain my concentration long. Sarah Jane needed to get her butt out of the Bug House now.

Then she needed to skedaddle.

Fast.

By the time the others reached me, the tower leaned

over the rubble of the fallen barn like a daisy stuck into the brim of a squashed straw hat.

As the others stared up at the contorted windmill, Gypsy stepped out of the Bug House, followed by Sarah Jane. I watched, hoping the Sundance newspaper princess would be smart enough to leave. I could almost make out the expression on Sarah Jane's face as she took in the warped and tortured mill; I was relieved when she didn't come to check it out.

Shouldering her backpack – *my* backpack – she followed a deer trail along the river towards the ridge instead of hiking up the access road, taking a sneaky way off the ranch. It made me twitchy with suspicion. But my diversion was successful; no one gave any indication that they had seen Sarah Jane.

'Now it's a windmill *and* a sculpture, Ledge,' Autry said after circling the bent-steel monstrosity half a dozen times. My uncle wiped his brow when he discovered that the windmill still worked. 'I'd like to think that this is progress.'

I couldn't meet Autry's eyes. He didn't know I'd

attacked the metal tower on purpose. Staring up at the surreal twist of metal, my stomach churned.

'Progress . . . sure,' I muttered. But I'd accomplished what I set out to do. Sarah Jane was gone and Autry and the twins would never have to know that she had been here. Not unless someone told them. And if I had anything to say about it, nobody would.

I went looking for Gypsy as soon as the fuss died down.

'I like what you did with the windmill, Ledge!' Gypsy said as she secured a crown of blue and yellow flowers in her hair a half-hour later.

'Forget the windmill,' I said. 'Grandpa said we had a visitor.'

Gypsy nodded. 'That's right! Your friend came looking for you.'

'Uncle Autry says we're not supposed to talk to Sarah Jane Cabot, Gypsy. She shouldn't have come here,' I blustered, folding my arms. 'She's *not* my friend.'

Gypsy smiled like a china doll with a Mona Lisa face. 'Okay, Ledge. Whatever you say.'

'You won't tell Autry or the twins she was here?' I narrowed my eyes at my cousin. Gypsy spun once, then adjusted her flower crown with a curtsy. I took that for a yes.

'So . . . what did she want?'

'Who?' Gypsy cocked her head, dropping flower petals on to one shoulder.

'SJ! I mean, *Sarah Jane*,' I answered through gritted teeth, trying not to lose patience with my flighty cousin. 'Did she – did Sarah Jane bring me anything?' I stammered, half hoping that Sarah Jane might have come to the ranch to return Grandma Dollop's peanut-butter jar. It was a slim hope, and a fraying one, but it was still strong enough for me to cling to.

Gypsy's thin brows shot up.

'What did you want her to bring?'

'Nothing,' I answered quickly. Too quickly. Gypsy's brows arched higher.

'She just asked a lot of questions. Mostly about you.'

I held my breath. 'What did you tell her?'

Gypsy spun again once, then answered. 'I told her

175

that you like to bathe in the river, that you live in Indiana, that you run really fast when you want to . . . and that someday you are going to be an artist.'

'An artist?' I snorted, trying not to look down the hill at the vomitrocious mess I'd made out of the windmill.

Gypsy's Mona Lisa smile returned.

'Did you talk about anything else?' I asked, redirecting the conversation. 'You didn't tell SJ about our family, did you? About savvies? You didn't tell her anything about –'

'Ledger, calm down,' Gypsy interrupted. 'You've gone totally doolally. I *almost* told her, because . . . well, she really deserves to know. But –'

'Deserves to know? Gypsy –!'

Gypsy's calm stare stopped me.

'But I didn't say anything, Ledger. I promise. I showed her the conservatory instead! And the Queen Alexandra's Birdwing chrysalides!' Gypsy sighed, as if sharing her private, glassed-in fairyland had made her happy.

I dropped my head into my hands, pressing my palms into my eyes. This wasn't as bad as Gypsy telling Sarah Jane our family secrets, but it came close. What would Sarah Jane do with a story about twelve of the world's largest butterflies taking up residence at the ranch – endangered creatures getting ready to emerge in Crook County, Wyoming?

She'd make it headline news in her paper, that's what she'd do. I thought of the free Super-Duper Humdinger issue Sarah Jane had threatened me with the week before. I was still waiting for it to come.

Now I was praying *extra* hard that it wouldn't.

Chapter 18

'YOU'VE REALLY GOT A KNACK FOR this, Ledge!' Winona declared three days later, after I stopped her from re-lacing wheel spokes wrongly for the second time. I was sure that if she continued as she was, the front wheel of the Knucklehead would never stay round.

'Are you sure you've never done anything like this before?' Winona continued. I snorted, casting my millionth wary look at the lathes, drills, band saws and brake presses that took up space inside Gus Neary's shop. To my surprise, I'd shown a talent for reconstructing the pieces of the bike on more than one occasion, discovering that I could spot a forgotten spacer the way my mom could spot a stain from fifty metres. Still, I sat in the doorway of the open bay as usual, half in and half out of the steel building, multiple escape plans ready.

'Trust me,' I answered. 'I'm a whole lot better at taking things apart.'

'I don't know, kid.' Winona glanced from me to the bike frame, then back at me again. 'You've obviously got some untapped skills. Heh, if Gus were here, you could be the son he always wanted.'

'I'd rather be the son *my* dad always wanted,' I mumbled. My throat tightened as I rotated a clamp on the Knuck's handlebars, but the wave of panic that usually followed thoughts of failure held back. For some reason, talking with Winona was easy, and working with my hands had a way of loosening my tongue. I often found myself saying things to her that I'd never said to anyone. Not Josh. Not Ryan. Especially not Big Mouth Brody.

'I'm supposed to be a runner,' I went on, double-checking the clamp.

'You run every day, don't you?'

'Yeah.' I shrugged. 'But I'm not fast – at least, not as fast as my dad hoped I'd be. I haven't even talked to him since he and Mom left. Mom and Dad called again yesterday but . . .' I trailed off, unable to tell Winona that the first time I'd tried to talk, I'd busted my uncle's mobile phone before Dad could even say *hello*. After a moment, I added, 'I'll never run the race of a lifetime like Dad did, and he knows it.'

'Those sound like your dad's dreams, Ledge,' Winona said, still working on the same spoke she'd been fiddling with for the last ten minutes. 'What're yours?'

'What are my what?'

'Your *dreams*, y'dumb lug!' Laughing, she threw the spoke at me. 'Surely you've got some of your own!'

'I guess I never really thought about it.' I caught the spoke and shrugged again, hoping Winona didn't see the way the thin metal rod curled into a corkscrew in my hand. A series of images flashed through my mind: Aunt Jenny's painting of a boat on the ocean, the infamous melting clocks incident in art class, the twisted arc of the windmill . . . Gypsy's Mona Lisa smile just after she'd said I'd be an artist.

While I'd gone to the salvage yard every day since meeting Winona, I still hadn't stepped into its sprawling steel ocean. 'Feel free to explore, Ledge,' she'd told me more than once. 'There's a lot more here than meets the eye. All kinds of treasures.'

'Treasures? It's a junkyard,' I'd snorted the first time she said it, imagining myself rising from the salvage yard the same way Eva Mae had risen from the river. Only, instead of stepping out covered head to toe in gold, I'd come out looking like a giant Transforminator toy or a goofball knight armoured top to bottom in rusted metal. I'd be a terrified and terrifying human sculpture – a piece of art, not an artist.

Now, as Winona rethought her approach to the wheel spokes, I shook those same images from my head once again. I glanced at a massive, mystifying shape that grew beneath a tarpaulin in the middle of the shop, wondering what it might be. The only bit visible was a curve of metal protruding from beneath the coverings like the foot of a giant beast. Whatever Winona worked on when I wasn't there, she wouldn't let me see, and I was dying to sneak a peek.

'Sarah Jane would look,' I said under my breath.

'Sarah Jane would do what?' Winona squinted at me, dropping a wrench with a clatter.

'Uh . . . nothing. I was just talking to myself.'

'About Sarah Jane Cabot?'

'Um . . . I guess. Do you know her?'

'Not personally, no. But I know her *work* – her father's too. Or haven't you seen the foreclosure sign out front?'

'But Sarah Jane doesn't have anything to do with the foreclosure. She's just a kid,' I replied, not sure why I was defending her.

'Sarah Jane featured Pops in one of her papers not too long before her snollygoster father decided to foreclose,' Winona said. 'Gus was so proud of getting in a newspaper, any newspaper, he hung it in the shop.' She rolled her eyes. 'I took it down. Every time I saw the headline: *Shiver Me Timbers! Gus Neary Be a Former*

Buccaneer! I started thinking Pops was a retired pirate: peg leg, parrot, scurvy – the works. He already had the eye patch, which is probably why Sarah Jane picked on him. But it's Sarah Jane's dad who's the real picaroon raider, not mine.' Winona stopped her ramble short, squinting at me. 'How do you know her, Ledge?' she asked, suddenly wary. 'Is Sarah Jane your –'

'She's not my girlfriend! Not, not, *not* my girlfriend.' I cut her off, but Winona only burst out laughing.

'Okay! Got it. But really, Ledge, I was only going to ask if she's your *friend*.'

I returned to the ranch that afternoon with more grease under my nails than river water could wash away. I'd been cleaning up the same way for days. No soap. No shampoo. Removing just enough stink to keep the girls from complaining, I got a hefty helping of wild-boy joy out of going uncombed and unscrubbed – knowing Mom would never let me get away with such a lack of hygiene.

But my new heights of grime were nothing compared

to the layers of red dust Fedora showed up wearing. Fe came back so filthy from her hunting trips with the twins that she practically needed her own high-pressure, outdoor kid wash to get the dirt off, while Marisol and Mesquite came back clean as Girl Scout whistles. It made me wonder if the twins had the ability to levitate the dust right off their skin, or if they were simply making Fedora do all their dirty work . . . whatever that might be.

Like me, the three girls kept their mouths closed about their secret daily missions and, for a while, I pretended not to care what kind of trouble Marisol and Mesquite might be getting my sister into. But that evening, when Fedora returned to the ranch tuckered out and sunburned, and with calluses and blisters on her hands, I began to worry.

'Tell me what you're doing with Mesquite and Marisol,' I demanded, catching up with Fedora before joining the others at the campfire. 'Where do the three of you go every afternoon?'

'Marisol and Mesquite say it's none of your beeswax,

Sledgehammer,' Fe answered, hitting me with the rotten nickname the twins had invented, then walking a little faster.

I clenched my teeth. Fe was spending too much time with the older girls.

'Don't call me that, Fedora!'

Stopping, Fe raised her pointy chin inside her helmet and crossed her arms over her dirty T-shirt. 'You're not Mom. You can't control me.'

'I am your brother though. Your *big* brother. Tell me what you've been up to or I'll pound you.'

'Careful, Ledge! Anger is only one letter away from *danger.'* Fedora started walking again, calling my bluff. She and I both knew I'd never do it. Pinch her, maybe. Pound her, no.

'Next time Mom and Dad phone, I'll tell them you're keeping secrets!' I hollered after her, feeling like a hypocrite and a tattletale too.

'You've got secrets too, Ledge!' Fe yelled back. 'Besides, I bet you don't even talk to Mom and Dad next time they call. I bet you'll be too scared you'll break the phone again! You'll be a big, fat phone-chicken . . . Bawk! Bawk!' She waggled her elbows, dancing in circles like a chicken.

'Fine!' I spat. 'Just don't expect me to tell you how I spend *my* afternoons,' I added, even though I was dying to tell *someone* about my time in the salvage yard.

'Fine!' Fe spat back. *'Sledgehammer Stupid-Head!'*

'Give it a rest, Fedora!' Both Fe and I turned at the sound of Rocket's voice. I hadn't heard him coming up behind us. Fe looked wounded at Rocket's rebuff. Her lower lip trembled. She wasn't accustomed to him siding with me instead of her. I wasn't either. But I didn't like it when someone else yelled at my sister.

Rocket moved past us to join the others at the campfire. I waited, every muscle tense, thinking he might turn round to ask again if we could talk. But he walked on, not looking back.

Fedora sniffed inside her helmet.

'Come on, Fe,' I said. 'Whatever you're up to, it's got to make you hungry.' I took my sister's hand and squeezed it. Then I led her towards the fire, wondering if Rocket had finally given up on giving me his lecture.

When the Super-Duper Humdinger issue of *The Sundance Scuttlebutt* came out, Sarah Jane mailed my copy directly to the ranch.

Two weeks had passed since Fish and Mellie's wedding. It was Saturday and Grandpa was dozing on the porch as usual. The colourful yarns of an old afghan blanket meandered across his lap despite the dog days of summer that panted hot breath at everyone else's heels. I felt a stab of guilt as I looked at Grandpa in his chair. I'd been so wrapped up in everything else – running, the Knucklehead, torturous lessons with the twins – I'd almost forgotten about Grandma Dollop's jar and the silent promise I'd made to get it back.

Rocket had left early that morning after losing an argument with Autry, making one of his rare trips off the ranch in his own truck – a rusty Ford F-1 that had a way of rolling away from wherever he parked it, the parking brake a goner. Autry sent Rocket into Sundance to collect the mail from the post office and, if there was any truth to Autry's teasing, to wave away the girls who buzzed around my cousin like honeybees to clover, the same way he waved away Fedora when she begged him to let her ride along.

My parents called just before the nonsensical newspaper arrived.

'Ledge? Fedora? Who wants to talk first?' Autry asked, holding his new mobile phone out over the picnic table.

'Me! Me!' Fedora shouted. I only half listened as Fe babbled to Mom and Dad. But I pricked up my ears when I heard her talking about the safest way to use a shovel.

'. . . and if you do that, you don't fall down if you hit something!' Fe was explaining. 'And we're hoping we hit something big! We're hoping to find –'

'Ssss! Fedora, shush!' Marisol hissed from her seat at the table.

'Yeah!' added Mesquite. 'You've talked long enough.

188

Ledger's turn!' Without giving Fedora the chance to say goodbye, the twins levitated the phone out of my sister's hand and zipped it my way.

I grabbed the phone before it could hit me in the side of the head, taking a deep breath as I raised it to my ear. Now Fedora would see that I wasn't a big, fat phone-chicken. But Fe still jammed her helmet back on her head and slid to the far end of the picnic table, just in case shards of phone went flying.

'Tell me everything, Ledger!' Mom's voice spilled from the phone in a tidal wave of mom-worry – so loud, Gypsy giggled from across the table, covering her mouth with her fingers. 'Are you eating, Ledge?' Mom asked. 'You need to eat. Are you brushing your teeth? Don't forget! Flossing? Don't forget that either! Remember to wear sunblock and don't let Autry give you too much pop or candy . . .'

I crossed my eyes at Mom's flood of concern, relieved that her savvy never worked well over the phone. I only felt vaguely compelled to brush my teeth, and had no impulse whatsoever to tell her everything.

'Are you doing all right, Ledge?' Dad asked when he came on the line.

'I'm running, Dad,' I assured him quickly. Unlike with Mom, I wanted to tell Dad about Winona and the Knucklehead and how I was good at knowing how things went together without even looking at a manual. I wanted to tell him about the windmill and how I'd twisted and bent the tower without destroying it. I wanted to ask whether Josh or Ryan had called or come by looking for me, or if Brody had told half the town that I'd been quarantined in Wyoming with mumps or measles or mad cow disease.

'I'm running, Dad. I'm running every day,' was what came out of my mouth.

'That's great, son,' Dad replied. 'But how're you doing? Are you okay?'

'I think I might be getting faster. But the air's thinner here, so –'

'Ledger –' Dad began to interrupt, but I never learned what he'd been about to say, because Rocket, just back from town and looking grumpier than ever, chose that moment to drop an envelope down on the picnic table in front of me.

I heard, 'Ledge? Ledger? Did I lose you?' Then Dad's voice was a crackle of static. I let the phone slip from my ear as Rocket pointed, jabbing with a single flashing spark at Sarah Jane's loopy handwriting:

From: S. J. Cabot, Editor
The Sundance Scuttlebutt

To: Cowboy Ledge,
AKA The King of Damage
c/o The Flying Cattleheart Ranch

It was the end of my conversation with Mom and Dad. Autry's new phone didn't stand a chance. Neither did the picnic table. This time the nails flew out of the table so fast, no one had time to push them down. After two weeks of holding strong, the picnic table collapsed into a pile of wood, my own hopes that Sarah Jane had given up on her humdinger newspaper collapsing with it.

I snatched up the envelope before any of the others had a chance to get a good look at it. What if Sarah Jane had written about my family and the wedding? What if our secret was out? All the rules broken? What if Sarah Jane had decided to tell the whole world I was *defective*?

Chapter 19

I DIDN'T OPEN MY MAIL UNTIL I'd run up to the birch-tree glade by myself, taking a seat in the shade after startling three or four white-tailed deer and an antelope or two that were nibbling at the peeling bark. I sat for a long time, staring at the envelope. I wasn't sure if I was brave enough to open it, even if I was dying of curiosity.

It was worse than I'd expected. I'd read Sarah Jane's last paper – the one about the aliens who liked strawberry-rhubarb pie. I'd also read every scribbled entry in her notebook twice. But what I held in my hands now was different. This time, Sarah Jane must've used every fancy feature available on the photocopier at Willie's Five & Dime. Two sheets of paper, printed on both sides, were folded and stapled together. And every headline had something to do with me, my family or the ranch.

Before sealing the envelope, Sarah Jane had attached a Post-it to the front page of the paper.

Ledge,

Here's your free issue! I thought you'd like to see it before it hits the stands on Monday!

- SJ

Grinding my teeth, I flipped through the newspaper. An article about Fish and his floating bride filled the front page, while Grandma Dollop's jar followed on the next. The centre pages held accounts of electrical storms and newfangled windmills, but my eyes popped when I saw a two-page spread describing the ruin of the

194

Knucklehead in front of the five-and-dime. Sarah Jane had written the article with a painstaking attention to detail, and Indiana boy Ledger Kale was the star of the story.

I couldn't believe the words emblazoned across the pages of *The Sundance Scuttlebutt*. No, actually, I *could* believe them. I did. And, for once, they were all true. What if Sheriff Brown read this stuff? My fear of being hauled to jail returned. Then a whole new worry hit me and my heart took a swan dive into my trainers . . .

What if *Winona* saw it?

I'd never be able to show my face at the salvage yard again.

I'd already disappointed my dad. I didn't want to disappoint Winona too. Turning to the last page of Sarah Jane's paper, my breath caught, making me cough and splutter as I read the final headline.

REPORTER CAPTURES WORLD'S LARGEST BUTTERFLY

'She didn't! She couldn't!' I cried aloud. Sarah Jane had taken one of the Alexandras! Didn't she know that the butterflies were endangered? Didn't she stop to think that my uncle might get in trouble for not protecting the butterflies from yet another smuggler – even if that smuggler was a sneaky thirteen-year-old girl?

I already knew that Sarah Jane was a thief, but this time I wouldn't allow her to get away with it. I crushed the newspaper into a tight ball. I may have been the first person to read the Super-Duper Humdinger issue of *The Sundance Scuttlebutt*, but I would also be the last.

'Hey! Get a wiggle on, Ledge! Marisol and Mesquite are looking for you.' I'd been so intent on Sarah Jane's paper, I hadn't seen Fedora march into the glade. Bitsy stood at my sister's side, tail wagging.

'Marisol and Mesquite want to get your scumbling lesson over early, before it gets too hot for us to –' Fe snapped her mouth shut quickly, remembering not to give away any secrets. I didn't care. Right now, I had much bigger secrets on my mind – a whole newspaper full of them.

'Tell Marisol and Mesquite I'm busy,' I snapped, hiding the wadded ball of paper behind my back. 'Tell them I don't want any more lessons. I'm done. Their lessons aren't helping.' I cringed at the memory of the fallen picnic table and the pieces of Autry's second phone. 'Nothing's helping.'

'Hey, what'd you get in the mail, Ledge?' Fedora removed her helmet and set it on the ground, picking up the empty envelope I'd dropped. I grabbed for the envelope but missed, dropping the balled-up paper I clutched in my other hand. The humdinger issue bounced against my heel and ricocheted off one of the juniper stumps. I lunged for the paper, but only succeeded in batting it into the air between me and Fedora.

'What is that? Let me see!' Fedora scrabbled for the paper as it flew towards her. I swatted it away. Then Fe and I hacky-sacked the crumpled ball between us as we each tried to be the one to catch it. Bitsy joined the game. Wagging her whole body, the dog got in my way and I stumbled, pitching forward towards my sister.

'Ow! My eye!' Fedora cried, covering one eye like I'd jabbed her. 'Eyes on safety, Ledge! Eyes on safety!'

Forgetting the paper, I leaned over her. 'You okay, Fe? Let me see –'

'Ha! Gotcha!' As soon as I got close, Fedora gave me a hard push – hard enough to make me lose my balance. As I windmilled my arms, trying to stay upright, she bent down and grabbed the newspaper. Then she ran down the trail towards the one place she knew I couldn't follow.

I was down the path in no time, chasing after her. Bitsy ran next to me. But when we reached the door to the Bug House, we both stopped. My heart thudded inside my chest as I looked up at the building. Autry had told me that if I thought about what scared me, I'd take my first steps towards scumbling. But so far, thinking about everything that scared me hadn't helped anything.

I fought to calm my nerves, counting backwards from ten to one – six or seven times – until I felt my pulse settle. All I had to do was make it in and out of the Bug House to get Sarah Jane's paper back from Fedora without knocking the entire place down.

Bitsy whined and lay down, her eyes darting between me and the Bug House, as if she, in all her doggy wisdom, understood exactly why I might be afraid.

'Stay, girl,' I commanded as I pushed in through the outer door of the conservatory. I paused briefly to wonder at the series of mirrors and fans in the space between the outer and inner doors, precautions to help ensure that no out-of-the-ordinary insects escaped to wreak havoc. The mirrors reflected my face back at me. In one glance, I could see myself from every angle – back, front, sides – making me feel strangely as though I were whole and broken into hundreds of pieces at the same time.

The air inside the Bug House was soupy with mist. Gently humming fans circulated soft breezes through the frondescent tangle of leaves, stirring up the smells of moss and peat. For a moment, the metallic tang I always tasted was replaced with the heavy flavour of moist, rich earth. I could almost forget the glass-and-steel roof over my head, crisscrossed with steam pipes and heavy cables supporting dense, flowering vines. It was easy to lose sight of the walls filled with nails and bolts, and the motors with their bazillion pieces that turned the blades of the fans.

I thought the Bug House was awesome . . . until

I spotted things crawling. And things *were* crawling. Crawling everywhere. Crawling, flying, buzzing, chirruping and droning. Suddenly, I got a rapid and ruthless case of the all-overs. The glass overhead rattled and the entire building shook as I moved further inside, jumping and scratching with every step, certain I could feel the tiny pinprick of insect feet on my skin.

I looked around for Fedora, not sure how I'd ever find her in the jungle of the conservatory. But beneath the murmuring *shush-shush-shush* of the fans, I could hear Autry talking with Rocket at the far end of the building. The barn shook again.

Moving carefully, I concentrated on Rocket's and Autry's voices. I was determined to find Fedora, retrieve Sarah Jane's paper, then get myself back outside into Wyoming's dust and dry heat before anything ludicrously large decided to land on me, sting me, or crawl inside my shirt.

I moved beyond a twist of flowering vines filled with the flutter of delicate, paper-like wings. Dozens of butterflies hovered close or flitted down from dangling tangles of trumpet-like flowers. Some of the butterflies were large, some small, some nearly camouflaged – hiding their colours by closing up their wings, and making me wish hiding a savvy were as simple. Others were non-stop bright and brilliant and reminded me of Sarah Jane, which only made the roof over my head rattle worse.

I found Fedora hiding behind an enormous cluster of prehistoric-looking fern fronds while trying to straighten the pages of *The Sundance Scuttlebutt*. When Fe saw me, she squealed and tried to stuff the whole thing down her shirt. I stopped her, grabbing the paper, then put a finger to my lips.

Autry and Rocket were arguing.

I clamped a hand over Fe's mouth, restraining her in the crook of my arm as she continued struggling and grabbing for Sarah Jane's paper.

'I told you it was a bad idea to make me get the mail,' I heard Rocket say, unable to forget the way he'd jammed Sarah Jane's envelope down at me with a spark.

'Now, don't blow things out of proportion, Rocket,' Autry tried to soothe him. 'It was a small accident.'

I bit the inside of my cheek, conscious of the way Autry endlessly forgave my smash-ups – big or small.

'These kinds of *accidents* aren't acceptable,' Rocket answered, his voice bitter. 'Not any more.'

I swallowed hard. I hadn't been at the ranch *that* long. I hadn't even been thirteen for a full month!

'A young man can't expect himself to be perfect, Rocket.' Autry's words backed me up.

'No, but that doesn't mean he can't be cautious or use some basic common sense!'

'Rocket.' Autry's sigh was audible. 'You've got to realize that boys grow into men, and men choose to learn from their mistakes and move on . . . and, hopefully, someday, *out*.'

Rocket's answer came fast and sharp.

'I don't think this boy will *ever* learn.'

Feeling like I'd just been stung by the Asian Giant

Hornet in a tank nearby, I let go of Fedora and took a step back. But as I turned and slipped, my right hand landed in a thick, sticky web – a web large enough to have been made by that Chihuahua-sized spider.

I leaped up with a shudder, every rafter shuddering with me. The entire structure of the Bug House began to buckle and heave as bolts spun loose and the walls began to lurch and sway. Not since the night of Fish's wedding had I felt my savvy come on so strong.

'Stop, Ledge! I don't have my helmet!' Fedora cried, wrapping her arms over her head. 'Falling objects can be brutal if you don't protect your noodle! My noodle, Ledge! My noodle!'

'Ledge?' Autry shouted. 'Ledger, are you in here?' I heard dampened footsteps heading in my direction, but I was already moving towards the exit. If I stayed any longer I'd destroy the conservatory. So I did the thing I'd trained for most in my life.

I ran.

Things flew and hopped and skittered all around me

203

as I made a beeline towards the door. Metal bolts rained down like hailstones and I wished in earnest that Fedora hadn't left her helmet in the glade.

Rocket was right. I would never learn.

Chapter 20

I HARDLY NOTICED THE CARS THAT passed me, or the heat radiating from the road as I ran east, tearing Sarah Jane's newspaper into shreds as I went.

Running straight into town, I passed a utility truck parked in front of the post office and slowed briefly to look up at the workman checking the transformer and the power lines overhead. The only other thing that curbed my speed was the new red-and-white foreclosure sign on the door of Willie's Five & Dime.

Just great. One more thing for Cabot to add to his collection.

Soon I was standing, out of breath and shaking,

across the street from the Cabots' hulking house and its forbidding spiked, iron fence. I wasn't going to let Sarah Jane Cabot continue to ruin my life or threaten my family.

Trying to decide if I should knock or break down the door, I ducked into the shadows of a nearby shrub, keeping a safe distance between me and the mailboxes I'd levelled on my last visit. Though right now a 'safe distance' might be somewhere in the eastern half of South Dakota, or the far side of the moon.

I stared at the fence surrounding the house and the forest of hodgepodge tree stumps inside its perimeter. The familiar metallic tang was in my mouth again, sticking to my tongue like I'd licked the iron posts.

My gaze settled on the single tall birch that leaned down to hug the house. I was surprised to find Sarah Jane beneath it. She lay on her stomach across a low marble bench, knees bent, ankles crossed behind her. Her hair hung free from its usual braids as she pressed her face against the cool stone, idly plucking at tufts of grass. Knowing Sarah Jane, she was probably dreaming up all new stories to further ruin my already wrecked-up life. I wondered if she had the butterfly chrysalis with her, or if it was upstairs in her room.

Moving out of my sheltered spot, I stepped on to the empty road. The thrum of grasshoppers on the hill behind the house sounded like the teeth of a thousand combs being dragged across cardboard. I kept my eyes peeled for any sign of Mr Cabot – or of the bug-eyed housekeeper. I'd promised Autry that I wouldn't put a shoe inside the Cabot house. With Sarah Jane outside already, I wouldn't have to break my promise.

'Hey!' I shouted as I crossed the road, stopping at a distance from the fence. Sarah Jane looked up. She waved and smiled like I was her best friend forever, come over to jump rope and put the braids back in her hair. Slipping from the bench she strode towards me, still smiling.

'I knew I could get you to visit me again, Cowboy,' she said as she drew nearer, her hair a jumble in the breeze. 'You got your mail?'

I balled my hands into tight fists, the truth dawning

fast. Sarah Jane didn't have one of the Queen Alexandra's Birdwings. How could she? Autry or Gypsy would've seen right away that one was missing. They would've said something. I would've known.

'Y-you tricked me with that article!' I sputtered. 'You don't have one of my uncle's butterflies, do you.'

'No, Cowboy. I don't,' Sarah Jane replied with at least enough decency to wrinkle her nose apologetically.

The girl would do anything to get a person's attention.

'Was the whole thing a trick?' I demanded, pulling a shred of the Super-Duper Humdinger edition of *The Sundance Scuttlebutt* from my pocket and holding it up. 'Because you can't put out this paper!'

'Relax, Cowboy! I just had to get you here. I won't put out that paper . . . not if you tell me what I want to know.'

'Sarah Jane –'

'*SJ*! Remember?'

I let out a long breath, trying to stay calm. 'Look . . .

SJ, there are things I'm not allowed to talk about. I'm not even supposed to be talking to you at all! You're going to get me into trouble. You're going to get my whole family into trouble! Would you please just give me back the jar you took and promise me no one will see that paper?'

'Oh . . . I can't give you the jar back, Ledge,' Sarah Jane said with another apologetic nose wrinkle. The tree branches shook behind her like a gentle scolding. A tremor ran through the fence.

'Why can't you give it to me? Did you break it?' I moved two steps closer.

'No.' Sarah Jane grimaced. 'I didn't break it. I . . . I kind of gave it to my father.'

'You did *what*?' I exploded, ignoring the full shudder that ran all the way round the fence. 'Well, get it back!'

'I can't.'

'Why not?'

'Daddy . . .' She hesitated, biting her lower lip before saying slowly, 'Daddy recycled it.'

'What?'

'I'm sorry, Ledge! I thought he'd like it for his collection. But Daddy took the jar away and told me I was being foolish. I should've known he wouldn't care about it if I gave it to him. He's always loved weird things, but he won't even let me tie my shoelaces in an unusual way. He wants me to be normal.'

I snorted. 'You're never going to be normal!' I hadn't meant it as a compliment, but my words made SJ brighten.

'Really? You think so?'

I threw up my hands and turned to walk away.

'Don't go, Ledge!'

'Why shouldn't I?' I asked. 'You're going to do what you want no matter what I do! Put out your paper! Nobody will believe it anyway.' Only, in my gut, I knew that might not be true.

'Wait! Ledge! Don't go! What if I checked the recycle bin?' Sarah Jane pleaded. 'Maybe Hedda the Horrible hasn't taken it out yet! Wait here! Don't go anywhere.'

I waited as she ran into the house, hope popping up

210

in me like breakfast table nails. But Sarah Jane was gone so long, I began to think she'd ditched me. Impatience added fuel to my ire. The iron fence shuddered in waves and I tried not to panic and run. This might be my last shot at getting Grandma's jar back for Grandpa. But the feeling of ants crawling underneath my skin always freaked me out. If I didn't like the way other people controlled me, I liked the way my savvy controlled me even less.

I was tired of everyone and everything else determining what I should do and who I should be – whether it was Sarah Jane, my parents, or my stupid savvy. I wanted to make choices for myself. Surely my Maker had had some plan when He put me together like this? The Ledger Kale schematics couldn't have been all wrong.

By the time Sarah Jane emerged from the house again, I'd calmed down. I even smiled when I saw that Sarah Jane had both hands wrapped tightly round a jar.

I took a deep breath.

You're the one in control here, Ledge, I told myself. *Just focus.*

Not willing to trust Sarah Jane one hundred per cent, I moved slowly towards the fence.

But as I reached between the iron bars, Sarah Jane tossed aside the jar, letting it land in the grass with a heavy *thud*. In the same movement, she reached behind her and deftly slapped one end of the antique shackles from her father's study round my wrist. Before I could pull back, Sarah Jane fastened the other half of the Sundance Kid's cuffs to one of the fence posts.

I'd been right not to trust her.

She'd tricked me again.

Chapter 21

'**DID IT EVER OCCUR TO YOU** that this might be the reason you don't have any friends?' I clanked the shackles against the fence as I looked at Sarah Jane.

Sarah Jane held up a rusty key and backed away, moving just beyond my reach.

'I'll let you go, Cowboy,' she said, all traces of remorse long gone, 'as soon as you tell me what I want to know.'

'What do you want to know?' I asked, working hard to keep from getting angry.

'*Ev-er-y-thing*,' she answered.

I squirmed, torn between keeping my mouth shut,

breaking free and running, and blurting out everything as fast and as loudly as Big Mouth Brody. I'd been keeping so many secrets – I was dying to tell someone *something*.

I struggled for a moment longer, then threw caution to the Wyoming wind.

'All right, I'll tell you,' I said, preparing to break *all* the rules now, not just the one about staying away from the Cabots. I'd got so good at breaking stuff, why not add a few rules and promises to my list?

Taking a deep breath, I started talking: about me, my uncle, Rocket, the twins, Samson. I skipped over the part about thirteenth birthdays – I didn't want to relive my own – but I still had plenty to tell. I even told her about Eva Mae. Sarah Jane stayed quiet, listening to my words like they were water and she'd just crawled out of the desert.

'My grandma captured the music in that jar,' I told her, nodding in the direction of the white lid nestled in the grass. 'It's full of radio waves she pulled out of the air. There used to be a whole bunch of jars like that. But I broke them all. All but the one you took. That's why

I've got to get it back. It means a lot to my grandpa, and Grandpa's not . . . he's not going to be around much longer.'

I waited for Sarah Jane to roll her eyes and laugh in my face. Or worse, to pull out a brand-new pad of paper and start taking down detailed notes, ready to call the Associated Press and syndicate the story in newspapers across the country. But she didn't do any of these things. Instead, she narrowed her gaze and said slowly:

'Prove it.'

Flashing a quick, wry grin, I canted my head towards the rusty shackles. With a click and a rattle of iron against iron, the antique cuffs slipped from my wrist and slid down the post to land on the ground in pieces. Puffed up with pride at this bit of control, I looked from the busted cuffs to Sarah Jane.

'How was that?'

Sarah Jane prodded the mangled manacles with the toe of one green trainer, kicking at the scattered, twisted links of chain.

'How did you do it?' she asked. *'Precisely.'*

'Precisely?' I shrugged. Then, with a grimace, confessed, 'I – I don't know. Usually it happens when I'm cranky.' But looking at the fallen shackles, I knew it wasn't anger or frustration that had forced the cuffs open. This time, I'd made the choice to do it.

'Cranky?' SJ lifted an eyebrow. 'Judging from the wreckage I've seen, Ledge, you must be the crankiest guy around . . . or the second-crankiest,' she amended with a grimace of her own.

A Cranky Cabot is bad for Sundance. I cringed. I didn't want to be like Noble Cabot.

'I didn't used to be this way,' I muttered, shuffling my feet as I thought back to better days – days *before* I'd turned thirteen. I shrugged again. 'It's not just when I get cranky. Sometimes it happens if I get startled, or hurt. But I think I'm finally getting better at controlling it,' I added quickly, looking again at the busted cuffs.

Sarah Jane squinted at me again; I could see her brain working.

'Do something else!' she commanded.

'I'm not your trick pony!' I snapped.

216

'Those shackles were old. They probably just fell apart,' she snorted. But her face was watchful now – curious – and her eyes never left me for a second.

Without missing a beat, I snorted right back. 'They *did* just fall apart. That's what I do. Haven't you been listening?' The bars of the fence shivered. Was she *trying* to upset me?

Yes, I realized. She was. I'd just told her all the things that triggered me. I breathed in through my nose, held the breath, then let it out slowly, wondering why Sarah Jane had to be so stubborn.

'Do something else,' she repeated. 'Do whatever it is you do again and I promise I'll give you this jar.' We both glanced down at the jar, its familiar white lid blinding in the sun.

'Okay,' I said at last. 'But if I show you one more time, you have to promise not to tell anyone about me or my family and destroy all traces of your humdinger paper. You have to promise! *Really* promise.' I knew I was digging myself deeper into trouble by the second. But for some reason, I couldn't stop shovelling.

'Eyes, needles, death, you got it!' Sarah Jane crossed her heart. When I frowned at her flimsy oath, she crossed her heart again, then put her hands together. 'I promise, Ledge! I do!' Then she asked excitedly, 'What are you going to do this time?'

'Just watch!' I raised my voice in exasperation, but I was more eager now than angry. Now that I wasn't keeping secrets, I wanted to do something cool. I flexed my fingers once or twice and puffed my chest up even more.

What could I do that would really impress SJ?

Something in my gut flip-flopped. At what point had I started wanting to *impress* Sarah Jane? If Josh were here now, he'd be laughing his head off . . . or maybe he'd give me some advice. I was beginning to think girls were as hard to figure out as a new savvy. But Josh understood way more about girls than I did. He knew that Misty Archuleta would like that necklace with the *M* on it before he gave it to her at the planetarium. Remembering that, I got an idea.

Taking another deep breath, I wrapped my hands

round the two closest fence posts and concentrated on the bolts and weldings that held them in place, trying to repeat my recent display of control. Repeat it, and, if possible, improve on it.

In seconds, things began to shift. The iron posts began to move and jerk, bending and twisting the same way the steel bracers of the windmill had done, only less out-of-control crazy. Quickly, I let go and stepped back, realizing that I didn't have to hold on, that I could feel my connection to all the pieces through the earth and the air between me and the fence. I let my vision blur, seeing only the shapes I wanted in the fence, imagining the ants under my skin crawling into the exact same patterns. The broken links of chain from the cuffs jumped at my feet like popcorn, and the spiked posts shimmied and began to snake into new shapes.

When I stepped back to look at my handiwork, the tips of my ears began to burn. Yet Sarah Jane's green eyes were bright as they reflected the twisted metal between us.

'Are those supposed to be my initials?' she asked with a grin.

Cramped and crooked, the letters *S* and *J* were bent into the fence, decorated with contorted curlicues and droopy flower shapes. All the picture needed was a lopsided heart with an arrow stuck through it, and my everlasting embarrassment would be welded in place forever. Half of me wanted to dig a hole and crawl into it. The other half was kinda proud. Crooked or not, I'd love to see Josh top *that*.

Sarah Jane was still smiling. I smiled back. Next to the house, the branches of the birch tree swayed in the breeze, its leaves shimmering like green glass in the sun. If a tree could laugh, I thought, this one was certainly doing it.

As Sarah Jane took a step back from her newly monogrammed fence, she accidentally kicked Grandma Dollop's jar, knocking it on its side. I looked down at the jar through my haze of embarrassment and pride, my brain slow to register what was wrong with the label.

The blocky yellow letters that spelled out *Peter Pan Peanut Butter* were missing. The label on this jar read: *Elmer Mann's Famous Pickled Herring*.

I looked back up at Sarah Jane, dumbfounded.

It wasn't Grandma Dollop's jar at all. This jar didn't contain any radio waves. This jar was full of nothing more magical than the lingering smell of fish.

Chapter 22

I SET MY JAW, THE CALM I'd felt gone. I'd told Sarah Jane everything! I'd broken family rules and embarrassed myself for her. And she'd conned me – *again*. Bent out of shape and seething, I was once again riding the storm on that boat in Aunt Jenny's painting. Only now that I was steering, I'd show Sarah Jane.

The Ledger Kale spectacular wasn't over yet.

Without lifting a finger or saying a word, I raised the fence in a tidal wave of iron, driving the force of my anger round the perimeter. Sarah Jane drew her arms up to shield her face as her initials fell between us, the bars of the fence toppling one after the next.

It was the sound of the screen door crashing that brought me to my senses. Hedda the Horrible stepped out on to the porch, a fireplace ash pan in one hand and a dry mop in the other, looking like she thought armies of aliens might be attacking. As soon as I saw the housekeeper, I reined in my savvy, shutting it down before Hedda could mistake me for an extraterrestrial and clean my clock.

Sarah Jane lowered her arms, running her fingers along a ten-centimetre scrape below her elbow where a fence spike had grazed her skin. The scratch wasn't deep. Not even bleeding. But my mind flashed back to the night of the wedding and the gash left on Fish's face after I destroyed the barn. Rocket had warned me then. He'd told me to be careful.

What use was the control I'd shown today if I couldn't use it to control my own reactions?

I took a step towards Sarah Jane. Her eyes went wide as she looked at me – no, as she looked *past* me.

Behind me a car door slammed shut.

Slowly, I turned. A long black Lincoln was parked

next to the kerb. White-walled tyres pristine. Black exterior spotless. Noble Cabot – red-faced, *cranky* Noble Cabot – was coming towards me.

'What in John Brown's britches is going on here?' he shouted. His eyes followed the line of fallen fence posts, then returned to focus, hawk-like, on me. 'You again!' he shouted. His cane was a jackhammer pummelling the ground. 'I thought I told O'Connell to keep you and everyone else like you away from my daughter!'

Cabot rapped the side of my leg with his cane as he hollered. It didn't hurt. Not really. But it did make me mad. And I couldn't afford to get any angrier than I already was. In hindsight, destroying the fence might not have been the best choice.

'Are you responsible for this . . . this *mess*, young man?' Mr Cabot dropped his voice to a low growl. He pointed his cane at my chest. The movement was so sudden it scared a stream of cuss words out of me. The grill on Cabot's Lincoln shuddered. The rims of the headlamps rattled.

Cabot glanced behind him at the noise. Turning back

to me, he raised his cane even higher, until the tip was a centimetre from my nose. I stared at it cross-eyed. I was caught. Just like one of Elmer Mann's pickled fish.

'Shall I call the sheriff, Mr Cabot?' Hedda the Horrible called from her defensive position on the porch.

'No, Daddy, don't!' cried Sarah Jane, jumping over fallen fence posts to shove her father's cane aside and step between us.

'This doesn't concern you, Sarah Jane. Go inside!'

'It does concern me!' she answered. She pushed her long hair from her face. 'None of this is Ledge's fault. It's – it's . . . it's mine!'

Cabot's whole body convulsed. He took an involuntary step back, a sudden panic painting his features.

I stepped back too, equally surprised.

'What did you say?' Cabot and I asked Sarah Jane at the same time.

'I told you. It's my fault!' SJ stood tall, chin raised. 'I knocked down the fence, Daddy! I-I have secret magical powers that break things. I just look at things and they fall to pieces. Like . . . like this! Watch!'

Mr Cabot turned to face his Lincoln as Sarah Jane held her arms out towards it.

'KA-POW!' she shouted, thrusting out her fingers. Naturally, nothing happened. Sarah Jane took a breath as if she was about to try again. Only this time when she shouted *KA-POW!* she stomped her heel down on my foot.

I bit back a cry as she smashed my toes with her shoe, but I couldn't stop the pain from triggering my savvy – just as she'd known it would. Less than a second after Sarah Jane's second *ka-pow*, the Lincoln's front fender was on the pavement, the radio antenna was an arrow in the sky, and Mr Cabot was ducking to avoid the hubcap that was sailing towards his head.

'See, Daddy?' Sarah Jane crossed her arms, ignoring the way I hopped around behind her. 'I'm *extraordinary*. More extraordinary than anything in that room of yours. You just haven't been paying attention! Y-you should've read my papers!'

'I've read all of your papers, Sarah Jane,' Mr Cabot

answered. 'And I thought I told you not to make those copies at the five-and-dime.' He looked from the fender to the fence posts, then back to his daughter, obviously confused.

Sarah Jane went pale at the mention of the five-and-dime. Her voice went from a whisper to a wail as she stammered, 'I-is that why you foreclosed on Willie's? Because Willie *let me use his copier*?'

'Of course not!' Her father stood up taller. 'I foreclosed because I own his deed and he owed me money!'

Sarah Jane shook her head.

Cabot looked at me, spluttering, 'This – this is your fault!' His face grew mottled and splotchy. I felt mottled and splotchy too. What was SJ *doing*? Why was she taking the credit for my damage instead of handing me over like a trophy to her father? Trying to follow Sarah Jane's thinking was like trying to follow a spinning top down a road full of hairpin turns. Every time I started to think I had her figured out, she'd change direction.

227

'This is your fault,' Cabot repeated, glaring at me again. 'Yours and your uncle's. You don't know how hard I've worked to keep my daughter from becoming like –'

'It's NOT his fault!' Sarah Jane screamed. Having exhausted every last shade of red and purple, Cabot's face went white. He gripped his cane, staring past Sarah Jane. Staring past me. Letting his gaze settle into the high branches of the tree next to the house.

'Hold your tongue, Sarah Jane.' Mr Cabot was no longer shouting, but his voice still held a dangerous, simmering rage. 'You know nothing about what you're saying.'

'You,' he said then, flicking his eyes away from the birch tree to level them again at me. 'Leave now. Or I'll have Hedda call the sheriff to escort you back to . . . back to that *ranch*,' he spat. 'Sarah Jane, go to your room. I have *things* to take care of.' He indicated the jumble of fallen fence posts. '*Lots* of things.' Cabot shot me another dangerous look.

It was a look I didn't like. Not one bit.

I tried to swallow, but my voice was tight with dread.

'Mr Cabot, I –'

'The *SHERIFF*, boy! I WILL CALL THE SHERIFF!' He didn't need to tell me again. I took off running. Away. Fast. Before any more pieces could fall off Cabot's car.

Chapter 23

IF I COULD'VE RUN AND KICKED myself in the head at the same time I would have. The grey matter inside my brain was unravelling, and my eyeballs felt sharp and treacherous, as sharp as the barbed wire that ran between the wooden fence posts along the road outside of Sundance. *Wouldn't my own dad be proud?* I thought as I split town. These days, I was always running. Running *away*. Disconnected and undone, I stumbled and tripped along the road.

A mile outside town, an old slug-bug Volkswagen Beetle full of teenage girls rattled up the road behind me, music cranked and thumping. I jumped as they laid on the horn, and their 2CUTE4U South Dakota licence plate fell off and flip-flopped into the ditch at the same time the rear bumper clattered to the ground. The girls drove on, oblivious. I didn't know if I'd made the bumper fall off, or if the punch buggy was simply ripe and ready for the salvage yard. But I did know that the time for that kind of sloppiness was over. It was just like Rocket said: I couldn't let stuff like that happen any more.

Glancing down at the bumper as I jogged past it, my shoe hit the edge of the pavement wrongly and I twisted my ankle, taking a classic Ledger Kale dive.

Lying on my side until my ankle stopped throbbing, I stared at my reflection in the chrome bumper. It was like looking into a funhouse mirror. But instead of being reflected into infinity as I'd been in the Bug House mirrors, in the bumper I was stretched out and squished – flattened sideways like a pancake. My nose was too long. My eyes bulged and colliding. My mouth a slanted comma.

'What happened to you?' I asked my distorted mirror image. 'Did you get caught in the doors of an elevator?'

No. My reflection shook his head. *Just caught between crazy Sarah Jane Cabot and her father.*

With nobody else there to do it for me, I picked myself up. Testing my ankle, I found that I could put my weight on it without too much pain. I dragged the fallen bumper from the road. Its edges were sharp and it was grimy with dirt and oil. But it was surprisingly light.

I hefted the unwieldy bumper over my head.

Then I clanged it down against the nearest wooden fence post.

Over and over, I smashed metal against wood, feeling the sharp edges of the chrome bite into my flesh and the vibrations in the metal ripple up my arms. I roared like a knight swinging a broadsword, fighting the windmills of frustration, venting my anger without unleashing my savvy for the first time since my birthday. Why couldn't I have done that back at SJ's? Why have control now, when I didn't even need it?

I thought about the way Sarah Jane had tricked me, and the way she hadn't ratted me out to her father. I also thought about the way her hair looked all loose and jumbled in the wind – shiny and wild. Thinking about Sarah Jane made my head a mess. But I found that as long as I pictured the bumper staying strong and straight, the thing didn't twist or bend, no matter how much I raged.

When I couldn't lift the bumper one more time, I dropped it.

Absolute silence had fallen around me as the earth waited for me to finish my tantrum. Then, as though some silent word sped out across the landscape that I'd run out of strength at last, a cricket chirped and the hum and drone of insects returned. Birds chittered back and forth like television news anchors reporting from the scene. Somewhere close by, a prairie dog barked out small, rodent alerts, warning its friends that there was a lunatic kid on the loose.

Behind me, someone cleared his throat.

'That's some progress, I suppose. At least the barbed wire's still intact.'

I turned my head slowly. Across the road, Rocket leaned against the side of his truck, arms crossed, one eyebrow raised. I hadn't heard his old F-1 arrive, or the

233

squeaky sound of the truck's door opening or closing. I wondered how long my cousin had been watching me.

A trio of noisy motorcycles sped up the road between us. Rocket rubbed his shaggy beard with one thumb, gazing after the bikes as they passed into the distance. Then he turned his electric-blue stare back at me and I guessed that I was done for. I might've been better off if Hedda the Horrible had called the sheriff to come and lock me up.

'So. Got it all out yet?' Rocket asked, his voice surprisingly calm, like he was asking me if I was done throwing up. Stomach churning, I thought I might start. Before my cousin had the chance to electrocute me on the spot, I rose to my feet and tried to make a break for it.

'Ledge!' I heard him call as I stumbled up the road on my sore ankle. 'Ledger! Hold up!' I already knew what Rocket thought of me. I wasn't going to stop now just so he could say it to my face.

But I did stop – *fast* – when a crack of blue sparks lit the air, and a single serrated line of electricity blocked my path in a lingering bolt, cutting through the air in

234

front of me and hanging there, filling my ears with static and making my hair stand on end. I turned to break left, and another crackling blue current reined me back. In every direction I turned, Rocket constructed a grid of jagged, glowing lines, boxing me into his very own savvy-powered electric fence.

'LET ME GO!' I dropped to my knees. 'Just let me go!' My shoulders slumped and began to shake. I didn't want my cousin to see me cry, but tears dripped down my nose before I could stop them.

As soon as Rocket let his electric snare drop with a sizzling hiss, I tried to make another break for it, scrabbling feebly on hands and knees. Exhausted, I didn't stand a chance.

'Ledger, just stop,' Rocket said as he grabbed the collar of my shirt, dragging me backwards and holding fast. I struggled, shouting wordlessly until Rocket got me pinned, one arm wrapped round my neck in a half-brotherly, half-nelson kind of way.

'I told Autry I'd find you and bring you back,' he said, not letting go. 'What happened, Ledge? Why'd

235

you take off like that? You're always running!' He shifted his grip on me, but didn't let go. 'Look, I don't care if you and Sarah Jane Cabot are pen pals – I don't care if the two of you are planning a trip to Mars to get married – but if Autry knew, he *would* care. It was a good thing I got the mail today, even if I did take out a transformer. There would've been some dark swarms over the ranch if Autry had seen –'

'That's not it,' I cut him off. 'I didn't take off because of the mail. I mean, that was part of it, but I . . . I . . .'

'You . . . you . . . what?'

'I know what you think of me,' I spluttered. The conversation I'd overheard inside the conservatory still stung. I swiped drips of sweat and snot from the end of my nose before blurting, 'You think I'll never learn to scumble!'

'What're you talking about, Ledge?' Rocket huffed.

'I heard you!' I shouted at him. 'I heard you talking with Uncle Autry in the Bug House. You said this boy will never learn.'

'What? You idiot!' Rocket rubbed his knuckles hard

236

into my scalp, then released me abruptly. He settled down in the dirt next to me, running both hands through his hair with a crackle of static.

'I wasn't talking about *you*, numbskull! I was talking about me.'

'You?' I stared at Rocket as his words sank in.

'Yes, me.' Rocket held his hands up in fists, then thrust all of his fingers straight. Ten thin fountains of sparkling blue electricity plumed from his fingertips, each sparking jet towering a half-dozen metres or more into the air before subsiding again with a sharp snap.

'Autry sent me into town to get the mail and I took out the power for five blocks around the post office! I'm a human firework, Ledge.'

'Yeah, but you're . . . *cool*.'

'Y'think?' my cousin snorted. 'I've done my share of damage, believe me. And not just to the Sundance post office after seeing mail arrive for you from a Cabot. I've made a mess out of power grids from Mississippi to Kansas. I can't even begin to tell you how many light bulbs I've blown apart since the day my savvy hit. My momma used to keep a dustpan in every room in the house. I nearly thought I killed my poppa once, and I –' Rocket stopped. I watched him curl his hands back into tight fists. 'I really *did* hurt someone else once, Ledge,' he said, then added quickly, 'Unintentionally, of course. Not on purpose. Not ever. I wouldn't do that. But still, I hurt someone I cared about.' He rubbed the back of his left hand as if the memory of someone else's pain burned him there. I hung my head, thinking of the mark the flying fence posts had left on Sarah Jane.

'I hurt someone too,' I said, my voice barely a whisper.

'I know you didn't mean to hurt Fish, Ledger,' Rocket tried to reassure me. 'I've been trying to talk to you about that for weeks.'

I hung my head lower yet. The gouge I'd left on my cousin had been an accident; I hadn't meant to destroy the barn and send all that shrapnel flying. But back at the Cabots', when SJ got hurt, I'd been angry. I'd been trying to make an impression. Just not *that* kind of impression.

'Who did you hurt?' I asked Rocket tentatively. 'Were you a kid when you did it?' Sitting in the dirt next to me, Rocket rested his elbows against his knees, once again rubbing his thumb absentmindedly against his beard. Behind the scruff, his face looked pained.

'It was a long time ago,' he answered. 'But I was still old enough to know better. I was showing off . . . for a girl.' He rolled his eyes, but the corner of his mouth turned up a little in an embarrassed half-smile. I squirmed.

'All this time, I thought you hated me,' I said, glancing nervously at my cousin.

'Hated you?'

'Yeah. I kind of thought you wanted to kill me.'

Rocket grimaced. 'Sorry, Ledge. I didn't realize I was making you that uncomfortable. It's been hard to watch you struggle.'

'So, does anything help you not *zap* stuff?' I asked, feeling braver now that I knew Rocket had no immediate plans to electrocute me.

Rocket snorted. 'Apparently, hiding. At least, that's

what our uncle claims I'm doing by living on the ranch so long.' He picked up a twig and began breaking it into pieces, tossing them over his shoulder one by one. 'I guess it runs in the family.'

'What? Hiding?'

'Haven't seen too much of Samson since you got here, have you?' Rocket raised his eyebrows.

'No . . . because he's invisible.'

'Sure. But he doesn't have to be. In fact, I think the whole world's better – stronger – when he joins in. Just look at Grandpa Bomba! It's like he's ten years younger whenever my brother casts a shadow next to him. When he actually shows up . . .' Rocket whistled and trailed off. I wasn't entirely certain what he meant, but I felt better knowing that I'd seen Samson after all, that I hadn't been imagining things.

'So why doesn't Samson just stay visible all the time?'

Rocket considered for a long time before answering. 'It can take a lot of strength to show up and be yourself . . . don't you think?'

I shrugged, not sure what I thought. I'd spent the last years trying to show up and be the kid my dad wanted me to be. Rubbing my sore ankle, I frowned, noticing how worn-down the tread on my shoes had become. It was no wonder I'd slipped and tripped. Maybe it was time to slow down a little. Or put on a different pair of shoes.

I laughed once – a short, sharp burst of air through my nose. 'I run. You and Samson hide. We're like outlaws,' I said. 'Fugitives.'

'Fugitives,' Rocket repeated. 'That sounds about right. Ever on the run from our own savvy talents.' Rocket smiled and punched my arm, careful not to shock me. It was the first real smile he'd given me since I'd arrived in Wyoming, but the expression was short-lived. His face grew dark as he looked up the road beyond me, his voice dropping to a low growl.

'I think we outlaws and fugitives had better keep our cool, Ledge, 'cuz it looks like the sheriff is headed this way.'

Chapter 24

WATCHING JONAS BROWN'S TRUCK APPROACHING FAST, I scrambled to my feet and stood next to Rocket, wondering if Mr Cabot had called the sheriff after all.

Sheriff Brown pulled over when he saw us, his truck repaired – door skilfully reattached. Stepping out of it, the sheriff placed a straw Stetson on his head, straightened his sunglasses, and hitched his gun belt higher. I half expected to hear the clink of spurs on pavement as he moved towards us.

'You fellas all right?' Brown asked. 'Is there a problem here?'

'Everything's swell, Sheriff,' Rocket answered, sounding overly chipper as he shoved both hands into his pockets. 'Right, Ledge?' He bumped me with his elbow and I nodded.

'I thought I told you to fix the brake on that old rust-bucket of yours, son.' Sheriff Brown pulled his sunglasses down his nose and peered over them at Rocket.

'Not a problem, Sheriff,' Rocket replied, pulling one hand from his pocket to point over his shoulder. 'My truck's not going anywhere, sir.'

'Have you told that to your truck?' Brown tilted his head down the road. The old Ford was already fifteen metres away and gaining ground, wandering off like Bitsy in search of a better spot of shade.

'Whoa! Get back here, you!' Rocket shouted, giving chase. Catching up to the truck, Rocket jogged alongside it. He leaped on to the truck's running board. The truck rolled faster. Even from a distance I could hear Rocket cuss as he tugged on the sticky door handle.

The truck veered right, towards the steep irrigation ditch next to the road. Rocket gave up on the handle.

243

He hoisted himself head first through the open window, struggling to get both shoulders into the narrow opening. I could hear the steel of the truck humming in my ears, mumbling rusty secrets.

'The cable's busted,' I said aloud, my voice sounding like it came from someone else – someone older.

'Might be.' Brown nodded. 'It could also be a rusted actuator.'

'No. It's the cable,' I insisted, not having a clue how I knew it. It was the same feeling I got whenever I helped Winona with the Knucklehead – I could see the problem clearly in my mind. The cable was definitely busted. Rocket needed to turn himself round. He needed to get his boot down on the footbrake fast, or the Ford was going to flip down the bank of the ditch. And if the truck rolled, Rocket was going to roll with it. He'd get crushed. Or drown in slow-moving water. Trapped beneath tons of steel.

'Rocket! Son! Get out of there!' the sheriff shouted, suddenly seeing the same fatal future. I yelled too. But Rocket didn't hear.

Sheriff Brown made tracks. He ran after the truck like his gone-to-jelly muscles had the strength to stop it.

If only Marisol and Mesquite were here! They might have lifted the truck up and set it down someplace safer. Or Autry! He could've built a barricade of bugs, or instructed spiders to spin a safety net over the water.

The sheriff would never get to Rocket in time. I couldn't either, no matter how fast I ran. I squeezed my eyes shut. All I could do was wish and hope and pray the truck's brake cable would fix itself.

The squeal of tyres made me open my eyes – just in time to see the truck lurch to a stop at the edge of the ditch.

Letting out all the breath I'd been holding, I watched Rocket pull himself the rest of the way into his truck, twisting to get himself right side up in the driver's seat. I jogged quickly to join the sheriff, ignoring the stiffness in my ankle. Sheriff Brown was already busy chewing Rocket up and spitting him back out. Behind the wheel, my cousin sank lower in his seat with every word. Eventually, Brown finished shouting, saying, 'You go

245

straight to Neary's place right now, son. No detours! I don't want to see this truck on the road again until it's fixed!'

'Yes, sir,' Rocket answered. 'Neary's. Got it.'

Rocket held tight to the steering wheel, letting the truck idle at the side of the road as he watched the sheriff leave. Then he turned the Ford round and headed for Neary's Auto Salvage Acres, one thumb tapping anxiously against the wheel as he glanced from the brake lever to me.

Still tense after the near-accident, neither of us spoke. As Rocket drove up the road, the wind carried the smell of sun-warmed sage and cowpats through the truck's open windows. It billowed hot air through our hair, and puffed up our T-shirts like balloons. Soon we both began to relax.

The interior of Rocket's old Ford was plain. Like the exterior, he hadn't done much to fix it up. He'd added a couple of rubber floor mats and a rubber steering wheel cover – simple precautions lacking free electrons to help protect the truck from any electric outbursts. But the only personal item inside the truck was a single faded photograph stuck to the dashboard.

The picture was old. Bent. Faded by the sun. The girl in the photo was pretty, with hair a darker shade of blonde than Sarah Jane's and a fringe that hung low over her eyes. The girl's smile, frozen in time, was playful and snarky, like she'd been joking around when the picture was taken.

'Is that the same girl who . . . you know? The girl you mentioned before?' I asked, nodding at the photo. I thought she might be the same girl in the photograph on his wall back at the ranch – the one with the gum bubble in front of her face. Looking down at the photo, Rocket drummed his thumb faster against the wheel. Then he pulled the picture off the dash, leaving a pink nugget behind; Rocket had used a chewed-up piece of bubblegum to stick the photo to the dash.

My cousin stared at the picture in his hand for the length of a heartbeat. Then, folding it once, he stuck it in his pocket and nodded, not taking his eyes off the road.

'Yeah, that's her.' He answered lightly, but I didn't miss the way his hands gripped the steering wheel even tighter.

'So . . . what happened?'

'It was a stupid mistake, Ledge, that's all.' At first I thought that he wasn't going to say anything more. Then the words started spilling.

'I went back home after my first few months here. I was still a teenager – though barely – and I was sure I'd got a handle on my savvy. Bobbi said –'

'Wait,' I said. 'Bobbi? You mean Will Meeks's sister?'

He shrugged. 'Technically, his aunt. But that's another story. Do you want to hear this one, or not?'

I zipped my lip.

'Anyway, Bobbi said she wished she could know what it was like to be able to harness lightning or shoot sparks. We'd known each other for a while – we dated – so she knew all about our family and what I could do.

'We were goofing around and I was feeling indestructible, forgetting that she wasn't. I thought I could show off. I thought I could handle my savvy well enough to

248

pass a bit of electricity from my hand through hers – you know, to let her shoot a few sparks of her own . . .' He trailed off, once more rubbing the back of his left hand.

'Did it work?'

The muscles in his jaw tightened. 'Oh, Bobbi shot sparks all right. She also got burned. Badly. She could've been killed.'

Thinking of SJ's arm, I wondered, 'Did she forgive you?'

Rocket took his time before answering. 'Yeah. She forgave me. She even tried to convince me it was half her fault. But I've never forgiven myself. After that, I figured her life might be better if I kept myself out of it. We've both moved on.'

Maybe Bobbi's moved on, I thought, looking at my cousin. But Rocket's still anchored in place.

My cousin was quiet again until we reached the salvage yard. But instead of turning immediately on to the access road to Neary's, he pulled the truck over and parked in front of the foreclosure sign, killing the engine.

Rocket turned in his seat and looked at me with a sigh.

'My mom paints.'

'Uh . . . yeah. I know,' I said. 'Your mom sent me a painting for my birthday.' Aunt Jenny was perfect and had been since the day she'd turned thirteen. The last thing I'd *ever* be was perfect. Why was Rocket telling me this now?

My cousin must have sensed my confusion.

'Did you know that the word *scumble* is a painting term, Ledge?'

I shook my head.

'Momma could explain it to you better,' he went on. 'But the way I understand it, scumbling is a technique painters use to tone down a colour so bright it jumps right off the canvas – so intense it takes over – making it hard to notice anything else about the painting. Scumbling doesn't get rid of that bright colour – it blends it better with the rest of the picture. It evens everything out. That way the painting feels more balanced.'

'Balanced?' I echoed. Rocket chuckled.

'Do you feel very balanced right now, Ledge? Or

250

does your savvy feel like it's going to take over? Like it's too intense to let you pay attention to anything else?'

I nodded, starting to understand.

'Think about it like this,' he went on, growing animated. 'If you compare scumbling a painting with scumbling a savvy, you have to imagine that *you* are the painting, the *whole* painting. The people and the world around you are not the painting. Scumbling is not about *you* trying to fit in with the rest of the world; it's about making your *savvy* fit in better with *you*. It's simply learning to balance all the different parts of yourself so that you don't let the one thing that feels most out-of-control take over and rule your life. Get it?'

'Simply?' I snorted. 'Did you really just say *simply*?' I raised an eyebrow at my cousin. Rocket caught my expression and laughed out loud. The sound filled the truck's cab and spilled out of the open windows.

'I suppose I'm the last person on the planet who should be giving you the "scumble talk", Ledge.' Rocket sighed. 'I'm just passing along what I've been told. What

I've been told over . . . and over . . . and *over* again.' As he said it, Rocket radiated a faint blue glow, painting everything inside the truck's cab blue as well – even the dried-up bit of bubblegum that was fixed to the dash like a hardened memory he'd never fully prise loose.

Chapter 25

SCOWLING PAST THE FORECLOSURE SIGN, ROCKET steered the truck into the salvage yard. But when Winona stepped out of the shop, he hit the brakes. Winona wore her grey-green overalls, as usual. She also had on a pair of heavy leather gloves and a welding mask tipped back on her head. I grinned. Fedora would've appreciated the safety gear.

'That's not Gus,' Rocket said as he watched Winona remove her gloves, his thumb now tapping a rapid short-long-short, Morse code SOS against the steering wheel. After learning about Bobbi, I understood why Rocket stayed so shy. From things Mom and Uncle Autry had said, I knew Rocket had been brushing off goggling girls for years. Even so, I guessed that Winona was like no girl Rocket had ever met.

'Gus is in Vegas,' I told him as I opened my door. 'That's Winona, Gus's daughter. Don't worry, she knows her stuff.'

'What? Ledger, wait!'

But I was already out of the truck.

'Hey, Ledge.' Winona met me with a grimy motor-oil high five. 'Decided not to run here today? Got your own chauffeur and limo now?' Pulling off her welding mask and tucking it under her arm, she winked at me, then thumped her hand against the Ford's side panel like she was greeting a giant dog. Still sitting inside the truck, Rocket was slow to join us, pulling on the stubborn door latch several times before it opened. Winona pursed her lips and raised an eyebrow as she watched him climb out of the ancient pick-up.

'Ledge says you're Gus's daughter?' Rocket gaped and gawped like he'd spent the last eight years in outer space.

'I'm Winona. Winona Neary,' she introduced herself with a crisp nod.

'Nice to . . . er, pleased to . . . uh –' Rocket struggled to choke out a proper how-d'ya-do. Elbowing him in the ribs, I coughed an instruction to him behind my fist: '*Your name!*'

'Rocket Beaumont!' he blurted, holding out a hand. Then, thinking better of it, he jammed his hand into his pocket. 'I'm Ledger's cousin. I-I didn't know Gus had any kids.'

Winona tilted her head to one side. 'I don't suppose Pops knows everything there is to know about you either, Mr Rocket Beaumont. Does he?' Rocket brushed at the front of his shirt with his free hand, trying to mask the way static electricity pulled it into crazy wrinkles. It was a relief to know that when Rocket got embarrassed, his savvy went haywire too.

'The sheriff told us to bring Rocket's truck here to get it fixed,' I explained. 'The emergency brake's busted.'

'Rolling away, is she?' Winona smiled.

'*She* almost rolled right over Rocket,' I answered,

smiling back. As Winona turned her back on us to look inside the truck, Rocket tucked in his shirt and tried to smooth his fork-in-socket hair.

Heat rippled the air above the salvage yard, making the place look distorted and unreal. In all my visits, I still hadn't worked up the nerve to explore the acres beyond the steel building. But after the day I'd been having, sailing through a sea of abandoned clunkers sounded positively relaxing. At least in there, the wreckage wouldn't be my fault.

'Wanna help me check out the truck, Ledge?' Winona's voice made me turn. But seeing Rocket's eyes still stuck to her like glue, I shook my head.

'No, thanks. I think I'll wander a bit – someplace less crowded.'

'Ready to check out the yard at last? Just remember: *You fix it, you buy it!*' Winona laughed. The salvage yard 'policy' had become a regular joke between us. 'You wander, Ledge. Your cousin and I will see if we can fix this old thing.'

'Check the spark plugs too!' I called over my shoulder, heading for the nearest path into the ocean of rusted cars and trucks. 'I don't think Rocket's engine is firing on all cylinders!'

Grinning, I ignored the single blue spark that missed my right ear by barely a centimetre. Then, taking a deep breath, I joined the rest of the wrecks.

As I moved deeper into the salvage yard I felt my palms warm and my fingertips buzz. Around me, steel and chrome shuddered and shivered. But I kept moving forward; one foot, then the other.

'Come on, Ledge, this isn't so bad,' I said out loud, my voice echoing across aluminium and glass. 'What are you afraid of anyway?'

The path twisted and I followed it round towards the back of the steel building. Stepping into a small clearing, I leaped back as I came face-to-face with an enormous, skeletal creature with eyes like headlamps and claws like pitchforks.

Real pitchforks.

Real headlamps too.

It was a sculpture. A bear-shaped, two-metre-tall sculpture built from bits taken from the salvage yard – scrap and car parts and other discards, recycled and reconfigured into something new. Something totally cool.

Looking around, I saw two more sculptures: a tortoise the size of a tank, with a shell of welded hub cabs; and a lion with a radiating mane of wheel spokes, radio antennae and metal dowels. On close inspection, I found the initials *WN* engraved on to the foot of each monster.

Winona was right when she said that there was more here than meets the eye. Someone at Neary's Auto Salvage Acres was more than *she* appeared. It made me even more curious what might be under the tarp back inside the repair bay. The shape was big enough to be a woolly mammoth.

I tried moving away from the metal beasts, back into the heart of the salvage yard. But Winona's creations wouldn't leave my mind.

'One more look,' I said to myself – three, four, *five*

times – returning to the clearing again and again to admire the way the sculptures had been put together. Thinking of the windmill and the fence posts I'd bent and twisted into less artful shapes, I wondered if I could learn to create instead of destroy.

Wanting to try, I found a spot away from the steel building – away from Winona's creatures – climbing up on to the bow of a rusted, tilting motorboat to get a better view of the materials around me.

'You can do this, Ledge,' I told myself, then called up every bit of savvy energy I could, recalling the sensation of the ants in their icy football studs, inviting each and every one to come on out to play.

It didn't take long before the wrecks around me began to shake. Cars and trucks began collapsing into pieces, and the boat rocked to and fro beneath me. I tried to keep my balance – I tried not to freak and run.

'Bricka bracka firecracker!' I called out Fedora's silly rah-rah cartoon cheer, trying to keep myself pumped up as pistons, carburettors and hubcaps jumped, and bumpers and nozzles jerked and spun.

'Bricka bracka – *yow*!' I hollered, ducking a flying transaxle. Then I leaped straight up with a 'Bracka . . . bricka – *whoa*!' avoiding the wheel spinning towards my shins. Sticking my landing on the boat's wobbling bow, I yelled, 'Oh yeah! Sis boom – *booyah*!' feeling kick-butt, ninja-action awesome.

Marisol and Mesquite had nothing on me. My lessons with them were *over*. I'd get to go home someday after all.

'Okay, Ledge,' I said, still trying to keep every rocking, spinning thing secure inside my savvy grip. 'You've got all the pieces. Now what're you going to *do* with them?'

A dozen different images rolled through my mind too fast to hold on to. The scrap heap rose in waves just as fast. Churning into a giant glass and metal whirlpool with me at its centre. Creating a hullabaloo loud enough to wake the dead. I imagined ol' Eva Mae Ransom rolling over in her golden grave at the sound – or her spirit standing next to me, cheering her own ghosty, spirited '*Sis boooo bah!*'

'Did ya have fun?' Rocket asked.

'Oh, yeah,' I answered, wiping the sweat from my face with the back of my arm, feeling like I'd just run an entire savvy half-marathon on my own. I batted at the dragonfly hovering near me.

'That would be Autry looking for us.' Rocket nodded towards the bug. 'He's probably worried. There are going to be spiderwebs and anthills everywhere when we get back.'

'Did Winona fix the brake?' I asked.

Rocket chuckled. 'She fixed the door latches. Didn't need to do a thing to the brake. She said it had already been repaired. Recently. Like, *today*, maybe?' He grinned. 'I see you're good at putting things together, Ledge, not just tearing them apart.'

'You think *I* fixed the truck?' I asked.

'Are you kidding? After the show you just put on – who else? Someone stopped the truck from going over in the ditch, and it wasn't me.' Rocket laughed again. 'Your new mechanic friend showed me the Knucklehead you've been helping her rebuild. Dude! She thinks you're some kind of genius!' Rocket grabbed my arm and pulled me towards him, grinding his knuckles into my scalp. 'But you're the knucklehead, Ledge. Seriously. Who would've guessed that pulling things apart was only the first *piece* of your savvy?'

'Not me.' I shook my head and laughed along with Rocket.

'Winnie's bringing the truck out now.' Rocket released me as he nodded towards the repair bay. 'I know you're stoked, but try to reel yourself in a bit until we're in the clear, okay? If Winnie hadn't had the radio on and her head buried in the truck inside the garage, she would've seen what a genius you *really* are.'

'*Winnie?*' I asked, still too super-charged to settle down. 'She's *Winnie* now?' I goaded my cousin, directing a mass of lug nuts into the shape of a heart at his feet.

'All right, all right.' Rocket went red as he kicked away the lug nuts. 'I know you're a happy camper now, Ledge. But don't push your luck.' As soon as Winona brought the truck out, Rocket shoved me into it, giving me one zinger of a zap as I got in.

'So, pick me up at seven?' Winona smiled as she leaned into Rocket's window.

'Seven?' Rocket repeated, the colour draining from his face.

'I thought we had a deal: I check the brake line on your truck, you take me out for dinner in Gillette.' Wiping her hands on the rag from her pocket, Winona winked at me. 'Ledge, make sure your cousin's here by seven.'

'You got it – *Winnie*.'

Rocket shot me a look. Driving back to the ranch, he gripped the steering wheel like a life preserver, yet he whistled all the way. He was happy. We both were.

But as we neared the towering steel sign of the Flying Cattleheart, Rocket's whistled tune died on his lips and he cussed, slamming on the brakes. Seeing what stopped him, I cussed too. Just inside the towering gate, a large red-and-white sign stood staked into the ground.

FORECLOSURE

A workman hoisted a post hole digger into the back of a CAD Co. truck, just finishing up his dirty work. Three metres away, Noble Cabot leaned against the hood of his Lincoln, tapping the earth with his cane. Looking at the sign . . . and smiling.

Chapter 26

I HADN'T TOLD ROCKET ABOUT WRECKING Mr Cabot's fence, or about anything else that had happened just before he'd found me outside Sundance. I didn't say a word to Uncle Autry either. After seeing the foreclosure sign, I didn't have the nerve to spill my guts – in case my uncle decided to feed them to his carnivorous beetles.

'I don't understand, Ledge!' Fedora cried as I stood in the middle of the river, scrubbing up before supper, Bitsy splashing in the water nearby. Still caked in dirt from her daily outing with the twins, Fe stood on the riverbank, her face scrunched in confusion.

'Ledge! Tell me what that big sign means.'

'It means Uncle Autry's going to lose this place!' I hollered over the sound of the river, trying not to aim my anger at my sister. 'It means the ranch is going to belong to someone else soon if Autry can't pay up.' I looked down at Bitsy, who stood, one paw up, balancing easily on two of her three legs as she tried to lick a crayfish. 'Then every last one of us defective misfits will be out of luck,' I murmured to the dog.

'Well, that's not going to happen!' Fedora crowed, her oversized motorcycle helmet making her look like an upside-down exclamation mark. 'Not if me and Marisol and Mesquite can help it!'

That night, dinner round the campfire was a sombre event. The evening sky was overcast, threatening rain. The fire barely crackled and never reached rip-roaring. I kept quiet about my triumphs at the salvage yard, wanting to draw as little attention to myself as possible, even though *not* telling was like trying to hold burning firecrackers between my teeth. But I knew it wasn't coincidence that made Cabot put up his foreclosure sign that day. Autry had told me to stay away from Sarah

Jane and her father, and I hadn't listened. I may have fixed Rocket's truck and been the hotshot of the salvage yard, but my successes were nothing in the face of my breach of Autry's trust . . . and the consequences.

Compared to the foreclosure, the fact that Cabot had recycled Grandma Dollop's peanut-butter jar should've felt trivial. Soon Noble Cabot would have every marvel on the ranch to do with as he pleased. But as I looked at Grandpa, slumped and weary in his chair, my pangs of remorse cut deeper yet. Fedora's old football helmet full of jar lids rested in their place on his lap, the lids catching and reflecting the dull campfire flames like they still had some magic buried somewhere inside them. But all those lids were now reminders – reminders of what had been lost. Of what had been destroyed. Maybe Gypsy had been right about me. Maybe I was an artist – a *con* artist.

Everyone moped around the fire. Marisol and Mesquite showed little interest in their lentil burgers, and Gypsy's gaze was faraway, watching the skies over her brother's house. The heavy clouds provided the perfect cover for Rocket to let loose; I imagined that the town of Sundance would talk for years about that night's electrical storm. Even knowing now that things between Rocket and me had changed – that I could sleep soundly in his house for the first time in weeks – the jagged forks of lightning made me flinch.

Twenty minutes after Rocket's storm finally ended, he joined us by the campfire. Autry looked up with an exclamation of surprise. And despite everything, a smile spread slowly across his face.

Rocket had shaved his beard and tamed his spiky hair as best he could, revealing a smooth face with a strong jaw and the good looks my mom had scolded him for hiding. He'd exchanged his wrinkled T-shirt for a crisp western one. And instead of cologne, my cousin reeked of Static Guard – a whole can of it, I guessed.

Gypsy raised a dimpled smile towards her brother. 'Now the whole world can see you, Rocket!' Rocket's newly shaven face bloomed in shades of red. Uncle Autry reset his own expression to neutral to keep from scaring Rocket back into hiding. But he couldn't keep the corners of his mouth from twitching as he asked:

'What's with the best bib and tucker, son? We're not having a funeral for this place yet.'

Rocket crossed, then uncrossed his arms, looking uncomfortable in his stiff shirt. 'I'm just going out for a while.'

'Out?'

Rocket cleared his throat, looking sharply at me before answering, 'I have a date.'

Crickets chirped.

Embers popped.

Then, 'Yes!' Startling us all, Uncle Autry jumped from his stump and cheered, filling the air with a swirl of dusty moths and a frenzy of shimmering, flying things. Autry swept Gypsy off her stump into a spinning jig. 'Your brother's going out, Gypsy. Out on a date!' Autry sang as they hopped and skipped around the fire.

The twins dropped their untouched food and got in on the act, whooping and spinning plates and cups into the air above us, clashing and crashing silverware together to make as much noise as they could. Hobbled by guilt, I didn't join in.

Soon, my uncle sat back down to catch his breath, still smiling. Just then, no one would have guessed that Autry O'Connell was a man walking a plank, moving closer and closer to the edge of losing everything.

'Thanks, man.' Autry held out a hand to Rocket. 'We needed something to make us smile.'

Even if I'd wanted more scumbling lessons from the twins in the following days, I wouldn't have got them. The morning after the sign went up, Marisol and Mesquite began disappearing with Fedora early and returning home late, all three coming back head to toe in dirt just before dark. Whatever the girls were doing, they were tripling their efforts.

'Can I help?' I asked at breakfast two days later, absentmindedly tying knots in the tops of all the nails protruding from the picnic table, which I'd recently helped Autry and Rocket put back together.

'No, you can't,' Marisol answered, not looking at me.

'You can help *me*, Ledge,' Gypsy offered. 'I'm in charge of watching the Queen Alexandra's Birdwings today while Uncle Autry goes into town.' Her face sparkled as she went on. 'They've nearly all emerged! Mostly males. But we're hoping the rest are female. Autry says the Alexandras don't usually breed in captivity. They need special plants. But if he can manage it, it could mean big things for the ranch, for the butterflies . . . for everyone! People need to see them! This world is so much better with them in it!' Gypsy kept talking, but I quickly stopped listening, getting up to look for my uncle instead. Autry hadn't joined us at the table.

I found him by his truck.

'You're going into town?' I asked.

'To see if I can talk to Noble,' he answered, his face drawn, all traces of cheeriness gone. I knew I had to tell him about the fence before he saw it for himself, or heard about it from Noble Cabot. I'd wanted to tell him for the last two days; the truth was eating away at me like termites. But for two days, I hadn't found the courage. And I wasn't finding it any better now.

273

'Y-you're going to SJ's? I-I mean, to Cabot's house?'

Autry shook his head. 'I'm going to his office.'

'That CAD Company place?' I asked, trying to swallow.

My uncle turned to look at me, reaching out to grip my shoulder hard. The gravel around his boots shifted and dozens of fat earthworms wriggled up out of the soil, all wiggling and waggling like scolding fingers, while a spider worked busily, building a web in the open window of the truck.

'Ledger. Please tell me you haven't been back to Sundance! Tell me you've followed my *one* rule and stayed away from the Cabots.'

I shuffled my feet. The morning sun wasn't yet hot and I hadn't gone for a run, but sweat still trickled down my spine.

'I-I haven't put a shoe inside their house. Just like I promised,' I answered, feeling lower than the worms at my uncle's feet.

Autry squinted at me, then nodded.

274

'Good boy,' he said. 'Keep that promise!' Releasing my shoulder, he slapped me on the back. The earthworms retreated, though the spider kept on spinning. And I was left wondering more than ever what the trouble between Cabot and my uncle might be.

'What's Mr Cabot's problem, anyway?' I asked as Autry climbed into the truck. I hadn't been able to get Sarah Jane out of my mind since I last saw her, or stop worrying about what might've happened after she took credit for my destruction.

'Did you turn fire ants loose at a Cabot family picnic or something? Or is this some old family feud?' I asked, plying my uncle with questions. 'Did Eva Mae Ransom refuse to share her gold with Noble's great-great-great-great-grandfather? Or does Cabot really just not like anyone who's different? He can't even know *how* different we really are!'

Autry hesitated before starting up the truck. He opened his mouth to speak, then closed it again as he watched his truck's radio antenna twist and bend – as he saw it shift from a corkscrew, to a pretzel, to a hook-like question mark as I held my ground. Instantly, I stopped my careless sculpting, realizing that I'd just shown precisely why Noble Cabot might know about – and dislike – our differences.

Uncle Autry turned the key in the ignition, making the engine roar and the spiderweb in his window shiver.

'Just keep your promise, Ledger,' he repeated. 'Stay out of Cabot's business!'

Chapter 27

WHEN AUTRY RETURNED TO THE RANCH, the lines in his face were etched deeper than they'd been before he left. Mr Cabot had refused to speak to him. Instead, he'd instructed two of his workmen to escort my uncle out of the CAD Co. building and back to his truck.

The next day, Autry left his beetle bolo tie behind and put on a proper suit and tie, headed to the bank, hoping to borrow enough to pay off what he owed.

'Cabot loaned Autry the money to build the conservatory after the twins were born and Autry's wife died,' Rocket had explained when we first saw the foreclosure sign. 'But Cabot's beef isn't only with Autry. It's bigger than that. He thinks he's protecting Sarah Jane.' Rocket snorted as he said it. He obviously knew more than he was saying. But when I continued to press him, all he said was: 'Wounded animals can be dangerous, Ledge. Some wounded people can be too.' He gave me an apologetic grimace. 'Listen to Autry, don't get too close to Cabot.'

No one needed to ask Autry how it went at the bank. He hadn't even parked his truck before dark swarms began hovering over the ranch. Autry sank into an uncharacteristic funk, disappearing into the conservatory for hours at a time, sometimes not coming out until well after dark. We found mealworms in our cereal and cicadas in our socks. The honeybees were lethargic. The lightning bugs didn't light. Even the grasshoppers wouldn't hop; they just sat, sluggish, in the grass.

Calls from Mom and Dad went straight to Autry's voicemail. So did those from Aunt Jenny and Uncle Abram. Uncle Autry battled a case of mule-headed pride, hoping to fix his foreclosure problems on his own, knowing that no one in the family was in high cotton.

I didn't mind that Autry never answered his phone. I hadn't gone for a run since the foreclosure sign went up. I told myself I needed to rest my twisted ankle. But in truth, I needed to figure some things out. I wasn't ready yet to tell my dad that I was building some new ideas for my future.

Fedora and I would probably be going home soon. I guessed Mom and Dad would come pick us up as soon as they found out about the foreclosure, whether they thought I'd learned something about scumbling or not. I was pretty sure I had enough control now not to wreck the van. Maybe, if I kept practising, I'd be able to go back to school in the autumn as well. But I couldn't help but wonder: what would Dad think if I told him I wanted to drop out of track and try something new – like art club? What would Josh and Ryan say if I dusted off my LEGO and Erector Sets? What if I bent the flagpole in front of Theodore Roosevelt Middle School into a lineman's knot and Big Mouth Brody told the world?

Rocket and I began spending more and more time at the salvage yard, driving there in his truck every morning after breakfast. I wanted to fix what I could before I had to leave. The Knucklehead was coming together nicely – even if we were rebuilding it bit by bit, the old-fashioned way. Even if, sometimes, Rocket and Winona got distracted.

'Hello? Kid here! Please keep all goo-goo eyes to a minimum!' I'd shout, shielding my own eyes whenever the two of them got too close. But sometimes, seeing them together, I couldn't help thinking about Sarah Jane.

I worried about SJ in that big old house, with only her father and Hedda the Horrible for company. Hiking down from Rocket's each morning, I'd catch myself thinking I'd seen a glint of green eyes or a flash of white-blonde braids in the shadows of the trees around the ranch. Then I'd realize that I'd only caught the glint of green in a magpie's wing or the white-and-tan flash of a running antelope, and I'd be surprised to find myself disappointed.

The chummier Rocket and Winona got, the more time I spent on my own in the salvage yard. The place rocked in my head like a symphonic scrap metal band, the buzzing, itching sensation of ants beneath my skin rarely bothering me any more. Like growing into a coat Mom bought on sale two years too early, or adjusting to the way my voice had started squeaking and croaking on its way to a lower register, I was getting comfortable with my savvy at last. It was becoming a part of me. A part I was actually starting to like.

Maybe when I got home, everything would fit together.

I practised as often as I could, trying out new things in the furthest reaches of the salvage yard, so far out I couldn't see the repair bay, hoping that, at such a distance, Winona couldn't see me either.

I took apart the frame of a '61 Corvair and put it back together three or four times – faster each time – wishing I had Dad's stopwatch to clock my speed. Beginning to wish that Dad were there to see me do it.

I created a bridge from the chassis of two dented Range Rovers and a reclining rhinoceros out of an old motorhome. I even stacked spark plugs like toilet-paper tubes to build the Eiffel Tower. This time my tower only leaned a little – my third-grade art teacher would've been so proud. But I still had nothing close to Winona's talent. My rhino looked more like a stepped-on roach, and my bridge wobbled when I walked across it.

After returning to Winona's sculpture garden a dozen times, I pleaded with her to let me peek under the tarp that hid her work-in-progress still inside the shop.

'Please can I see what you're building now?' I begged.

'Okay, okay!' she sighed, giving in at last. 'But you have to promise to be nice and not make fun – *both* of you – because it's still in pieces. I keep taking it apart and putting it back together. I can't quite get it right.' Rocket knew all about Winona's artwork; I'd dragged him out to see her sculptures as soon as he joined Team Knucklehead.

'We won't make fun!' Rocket assured Winona. Then he grinned. 'Unless it's funny.' Winona thumped Rocket in the chest with a wrench, but he didn't let a single blue spark fly.

'Don't make me take you apart, mister!' Winona threatened.

Rocket and I exchanged glances, then exploded in an eruption of uncontrolled laughter that doubled me over and brought tears to Rocket's eyes. Winona gripped the edges of the tarp, ignoring us.

'Hey, sometimes things have to come apart before they can become something *new*.' So saying, she pulled the covering aside with a flourish. Still chuckling, Rocket moved next to Winona, standing close and gazing up at her creation. Putting on a serious face, the corners of his mouth only twitching a little, he tilted his head to one side, trying to discern a recognizable shape in the hodgepodge of spare parts.

'Wow! It's a . . . It's a . . .' Rocket scratched his head.

'You can't tell?' Winona gave him another thump with her wrench.

'*Oof!* Ow! Is it a donkey?' he asked, laughing again as he wrestled the wrench out of Winona's hand. I stared up at the sculpture too. I didn't laugh. I recognized

283

the shape immediately: rounded back end, tufted tail, branching antlers sprouting from between two long ears . . .

'It's a jackalope!' I said, remembering the broken magnet Fedora bought at Willie's Five & Dime.

Winona nodded at me, beaming.

'See?' she said to Rocket, grabbing back her wrench and jabbing him in the stomach with it. 'Another *artist* can see my vision right away!'

'Is that what you are, Ledger?' Rocket asked. I looked up, thinking Rocket was razzing me the same way he'd razzed Winona. But even though his smile was wicked and toothy, I could tell from the look in his eyes that his question was no joke.

I shrugged, even as my face went red.

'Don't worry, Ledge.' Rocket winked. 'You've got a long life ahead of you – you'll figure out how to put yourself together.'

The following Monday, the last giant butterfly emerged from its chrysalis, and Rocket brought me another

284

envelope from the post office. My pulse raced as I recognized SJ's handwriting.

To: Cowboy Ledge, Escape Artist
and Master Fence Bender

Rocket didn't glower like he had when he'd handed me Sarah Jane's first envelope. But he didn't look Green Giant jolly either.

'Is there anything you want to tell me, Ledge?' he asked, pointing to the words *Master Fence Bender* on the envelope. I paused before answering, watching the others go inside the Bug House to see all the butterflies. The twins floated Grandpa into the conservatory in his comfy chair, while Samson's thin outline followed. Next to Samson's shadow, Fedora bounced like a jumping bean soaked forty days in Red Bull and then set out in the sun.

The successful appearance of seven male and five female Queen Alexandra's Birdwings had improved Uncle Autry's mood substantially – enough to make the rest of us stop checking our breakfast for bugs. But I still didn't think it wise to say anything about the Cabots' fence.

I crumpled the envelope. 'This is probably just one of Sarah Jane's newspapers. I must have won some kind of free subscription or something. I'll throw it away.'

Rocket looked down at the envelope, raising his thumb to his jaw in his old nervous habit, trying to rub at the beard he no longer had. Dropping his hand, he murmured: 'Just be careful, Ledge.' But he said nothing more.

I held my breath until Rocket joined the others in the Bug House. Then I ran to sit on the far side of the potting shed, where I'd be out of sight of everyone – everyone but Bitsy, who followed me, tail wagging.

I stared at the crinkled envelope for several minutes before tearing it open. I'd been wondering if I'd ever hear from Sarah Jane again. Even if it was only one of her newspapers in the envelope, it reassured me that she must be okay. Besides, as long as this new edition of *The Sundance Scuttlebutt* was not about my family, it would be good to have something new to read. I still carried SJ's notebook in my pocket; I'd practically memorized every story in it. I'd finally given in to the fact that, somewhere along the way, I'd actually started liking Sarah Jane – despite all of her cheats and sneaks and tricks.

But the envelope didn't contain a newspaper. Instead, it held a letter.

Ledge!
My dad is so MEAN! I'm totally grounded. He <u>locked me in my room!</u> I know he's trying to take away your uncle's ranch. What he's doing isn't right. Maybe we can prove it. Only, I need your special talents to get me out. You need to come <u>NOW!</u>
SJ

Sarah Jane had signed her initials in the same crooked way I'd sculpted them into the iron fence before blast -ing the fence to pieces. Her words, underlined and capitalized, jumped off the paper and climbed into my brain. Adrenalin made my heart race faster; my blood pounded in my ears. Even sitting where I was behind the potting shed, my knees began to hammer up and down. My legs were restless. Itching to run.

Gah! Sarah Jane's dad was so mean!

He'd locked her in her room!

I had to get there *now*!

I leaped up, tripping over Bitsy. Completely under the spell of Sarah Jane's urgent letter, I didn't see the twins coming round the side of the potting shed until we collided. Fedora ran past the rest of us, oblivious, and disappeared into the shed.

I stuffed SJ's letter back into its envelope. But before I had time to jam it in my pocket or hide it behind my back, Marisol levitated the envelope out of my grip.

'Did you get a love letter, Ledge?' Marisol baited me irritably as she dangled the envelope a metre above my head.

'Ooh! Do you have a girlfriend now too, *Sledgehammer*?' Mesquite made kissing noises as she swished the envelope back and forth with a flick of her little finger. 'Are you and Rocket going to double-date?'

I didn't have time for the twins' half-hearted attempts at torture. Sarah Jane needed me now! Her letter said so. I flicked a finger of my own, startling Marisol and Mesquite by nabbing the envelope, easily creating a lunging snare from the chicken wire strung around Rocket's garden. The wire snapped up to grab the paper from the air, like a giant frog's tongue snagging a hapless fly.

'Whoa! Ledge! When did you learn to do *that*?' Mesquite took a step back, dropping her ornery attitude in a flash. Marisol also forgot to be snippy and whooped out loud.

'Whoo-hoo! Our lessons worked! Good karma, here we come! Just in time too! We needed a solid turn in our luck.' Marisol and Mesquite both rubbed my belly like I'd turned into the golden Buddha laughing in the entryway of Mr Lee's Panda Palace.

Fedora came out of the potting shed just then, clutching a mud-caked shovel and eyeing the sharp edges of the chicken wire warily as I unwrapped Sarah Jane's envelope from its snare.

'Look sharp, Ledge!' Fedora said. 'Don't get cut!'

As I took off running towards the south ridge, heading straight for Sundance, I wondered what safety advice Fe would've offered had she known where I was going.

As if she could read my mind, my sister shouted after me:

'Don't learn safety by accident, Ledge! Think through it before you do it!' But the morning breeze caught Fedora's words and blew them away.

It hardly mattered – I couldn't listen. Sarah Jane's letter was still in control of my brain.

Chapter 28

FUELLED BY THE URGENCY WRITTEN INTO every compelling vowel and consonant of Sarah Jane's letter, my legs flew on autopilot. I was halfway to Sundance before my head cleared and I started thinking for myself. Still, I didn't stop. Maybe I'd needed to take a break from running for a while to realize how much I missed it. Wherever my savvy talents were taking me, I was glad to know I could still run if I had to – or if I wanted to. Who said I couldn't run the half-marathon with Dad *and* join the art club at Theodore Roosevelt Middle School?

It wasn't long before I was leaning against my knees, trying to catch my breath as I stared at the fence posts stacked in a pile on the Cabots' front lawn. How was I going to break Sarah Jane out without alerting Hedda the Horrible to my presence?

I knew Mr Cabot wasn't home. All of Sundance knew it. Mr Cabot was the Big Boss of the Bulldozer, standing tall in his gleaming yellow hard hat as he supervised the total destruction of the T-shirt shop down the street from Willie's Five & Dime. Now that the five-and-dime had its own foreclosure sign, I wondered how long Willie had before his shop got torn down too.

I could hear the noise of the CAD Co. demolition vehicles from where I stood in front of the Cabot house. I could see the cloud of dust that rose above the town. I hoped that Sarah Jane was correct about being able to prove her dad was doing wrong by coming after the Flying Cattleheart. The image of those wreckers finishing what I'd started on the night of Fish's wedding wasn't one I liked.

The sound of a TV drifted from the rear of the house. Cautiously, I circled the building. Peering carefully through an open window, I saw Hedda with her feet up in a small room off the kitchen. She was eating popcorn while watching a daytime talk show.

'*Tell me again, Mr Rojenski,*' the talk show host was saying. '*You claim you visit a different solar system every time you eat your wife's mashed potatoes?*'

Engrossed in her programme, Hedda sat motionless, holding a piece of popcorn in front of her open mouth as though she'd been frozen by a freeze-ray until the next commercial break.

I let out a breath. It would be a whole lot easier to break Sarah Jane out of her tower room with Cabot gone and Hedda the Horrible hypnotized by hogwash. Still, I was scared of getting caught. Scared of causing more damage for SJ to take credit for.

Fedora's last safety warning drifted back to me with the breeze: *Think through it before you do it!*

'Okay, Ledge, listen to your sister for once,' I said to myself as I moved back around the house, trying to breathe normally and keep my savvy under control. Determined not to simply react, I started thinking through my options.

I could sneak inside . . . climb the stairs . . . and take apart the lock with a single finger snap. Easy! Only, I'd promised Autry I wouldn't put a shoe inside the house. One wrong creak going up the stairs – one crashing, falling door – and Hedda would be on the phone to Cabot or the sheriff lickety-split.

'Not a good plan,' I told myself. I needed something better. If only those braids of Sarah Jane's were long enough, she could toss them down like rope.

I thought about scaling the tall birch tree that slanted towards the house. I'd climbed the birch trees at the ranch a bunch of times; this one didn't look too different. And its branches stretched close to Sarah Jane's window.

Careful not to trip over a dozen different stumps, I hustled to the base of the tree. Moving around it, I stared up, trying to gauge the strength of its branches.

'Well, Ledge, you might be able to fix things now as well as break them,' I murmured, thinking. 'But you can't fix your own bones if you fall out of this tree.' Still looking skyward as I considered the birch, I banged hard into the marble bench that rested in its shade.

294

'Ow! Shhhha*zam*!' I covered my mouth with both hands to stop myself from cussing, to keep from alerting Hedda to my presence. Bending down to rub my shins, I looked more closely at the bench. There was writing carved into the stone.

IN MEMORY
SUMMER BEACHAM CABOT
WIFE AND MOTHER
BESIDE US FOREVER

Summer Cabot was SJ's mom's name. I remembered Autry telling me. I read the inscription again, staring at the name.

Summer Beacham Cabot

Beacham . . . Beacham . . . I'd heard that name before too. I tried to remember, but I had other things on my mind. Crucial, clamorous things. As my eye fell back on the enormous pile of iron bars that had once been Mr Cabot's fence, *Mrs* Cabot left my mind, warp speed. I suddenly knew exactly how to get Sarah Jane out of her room. And I wouldn't have to put a shoe inside the house to do it.

'*Your uncle took a wasp nest down from outside my bedroom window . . .*' Sarah Jane's voice came ringing back to me. Uncle Autry had climbed a ladder. I would too.

But when I looked again at the jumble of iron bars, I baulked. Doubt hit me like confidence kryptonite. Sure, I could do stuff like this all I wanted in the safety of the salvage yard, where no one else could see me. But what if someone here was watching? A neighbour . . . someone driving by . . . Hedda coming out to sweep the porch between shows?

'Come on, Ledge. You didn't think about stuff like that the last time you were here,' I said out loud.

Then I thought: *Maybe I should have.*

Checking to make sure no neighbours were outside watering lawns or walking dogs, I took a deep breath and stepped towards the pile of iron bars. Looking up at Sarah Jane's window ten metres above, I swallowed my anxiety. To keep myself steady, I crouched down low. I splayed my fingertips on the ground between me and the pile of fence posts, like I was at the starting line of a hundred-metre dash.

Shoving memories of falling barns and bumpers from my mind, I closed my eyes and pictured the iron bars lifting and coming together. Bending where they needed to bend. Fusing where they needed to fuse. My hands tingled and my nerves pulsed, and all the while the iron hummed, and my mouth filled with the metallic tang I'd got so used to.

Clinks and clangs filled the air, but softly. As if the metal bars knew they needed to be quiet.

I added rung after rung.

I telescoped rails up and up and up.

From the town below, the crashing and scraping and crunching and beeping of the demolitions equipment easily covered my own construction noise.

When I opened my eyes at last, I saw that no one had come running. Hedda's TV continued to blare babble. SJ's window was still closed.

I stood and stretched, a warm, satisfied feeling replacing my earlier doubts. Reaching from the ground at my feet to the sill of Sarah Jane's high window, a crazy ladder spiralled upward, like a strand of DNA.

I'd done my thinking. I'd done my building. Now I didn't hesitate. I didn't stop to test my weight against the first few twisting rungs. I didn't shake the ladder to see if it would fall apart. Instead I clambered to the top, confident that my savvy was sound and my creation would hold me up.

I tapped gently on Sarah Jane's window. When she opened it, her eyes were wide – though not dis-believing – and she smiled as she looked down at my impromptu climbing structure.

Her hair was loose again today. It flowed out of the window and down the ladder in a clean and shiny swish of white-gold, making her look like that fairy-tale girl Rapunzel. Making me aware that, after bathing only in the river for over three weeks, I was probably far from charming.

I scrubbed my fingers through my hair. Yep. Sure enough, it was full of grit. But SJ didn't seem to care.

'Got my damsel-in-distress call, did you?' she said with a grin. I pulled her letter from my pocket and waved it in answer.

'Does this mean you forgive me?' she asked.

I shrugged, glad to see no trace of the fence post scratch left on her arm. 'I'm still considering my options.'

Sarah Jane peered over the window ledge again. 'Well, consider fast, Cowboy. There's someplace you and I need to go.'

Chapter 29

'YOUR TIMING IS PERFECT, LEDGE!' SAID Sarah Jane, tying her hair back and zipping down the ladder after me before Hedda the Horrible's TV show could end. 'Daddy is supervising the demolition and there'll be nobody at his building. We'll be able to get into his office easy.'

Pulling me away from the house, SJ dragged me down streets that bypassed downtown Sundance, steering us clear of the demolition. She jogged at a swift pace I easily matched. And she only tripped me twice.

Just as she'd said, the Cabot Acquisitions & Demolitions building was empty when we reached it. It was also locked up tight. I acted as lookout as SJ checked the

300

doors. Though, mostly I stood and stared at the filling station across the street and at the CAD Co. equipment yard still half-full of excavators, trucks and forklifts, trying not to picture myself blasting bulldozers into petrol pumps. I could practically smell the spark from metal hitting metal, almost feel the wave of heat from a giant, exploding fireball.

'Don't you have a key or something?' I asked after Sarah Jane had circled the building three times. The collar of my T-shirt felt too tight. My throat felt even tighter.

'I've got *something*, all right,' SJ answered. 'I've got you!' She raised her eyebrows, then smiled. I looked from her to the forklifts to the petrol station, sucking in my breath.

'Don't freak out now, Ledge.' SJ saw my worry. 'You've got mad skills! I bet you can unlock the back door easy.'

'I could blow up this entire block easy,' I answered. Maybe I'd seen too many movies, but I knew I could never do the cool-guy walk away from any destruction I caused. Instead, I'd be on my knees, watching in horror, just like I had been when I took down the barn. Or I'd be running, same as always.

'Ledge! Hello?' Sarah Jane waved her hand in my face, breaking the stare I'd fixed on the petrol station. 'Good golly, Cowboy, get a grip! I lost you there for a second.'

I scrubbed my face with one hand. First at SJ's house, now here. No matter how many scumbling successes I had, doubt still followed me everywhere like a three-legged dog. Autry had warned me that fear had a way of coming back around. I understood now that he was right: this fear-thing had no finish line. The realization made me cuss out loud.

'Save it for the deadbolt in the back, Ledge,' said SJ. Then she pushed me into action.

The deadbolt securing the back door came apart quickly and easily, falling into pieces at ten paces. 'Did I tell you my mom stopped a bank heist once?' I popped my knuckles nervously. 'Now look at me . . . breaking and entering. Wouldn't Mom be proud.' Sarah Jane

302

laughed nervously, but I couldn't even crack a smile. For a moment I wondered if I was going to turn out like Aunt Jules and Grandma Dollop's sticky-fingered younger sister, Jubilee, who could open any lock and felt free to take whatever she wanted, whenever she wanted it.

'I'm going to go to jail,' I muttered, shaking my head as I stared at the broken bolt. I remembered the feeling of the Sundance Kid's shackles round my wrist and it wasn't something I wanted to feel again. Sarah Jane seemed to have no problem with the fact that I had unexplained abilities. Nor did she have any problem taking advantage of them. This wasn't the me I wanted to show the world, I thought. This wasn't what I'd been made for. If it was, then I really *was* defective.

'Don't be such a drama llama, Ledge. It's my dad's building, and you're here with me. How much trouble can we get into, really?' But even as Sarah Jane said it, her voice caught, hinting that her brash confidence might be mostly bluster. 'Let's just hurry.'

I steeled myself, knowing I had to do whatever I

303

could to help Autry and the twins keep their home. Still, if the CAD Co. building hadn't belonged to SJ's dad, I never would've busted that lock.

'Are you sure we can find something here to prove that what your dad's doing is wrong?' I asked in a whisper as we stepped inside. 'I mean, my uncle does owe your dad money . . .'

'I'm not *sure*, no,' SJ answered, rattling locked doorknobs as she moved down a dim hallway.

'Then, why are we doing this?' I croaked. 'Why do you even care what happens to the ranch?'

'I care because your uncle's place is special,' she replied. Then, not looking at me, she added quickly, 'And because *you're* . . . er, my friend.' For a moment I thought SJ had been about to say that I was special too. I wasn't sure how to answer, so I just swallowed and said nothing.

'Come on.' She grabbed my hand and pulled me further down the hall. 'We have to find Daddy's office.' Reaching a place where the hall branched in two directions, she nodded to me. 'You take the doors on the left, I'll get the ones on the right. But first, can't you do something about *these* locks?'

I sighed heavily, feeling my brow furrow as I debated how far to take this break-in. But trying to think things through with SJ's hand in mine was difficult. Trying to *breathe* with her hand in mine was difficult.

'Don't you know which office is his?'

'Daddy's never been the Take-Your-Kid-to-Work-Day type. Just break *all* the locks!' Sarah Jane thrust the fingers of her free hand out at me in an impatient gesture. 'What are you waiting for? Get your magic on!'

'It's not magic!' I said, mimicking her gesture. Only, when I thrust *my* fingers out, every doorknob, left and right, fell clattering to the floor, and every door, left and right, swung inward on loosened, groaning hinges.

'Looks like magic to me, Ledge.'

'It's just a talent. Like I told you before. . . a *savvy*.'

'Well, get your savvy tail in gear, Cowboy!' she said, letting go of my hand. 'I don't know how long we have!'

305

We split up. SJ turned her newshound nose towards anything that might smell fishy, looking for a file room. I looked for a door that might lead to a washroom, thinking I might throw up. I didn't have the stomach to be a criminal. How did Grandma Dollop's sister do it? How had the Sundance Kid and the Wild Bunch gang not puked their guts out before robbing trains and stealing horses?

I stepped through a door marked PRIVATE. But it wasn't a washroom, it was Mr Cabot's office. I knew it by the albino squirrel stuffed and mounted and holding a pencil jar on the desk, and the cuckoo clock collection on the wall behind it.

A tall, steel safe stood against the wall to my left. It had a gold-plated five-spoke spinner handle and an electronic lock. The wall on my right showed off an antique, eight-kilo circus-tent sledgehammer and a black-and-white photograph of Baz the Able Elephant wielding it.

'Ha!' The combination of safe and sledgehammer

made me laugh out loud – it was like Mr Cabot was daring someone to try to bust open his safe.

I turned to call to SJ but leaped back, startled by a life-sized cardboard cut-out of Mr Cabot. The cut-out was dusty and bent and had a sign offering low rates on private loans, but it looked enough like SJ's dad to scare the living daylights, night-lights, light fixtures and light sockets out of me . . . not to mention a spasmodic surge of savvy blasting power.

I may have been scumbling better than ever, but my startle response still needed work. I ducked as the heavy hammer head flew off its handle – and off the wall – soaring across the room and putting a dent in the front of the safe.

The electronic lock exploded.

The locking bolts broke loose.

The stuffed squirrel on Mr Cabot's desk dropped its pencils, its glassy eyes watching with mine as the door to Noble Cabot's safe swung open – then fell off.

Chapter 30

'OH . . . CRUD,' I SAID OUT LOUD, feeling the weight of my understatement hit like its very own circus sledgehammer. Maybe the twins' nickname for me was spot on after all.

I moved quickly to hoist the safe's heavy door up off the floor. To try to meld it back in place. But seeing a gleam of light reflect off glass, I stopped before finishing the job.

I stared in at the contents of the safe: stacks of cash, papers, file folders . . . and Grandma Dollop's Peter Pan Peanut Butter wedding jar.

Either Mr Cabot had lied – or Sarah Jane had. Her

father hadn't recycled the old jar. He'd locked it in this safe.

I reached past jewellery and money and pulled out Grandma's jar, knocking papers and books on to the floor. Ignoring the mess at my feet, I spun the white metal lid to see if the symphony of sound was still safely trapped inside.

As the familiar music filled the room, a heavy weight in my chest hoisted anchor and skirred away. Grandpa Bomba wouldn't need the twins' help after I got back to the ranch – he'd be floating on air all by himself. Aunt Jules, Mibs and Will . . . the whole family would be happy to have Grandma's jar back ready for future weddings. Grinning, I tightened the lid, but not before the canned trumpets brought SJ running.

'You found it!' she cried, wrapping her hand round my arm. 'I didn't think Daddy would bring it here!'

I squinted at SJ, trying to decide if she was lying, doing my best to ignore the little zings that ran beneath my skin where her skin touched mine.

'You have to believe me, Ledge!' she said, getting

right up in my face, her green eyes imploring me to trust her. 'Daddy really *did* tell me he was going to recycle it. I swear!' Her face was so close I could smell her fruity watermelon lip balm. My palms began to sweat. It would've been easy to lean forward a few centimetres, tilt my head, and . . .

Ack! No! What was I thinking? I moved quickly away from Sarah Jane, slipping on the books and papers scattered on the floor.

'Yeah, yeah,' I told her, cringing as my voice squeaked. 'Put it in writing, SJ. Then I'll believe you.'

My pal Josh would've whapped me upside the head if he'd been next to me. I could hear his howl: 'You should've gone for it, you chicken!'

I crouched down and began shoving the mess of fallen papers back into the safe. SJ knelt beside me, pulling a sheet of paper from her pocket.

'Maybe this will help, Ledge. Look what I found in the file room!' She waved the paper in my face, adding, 'It was alphabetized under *O*. I think it's a deed or a loan document from your uncle to my dad. It's definitely

paperwork for your uncle's place. It's got original signa-
tures and everything!'

I glanced at the paper. 'So what? It looks pretty
official to me.'

'Ledge, if it's here, then maybe it hasn't been filed! And
if it's never been filed, we could tear it up! Then it would
be like it never existed, right? Ledge? Are you listening?'

I wasn't. Instead, I was staring at a thick, leather-
bound scrapbook fallen open next to me on the floor.
Mr Cabot didn't strike me as a scrapbook kind of guy.
I flipped through the book, expecting to see pictures
of shrivelled Wyoming mummies or find a two-tailed
lizard pressed flat between its pages. But the scrapbook
held another type of collection – a *normal* one.

There were photographs from every 4-H youth-club
contest, Thanksgiving pageant and school spelling bee
in which Sarah Jane had taken part. There were stories
she'd written in kindergarten and drawings she'd done
in fourth grade. Aced history tests, report cards, even
'Great Smile!' stickers from the dentist.

'Check it out!' I nudged SJ with my elbow. She

sucked in her breath as she looked at the slices of her life spread before her. Immediately taking over the job of turning pages, she ran her fingers lightly down each one, as if she needed to use at least two of her senses to absorb what she was seeing.

There were pictures of SJ's mom in the book too, and of Noble and his wife together – boating, fishing, waving from the Grand Canyon. As SJ lingered over the pictures, I pulled out a folder that had been tucked into the back of the book.

'SJ, look!' The folder was filled with laminated copies of *The Sundance Scuttlebutt*. The Gus Neary pirate edition was there, and the Selma Witzel alien abduction issue too. There was even one about ghosts of outlaws haunting the T-shirt shop. I shivered, glad I'd never gone into that shop before it closed.

'That was my first paper!' SJ nodded to the story about the ghosts. 'Dad wouldn't take me out or let me have a party for my birthday. He wouldn't even let me go outside. So I spent all day getting *The Sundance Scuttlebutt* up and running.'

Something nagged at my brain as I listened to SJ talk about her birthday. Something familiar. But I was too busy shuffling through Mr Cabot's collection of SJ's papers to concentrate. Mr Cabot may have thrown away the news SJ printed to sell, but he'd saved at least one copy of every edition for himself.

Every edition but one.

I sighed with relief when I realized that the Super-Duper Humdinger savvy-family edition of *The Sundance Scuttlebutt* wasn't in the folder. SJ had promised not to show that issue to anyone, and it looked like she'd kept her promise.

'I think you were wrong, SJ,' I said, flipping through the laminated papers. 'I think your dad *has* been paying attention.' Sarah Jane didn't answer. She'd turned the scrapbook to the beginning, and was looking at photographs from her parents' wedding. I watched her slowly turn the pages.

'Wait!' I stopped her. Swivelling the scrapbook towards me, I flipped back and forth through the same three pages. The same three pictures.

Normally, I wouldn't have given a thundering toot about the wedding photos. But something about these caught my attention and held it. I stared at them without blinking until it hit me:

'This is the glade at my uncle's ranch . . .' I said slowly. 'The one my cousin Fish got married in.'

'No way! Why would my mom and dad get married there?' SJ tried to grab the book back, but I wouldn't let her.

'See the juniper stumps?' I pointed. 'They're the exact same ones!' I nodded at the first picture. There, in full colour, Noble and Summer stood together between two twisting juniper stumps, exactly like Fish and Mellie had only weeks ago. These had to be the same stumps – I'd stared at them for too long when I was frozen by Mom's savvy not to recognize them now.

'It can't be the same glade,' SJ answered, yanking the scrapbook away from me and pointing at the picture herself. 'There aren't any trees behind these stumps.'

I squinted. She was right. In this photograph, there were no towering, interlacing birch trees behind the couple, just an open grassy meadow. I turned the page and jabbed the next picture with a grin.

'Look again!'

The second picture showed the same stumps and the same gooey-eyed couple holding hands. But now the two birches were there as well – small and leafy – each no taller than the bride. Next to me, Sarah Jane shook her head, mystified.

I turned to the next page and pointed again. Sarah Jane's mom and dad were kissing – husband and wife. Only, the birch trees behind them were suddenly high and lofty, branches intertwined just as they were now.

Sarah Jane blinked at the photos in the scrapbook. I sat back, leaning against the safe, thinking suddenly of another tall birch tree I'd met recently, and of the engraved marble bench beneath it.

On the far wall, the cuckoo clocks all struck the hour, breaking the silence that had fallen between us. How long had we been in Mr Cabot's office? I wondered. We couldn't afford to sit around all day looking at these pictures. Mr Cabot might come back at any moment!

A final *cuckoo* echoed the hour through the room. With time on the brain, I remembered time-hopping Aunt Jules's words as Fish's blustering savvy storm made the birch trees in the glade crack and bend at his wedding.

Trees this size don't grow back overnight, you know. At least, not since we lost the last Beacham with any talent.

The last Beacham with any talent . . .

Sarah Jane continued to stare at the bewildering photos. Despite her fondness for far-out stories, SJ hadn't grown up knowing about savvy talents – having cousins disappear, read her mind, or trigger storms or lightning. I couldn't blame her for not putting two and two together quickly. When it came to savvy families, she'd never learned the maths.

But I had. And things were adding up fast.

Dollars to doughnuts, Summer Beacham Cabot had been the one to make the birch trees grow in *seconds* in the glade. I was willing to bet she'd also grown the one next to the house in Sundance. And if Sarah Jane's mom had had a savvy, that might mean that Sarah Jane had one too . . .

A chilling thrill ran through me at the prospect, until a new thought struck. One even scarier than the idea of a Sarah Jane with larger-than-life powers. What if SJ were my *cousin*, or some other relative I didn't know about?

I stood up fast, riddled with heebie-jeebies. I'd locked lips with her! And I'd considered doing it again!

'You okay, Ledge?' SJ asked, standing up as well.

I didn't answer. I could only stare. I stared at Sarah Jane so long I felt like I was trying to see right through her, trying to see if I could spot any trace of a savvy, or any family resemblance: Grandma Dollop's nose, Aunt Jenny's eyes, Fish's cockeyed grin. When SJ waved a hand in my face to break my gawping gaze, I ducked under her arm and dodged right, sure I'd catch kissing-cousins cooties if we got too close again.

'Uh . . . you're thirteen, right?' I asked, continuing to back up.

'For, like, six months now,' she answered, regarding

me cautiously as she clutched her father's scrapbook in one hand and Uncle Autry's deed in the other. I could see the gears in her brain moving, though they still hadn't clicked into the same rhythm as my own. When I'd spilled family secrets outside her house, I hadn't told SJ about thirteenth birthdays. I'd left that part out.

'So did anything . . . you know, *extra-weird* happen on your birthday?'

SJ narrowed her eyes.

'No, just what I told you. Daddy wouldn't even let me go outside. That's the day I starting writing my paper. What are you trying to get at, Ledge?'

Her writing! Sarah Jane's persuasive stories had been staring me in the face for the last three and a half weeks. I opened my mouth to speak, to share my savvy-SJ suspicions. But I never got the chance.

'What in blazes do you kids think you're *doing*?' Sheriff Brown stood in the doorway, thumbs hooked over his gun belt, pointed badge shining.

Jonas Brown stared at us. Then he glowered at the cracked-open safe. The man looked like he wished he'd

318

called in sick that morning, or chosen not to respond to whatever silent alarm or tingling sheriff-sense had brought him to the CAD Co. building.

Unhooking his thumbs from his belt, he took off his hat and scrubbed his forearm across his face. I quickly tucked Grandma's jar into one of the gusseted pockets of my cargo shorts. Sarah Jane shoved the scrapbook into the safe. Then she jammed the deed she'd found down the back of my shorts, making my eyes bug out and my face burn red.

When the sheriff dropped his arm and looked at us again, the end of the world, my world, was written across his face as clearly and believably as if it were a headline in one of Sarah Jane's papers.

I only prayed they offered art classes in prison.

Chapter 31

IF SARAH JANE COULD'VE MADE A *written* statement, it would've been easy for her to convince the sheriff that we'd stumbled on to the scene of a break-in at her father's building, scaring away who-knows-how-many nameless, faceless robbers before they'd had the chance to steal anything. Though it was soon plain enough that Sheriff Brown didn't believe two kids could bust into a safe using a circus-elephant's sledgehammer. The sheriff didn't know what I could do.

'You kids have put me in a pickle.' Brown scowled as he loaded us into the backseat of his truck. 'Mr Cabot has a right to know you were both here. But telling your dad about this now, Sarah Jane, while he's already sailing his destroyers through Sundance . . . well, that wouldn't seem to be in the best interest of the town. Who knows what else your daddy might flatten if he found out how close you got to danger?'

'I won't tell if you don't, Sheriff,' offered SJ. 'Daddy does have a way of flying off the handle.' Then, casting me a quick, I've-got-no-other-choice grimace, she raised her hand to her mouth and said, 'Doesn't Daddy hold the deed to your wife's beauty shop, Sheriff?'

I shook my head. Sarah Jane had no shame.

The sheriff chewed that tidbit for a time, before saying, 'I think we can leave you out of this, Sarah Jane. I wouldn't want your daddy thinking I can't keep the kids in this town safe.'

SJ may have got off scot-free, but I wasn't as lucky. Sitting in the Crook County Sheriff's Office twenty minutes later, I waited for Uncle Autry to come for me, praying every prayer I could think of, hoping God might intervene with my uncle on my behalf. Sheriff Brown

321

hadn't locked me in a cell, or put me in handcuffs either. But he did make me sit for an eternity on an uncomfortable chair next to his desk. I listened as he dispatched one deputy back to CAD Co. to seal the crime scene, and another to notify Mr Cabot about the break-in.

When Autry arrived, he was mad.

Really, *really* mad.

If God had put in a good word for me with my uncle, it didn't show. I knew how mad Autry was, not by his expression, or by anything he said, but by the sheer number of enormous yellow-and-black wasps that flew into the building with him, an entourage of angry wings and stingers. Once inside, the wasps all scattered, bumping against the windows and circling coffee mugs and soda cans. They hovered in the glow of computer monitors and strafed past stacks of Post-its.

Somewhere, a woman shrieked. A clerk across the hall scattered a full ream of white copy paper as he swatted at the intruders. Autry's silent upset was so strong, he didn't raise a finger to control the hordes of flying things. As far as I could tell, nobody was getting stung. But when one of the wasps landed on the end of my nose, I guessed I might be first.

'Um, a little help here?' I looked up at my uncle, moving nothing but my eyeballs. Autry stared back at me. Then he canted his head towards the wasp, a warning look darkening his features. He might've been warning me, or he might've been warning the wasp. Either way, both of us snapped to attention. The wasp lifted from my nose and flew away fast, while I jumped to my feet like the sheriff's chair had grown a stinger of its own.

Autry spoke with the sheriff in another room as the chaos with the wasps continued. When he finally came back, he was grim and unsmiling. The sheriff nodded my way once, then Autry ushered me out of the building, two hundred wasps following in our wake, the Pied Piper of Pests taking us all with him.

I wanted to tell Autry about all the good stuff I'd managed lately: getting Grandma's jar, the ladder I'd built, my sculptures in the salvage yard, and how I'd begun to deal with my fear and finesse things a little – no, how I'd begun to finesse things *A LOT*. Just as he'd imagined for me back when I was unable to imagine it for myself.

More than anything, I wanted to ask him about Summer Beacham, about Mr Cabot . . . and about Sarah Jane. I didn't understand; if Mr Cabot had married into a savvy family, why did he hate us? And why did he keep so many secrets – important secrets – from Sarah Jane?

But, climbing into Autry's truck outside the sheriff's office, my uncle still hopping-hornet mad, I knew that this wasn't the time or the place for any of it.

It wasn't long before I missed the buzz from the wasps we'd left behind; driving out of Sundance, Uncle Autry's voiceless fury became sheer torture. By the time we neared the ranch, the silence between us had grown unbearable – so unbearable, I decided to break it.

'I think Sarah Jane Cabot has a savvy.'

Autry hit the brakes so hard the truck fishtailed before coming to a stop, engine stalled, facing the fore-closure sign.

'What are you talking about, Ledge?' Autry spoke without looking at me. His tone was flat. Too flat to pretend he didn't know what I meant.

'Sarah Jane's mom, Summer. Her last name used to be *Beacham*.'

Autry said nothing, so I kept hammering.

'The Beachams used to come here too, right? Mom said you wrestled one of them in a pile of cactuses –'

'Cam.' Autry nodded once, still staring forward. 'Cam Beacham was Summer's older brother.'

'So . . . does that mean we're related to Sarah Jane? Are the Beachams Eva Mae's descendants too?' These questions seemed to wake my uncle up. He snorted and a crooked half-smile touched his lips.

'I hate to break it to you, Ledger, but your grand-father invented that whole story. There was no Eva Mae El Dorado Two-Birds Ransom.' He waved one hand in a dismissive gesture. 'When your mom and Aunt Jenny and I were kids, the first savvy ancestor was a buck-toothed man named Bullthorn Johnston who dropped a dozen hot biscuits that rolled away across the plains. By the time those biscuits trundled to a stop, they'd picked up so much dirt and so many stones, they became the Rocky Mountains. According to your grandpa, old Bucktooth Bullthorn, still hungry, took a bite out of the top of Little Bear Peak and had extraordinary talents ever after, talents that he passed on to his children . . . and his children's children . . . and so on.' Autry rattled off the story like he was dumping rocks out of his shoe.

'There was no Eva Mae?' I must've sounded disappointed, because Autry turned towards me at last. His face remained stern, but a flicker of regret softened his eyes.

'Who knows, Ledge?' he said on a sigh. 'I mean, who knows *really*? For all I know, Bullthorn Johnston was one of Eva Mae's long-lost brothers. But neither of them ever lived here – even if this land *has* been in our family for years.'

'So Sarah Jane's not, like, my *cousin* or anything, is she?' I asked, sweat beading on my forehead.

Autry stopped short of laughing. 'No, Sarah Jane's not your cousin, Ledger. And her mother wasn't mine.'

326

I wiped the sweat from my brow, relieved.

'As for the Beachams,' he continued. 'I suppose they could've been kin once, way back when. But no, these days the Beachams are just another savvy family, like the Danzingers or the Kwans or the Paynes. There're a lot of us, Ledge. Sometimes we know each other, sometimes we don't. But this ranch has always been a safe place, even for those who aren't kin.' Autry shot a hard look at the foreclosure notice before adding: 'At least, it *was*.'

I wanted to tell Uncle Autry how sorry I was for making everything go south. But he wasn't done talking, so I stayed quiet.

'I met Summer and Cam here when we were kids. June to August, your great-uncle Ferris ran this place as a lodge and had it filled with old ramshackle cabins.'

'Great-uncle Ferris. Really?'

'That man could turn snot into icicles in ninety-degree weather!' Autry couldn't help smiling at the memory. 'Your grandpa may have fixed this place up and made it bigger, but Ferris owned it. Whenever we'd visit, us kids would head for Sundance whenever we could get away with it . . . same as someone else I know.' He cleared his throat, flashing me a look that was half reprimand, half sheepish confession.

'That's how Summer and I first met Noble,' he continued, fixing his eyes back on the foreclosure sign. 'Noble was actually a good guy when we were kids. A little odd maybe, but who was I to judge? I was still learning how to keep caterpillars out of my pockets and no-see-ums out of my underpants. Noble caught on quick to the fact that we were different. Summer's savvy was astonishing. She could turn anything into –'

'A tree?' I cut in. Autry looked at me, surprised.

'Figured that out, did you?' Then on a sigh, he added, 'Me with the bugs . . . Summer with the trees . . . Noble's always had a talent for collecting unusual things. Even when it came to friends.'

Picturing my uncle as a kid, squished flat under glass, I shivered.

'Back when Noble married Summer, his collections were pretty tame,' Autry went on as though he'd read my mind. 'Rocks, stamps, coins. But he really did love her. And Summer loved him too.'

I made a face.

'Everything changed after Summer got sick, Ledge, *really* sick. She made a decision Noble couldn't understand, hoping that in some way she wouldn't have to leave him and Sarah Jane. Noble got so angry then – angry at her for being sick – angry at her for –'

'For turning *herself* into a tree?' I knew it was true, even as I asked it. The big white birch tree that held the old house on the hill in Sundance inside its branches . . . that tree *was* Summer Beacham.

If Autry was surprised that I'd figured this out on my own, he didn't show it.

'I supported her decision,' he went on. 'What else could I do? Summer was dying. Noble wanted her to wait, to keep fighting. But Summer knew that if she waited any longer, she'd lack the strength to make the change. She didn't even know if she could do it. Summer could change just about anything into a tree . . .

329

a tin can, a stone, even her brother Cam's lucky baseball glove. You know that big cottonwood down by the river?' Autry watched my eyes go wide, then chuckled wistfully. 'But change herself?' He shook his head, smiling even as his eyes grew moist. Several moments passed before he went on.

'I was there until Summer's last leaf shivered and unfurled, breathing in the sun. Then Noble kicked me off his property, and that was that. He made it plain that he didn't want Sarah Jane to have anything to do with me, my girls, the ranch, savvy folk, savvy *anything*, and that I'd do well to remember it, since I'd signed over a deed to him for my land when he loaned me the money to put up the conservatory. We'd been friends when I signed the paper. It just seemed like a formality. But as soon as Summer made her last boughs, I took one look at Noble and understood that borrowing from him had been a mistake – one which, someday, might come back to bite me.'

Autry turned in his seat to face me.

'Did you know, Ledge, that in all the years I've been surrounded by spiders, bugs and insects, I've never been bitten once? Not once! I guess I thought my luck would hold.'

'Rocket said wounded animals can be dangerous,' I murmured, still digesting Autry's story. 'Wounded people too.'

'And losing someone you love can tear your heart to pieces,' Autry added. 'I know.'

'But you didn't turn rotten when your wife died,' I replied.

'Everyone puts themselves back together differently after things fall apart, Ledge,' said Autry. 'You of all people should know that.' He laughed then, but his short burst of humour died quickly and, staring again at the foreclosure sign, his smile decomposed. 'You stepped right into it, coming here.'

'I-I'm sorry, Uncle Autry.' The words sounded lame, but Autry accepted them with a dip of his chin.

'So, you think Sarah Jane takes after her mom,

Ledge?' Autry glanced at me out of the corner of his eye as he finally restarted the truck. 'You think she's got a savvy?'

I nodded.

'Do you know what it is?'

I felt inside my pocket for Sarah Jane's notebook. 'Yeah, I think so.'

'I think I might too.' Autry chewed at the inside of his cheek as he drove us up the gravel road. 'I'll tell you something else I've not told anyone, Ledge. Just before Sarah Jane turned thirteen, Noble came to talk to me.'

'He did? What for?'

'He wanted to know if there was any way to *stop* someone from coming into a savvy.'

'What did you say?'

'I told him it would be like trying to keep someone from growing up.' Autry frowned. 'It wasn't what he wanted to hear. I think he was convinced that if Sarah Jane weren't exposed to us or the ranch or anyone different, she'd manage to get through her birthday without any fuss. Then he wouldn't need to worry about losing another person he loved.

'That's when foreclosure signs began going up,' Autry continued. 'Anyone too odd was swiftly threatened or removed – even though Noble himself is one of the oddest ducks around.' Autry gave a snort, parking the truck in the thin, twisted shade at the base of the windmill. 'And when Sarah Jane started selling her papers . . .'

'She wrote all those crazy stories about the people in town!' I exclaimed. 'Then Mr Cabot read them and believed them and . . . and . . .' I slammed my palm against my forehead. 'SJ was trying to get his attention. But she just made everything worse.'

'Who knew Sarah Jane's savvy has been staring everyone in the face this whole time?' Autry chewed his cheek again. 'That girl doesn't even know how powerful her talents are. Or how much damage she can do.'

I shifted uncomfortably in my seat, wiggling as something scratched my back beneath the waistband of my shorts.

Autry's deed.

It was the first time since the sheriff nabbed me and SJ that I'd thought of the document SJ had found in the CAD Co. file room.

'Sarah Jane found this,' I said, pulling the paper from my waistband and handing it to my uncle. 'She wanted to help fix things.'

Autry took the document from me and stared at it.

'Is this why you and Sarah Jane broke into Noble's building, Ledge?' he asked, holding the paper between us, his voice rising again. 'What did the two of you think you were going to do with this?'

'Rip it up?' I offered. 'Destroy it so that Mr Cabot can't take away the ranch?'

Autry bit back his words three times before he spoke again. When he did, his voice was taut, but controlled – just like his savvy. I didn't see a single wasp or spider anywhere.

'I know you kids thought you were helping, Ledger. But breaking into other people's buildings and destroying legal documents isn't the way to do it.' His tone remained hard as he continued. 'I hate to break it to you, Ledge, but ripping things up won't *fix* anything. I signed this paper and agreed to Noble's terms. The consequences are mine.'

I hung my head. I'd been stupid to think I could patch up my uncle's problems, dumb to believe SJ's letter. Though, now I knew I couldn't NOT believe anything Sarah Jane wrote. Her savvy wouldn't let me.

Chapter 32

As SOON AS I COULD, I went looking for Grandpa, finally able to give him Grandma Dollop's jar. I found him sitting in his overstuffed chair by the river, shaded by the giant cottonwood that had once been Cam Beacham's lucky glove.

'Here, Grandpa,' I said, handing him the peanut-butter jar and watching the old man's wrinkled face light up.

'Look what you brought me, Ledger!' Grandpa murmured as he turned the lid, listening to the canned symphony like it was the first music he'd ever heard.

'I-it didn't get broken, Grandpa. It just . . . it just got kinda lost for a while.'

Grandpa stood from his chair and hugged me with more strength than I thought he had left in him. He kissed the jar, gave the lid a little twist, then held it high, waltzing in slow, shuffling steps to the music, as if Grandma Dollop were there dancing with him. Bitsy tipped back her head and howled in doggy harmony. Birds chittered and chirped. Insects added percussion. When I saw tears travelling down paths worn deep into Grandpa's cheeks, I quickly turned away, hoping I'd somehow said and done enough.

'Ledger!' A voice I barely recognized stopped me. I looked over my shoulder but couldn't see anyone. A shadow brushed past me and, for a minute, Samson was there, having got up from his own chair next to Grandpa's. I could still see the river and the cottonwood tree through my cousin, but he was definitely there, one hand holding a book, the other stretched out as if he'd been about to grab my shoulder and changed his mind at the last moment.

'Take my seat for a while,' he said, his voice dusty with disuse. 'There's something I need to do for Uncle

Autry, and Grandpa shouldn't be alone.' Then he was gone – *poof* – just like that. Yet, somehow, I felt better for having seen him at last.

Dancing tired Grandpa quickly. His tears slowed, then stopped. But as soon as he sat back down with Grandma Dollop's jar, he started pitching all the jar lids from Fedora's helmet into the river one by one, watching them skip and splash *kerplunk*!

'Grandpa!'

'It's all right, Ledger. All things pass. My Dolly-Dollop's gone and it'll soon be time for me to join her. I've been living on borrowed strength too long already.' Grandpa gazed past me as if he could still see Samson's shadow in the distance. Then he patted Samson's empty seat. 'Sit down and keep an old man company.'

Bitsy hobble-bobbled at my feet, pushing her wet nose into my hand. I scratched the dog once behind the ears, then sat down. Grandpa gave me my own handful of jar lids and, together, we tossed them into the river.

Soon all the lids glinted from beneath the water like wishes in a fountain.

Squishing deep into the cushions of Samson's high-backed chair, I realized how comfortable I'd grown sitting on the hard, unbreakable stumps by the fire. For weeks, I'd wanted to go home. Now I knew I was going to miss those sawn-off trunks when I went. I was going to miss a lot of things. A lot of people too.

Autry had felt obligated to call my parents when we got back from the sheriff's. Mom had totally freaked out. She freaked even more when Autry shared the news of the foreclosure at last, convinced that she and Dad needed to head for Wyoming straight away.

I sighed and pitched the last of the jar lids into the flowing river, thinking about the long list of punishing chores I knew Autry was compiling. I guessed I'd soon be weeding the garden or scrubbing compost buckets. Or worse, feeding budworm larvae to predatory stink bugs.

'Tell me, Ledger.' Grandpa rested one hand lightly on my arm. 'Tell me the story.'

'What story, Grandpa?' I looked at him, confused.

'Tell me the story of how the jar got lost, and how it found its long way back.'

'But –'

'Just tell me the story, Ledger.' Grandpa Bomba closed his eyes, settling back into the cushion of his own tall chair, the sound of the river like a great-great- and greater-than-that-grandmother whispering to us from the past. 'And, Ledge,' Grandpa added, letting just one eye pop back open.

'Yes, Grandpa?'

'Make the story really good.'

I tossed and turned all night, wondering if SJ had got into trouble – if she was all right. Wondering if Jonas Brown had ignored his sheriff-duty and kept our presence at the CAD Co. building secret. Wondering, too, what Mr Cabot had thought of the brand-new ladder spiralling up to his daughter's window.

The next morning, I was bleary-eyed and tired, while my uncle Autry looked like an all-new man –

or an all-new *kid*, judging by the way he was acting. He woke us up early, before dawn, thrusting an email under our noses and spinning like a Frisbee between the truck, the Bug House and his office inside the house.

'What's going on?' I yawned under the grey-pink sky, watching Fedora kick the tyres on Autry's truck, checking that everything looked safe and sound and up to snuff.

'Uncle Autry's leaving,' she said.

'Only for the day!' Autry called from behind the stack of charts and papers and photographs of butterflies he was busy loading into the truck.

'There are people who've heard about the butterflies and want to give Uncle Autry money to save the conservatory!' Gypsy clapped her hands, the only one besides Rocket who didn't look ready to crawl back into bed. 'But –'

'But only if I'll consider opening the place up,' Autry finished for her, coming round the side of the truck to stand with the rest of us.

341

Marisol and Mesquite both woke up at that.

'Like some kind of zoo?' Mesquite asked, uncertain.

'You want to let total strangers into the conservatory, Papi?' Marisol chimed in. 'Little kids with lollipops and grown-ups with great big clumsy feet?'

'I don't know yet!' Autry answered. 'I have to go to Cheyenne for a meeting today. To show off the results from the work I've done. To prove we've got honest-to-goodness Alexandras here, surviving and thriving.

'This could be it, girls!' He grinned at the twins. 'This could be what saves this place! And people would learn something coming here, no matter how big or small their feet might be. No one can look at a Queen Alexandra's Birdwing and not be changed! I suppose we might have to think about relocating some of the bigger spiders . . .' Autry scratched his head.

I stood back and watched as Marisol and Mesquite hugged their dad goodbye. Then Autry turned and ruffled Gypsy's hair.

'You're in charge of the butterflies today, okay, Gypsy? Rocket's in charge of everything else.'

Rocket nodded. Gypsy gave a barefoot, twirling salute, before adding, 'I'll watch over them, no matter what!' The enormous butterflies were a big success for Uncle Autry. He hadn't lost a single one.

Before leaving, Autry turned last to me and Fedora.

'Whatever you two do, if your mother phones, don't tell her I'm in Cheyenne. She'll tan my hide. Besides, I'll be back tonight. I think I've convinced your folks that they don't have to come for you right away. But if Dinah calls and finds out I'm not around to keep you out of trouble, she'll savvy-talk the Indiana Air National Guard into flying her here in a fighter jet.'

Fedora and I both nodded as Uncle Autry climbed into his truck. Autry hadn't warned me again to stay away from Mr Cabot. He hadn't said two words about Sheriff Brown. In the end, it was my mom who worried my uncle most. Thinking about it almost made me laugh.

'Ho, Ledger!' Autry had already begun to pull away when he stopped the truck and called to me from his open window. I jogged towards the idling truck and looked up, wondering if he was going to add to my list of punishments for breaking into the CAD Co. building. But my uncle had something else on his mind.

'Be a sport, Ledge, and don't tell the others what I said about the Eva Mae story, all right? The girls have been working too hard these past weeks looking for her treasure.'

'Treasure?' I repeated, my mouth hanging open. That was what Marisol and Mesquite had been doing with Fedora all this time? Digging for *buried treasure*? It explained everything: the dirt, the shovels, the need for extra doses of good-karma luck.

Autry winced. 'The girls don't think I know what they've been up to. Let's not spoil their fun, all right? Sometimes the searching is the best part of any quest. Oh, and I almost forgot,' Autry called over the sound of the truck's engine. 'I've got something for you.' He shuffled through a bag next to him. It was from Willie's Five & Dime.

'Something for me?' I asked, surprised. I'd expected chores, not presents.

Autry handed me a heavy bar of novelty soap, marked down for quick clearance. On the wrapper, the Sundance Kid sat behind bars, the words *You're in Sundance Now – Keep Your Nose Clean* printed just below the picture.

'You bought me soap?'

'Do us all a favour, Ledge, and take a real shower for a change? Eva Mae Ransom may have bumped and tumbled down the Big Muddy for a good long time, but she probably didn't know the magic of hot water and indoor plumbing the way we do.' Autry winked, then hit the accelerator, disappearing over the ridge, followed by jet streams of dartling, flittering, flying things.

I ran a hand through my grimy hair, realizing that, for the first time in my life, it had grown long enough to touch the tops of my ears. Looking at the soap, I lifted my shirt to my nose and took a whiff – I didn't smell that bad, did I? I considered giving the bar of soap to Samson to help him stick his shadow to something a bit more solid, but in the end, I went back up to Rocket's house and made the choice to take a shower.

Chapter 33

THAT AFTERNOON, AS GYPSY WATCHED THE butterflies, Samson watched Grandpa, and Fedora and the twins continued their going-nowhere treasure hunt, Winona, Rocket and I put the last spit and polish on the Knucklehead. Headlamp to harness – the bike was done.

We were all sitting back, admiring our work, staring happily at the awesome bike and at Winona's gleaming, scrap-yard jackalope, when Winona let out a sudden noisy whoop.

'Unless I'm wrong, I think we've still got time, boys!' In an instant she was up, grabbing a calendar and digging through a stack of papers on Gus's desk. 'I can't

346

believe it! We do!' Winona looked at a clock on the wall. Rocket and I looked at each other, clueless.

Winona explained, rapid-fire: 'The motorcycle show in Spearfish! The one with the big, fat prize that Gus and I planned to enter. It's this weekend! Today's the last day to register. The last day to deliver this baby for the show.' She leaned over and kissed the bike's handlebars, then polished them back to perfection with her rag.

'Well, what are we waiting for?' said Rocket. 'Let's get this Knuck in the truck!' He clapped his hands together, showering harmless sparks.

Rocket went pale. But Winona hardly paused before she pointed at Rocket and said, 'Okay, *that's* something you're going to have to explain to me a little later. In fact, I think you both have some explaining to do.' She cocked one eyebrow at me. 'I've been out in the yard. I want to know what's going on. Only later! Right now, we've got a motorcycle show to enter.'

'Won't Autry get mad if he finds out we went to South Dakota?' I asked Rocket as Winona gathered what we

347

needed to get the bike to Spearfish. 'He did leave you in charge of the ranch.'

'When did you start worrying about what will or won't make Autry angry, Ledger? This morning after breakfast?' Rocket gripped the back of my neck and gave me a joggle. 'Because I know you weren't trying to throw him a party when you were breaking into Cabot's place with Sarah Jane.'

I swallowed hard. 'He told you?'

'He told me,' Rocket answered. 'But he also told me that you were trying to help. So, I get that. Still . . . dude. Stupid.' He let go of my neck and knocked his knuckles into mine. And since I didn't get electrocuted, I guessed I'd been forgiven.

Rocket squared his shoulders. 'As the adult in charge today, I'm giving us permission to drive to South Dakota,' he declared. 'Spearfish isn't far, Ledge; it's not like we're travelling to a galaxy far, far away. And Autry's been harping on me for years to get *off* the ranch more often. We won't be gone more than two hours. Besides, it's not like there isn't another adult at the Flying Cattleheart . . . Grandpa Bomba's there.'

I gave Rocket a dubious look. I was pretty sure Grandpa's waltz by the river had been his last dance. If something did go wrong at the ranch – flood, fire or fruit fly rebellion – Grandpa Bomba would probably snore right through it, the same as he'd done through my story about Grandma's jar.

Soon the Knucklehead was secure in the bed of the truck, held upright in a web of tightened ratchet straps, the three of us jammed together up front. As we drove through Sundance, headed towards Spearfish, I couldn't keep from leaning out the window, craning my neck to look behind us. I wasn't staring at the golden bike. Instead, I was looking towards the house on the hill, picturing Sarah Jane locked in her room, still totally unaware that she had a savvy of her own.

'Ha! Some people will believe anything.' Winona laughed next to me.

'Huh?' I grunted, pulling my head back inside the truck. Winona pointed at the car in front of us. Its rear bumper, still attached, was plastered in stickers:

MY OTHER CAR IS A UFO
BIGFOOT RESEARCH UNIT
I ♥ AXEHANDLE HOUNDS

I smiled, thinking of *The Sundance Scuttlebutt* and all of SJ's crazy stories. Then my stomach lurched as I was struck by a sudden thought . . .

If my parents arrived to take me and Fedora home as soon as Mom had said they would, I might not get to see Sarah Jane again. My palms itched. My knee hammered up and down even as I tried to get my head and shoulders out the window, straining to see SJ's house again. I couldn't leave Sundance without seeing Sarah Jane. She knew the truth about me. Now she needed to know the truth about herself.

'Hey, Ledge! You doing okay?' Rocket asked, his voice vibrating as he held tight to the shuddering steering wheel. Winona dragged down on my T-shirt.

'What're you trying to do, Ledge? Get your head taken off?'

'Stop!' I bellowed, reaching for the door handle. 'You've got to let me out! You two take the bike to

Spearfish without me. You have to get it there before it's too late. I've got to stay here – there's something I have to do.'

'Whoa, Ledge, slow down!' Rocket pulled the truck over as quickly as he could to keep me from jumping out while it was still moving – and to stop my distress from undoing all our work on the bike in one cataclysmic savvy blow.

'Just get the bike to Spearfish!' I said, leaping from the truck. 'Get it there so it can win that money. You can't let Mr Cabot have the salvage yard!'

The Cabots' housekeeper was outside when I got there, sweeping a single spot on the front porch over and over as she stood engrossed in the colourful supermarket tabloid she held up in front of her broom.

Even from across the street, I could hear Sarah Jane throwing a pitching, screaming fit inside. She wasn't just crying. She wasn't just yelling. Sarah Jane was *breaking* things. It sounded like she was hurling objects – large and small – against the locked door of her room.

Hedda the Horrible didn't even flinch.

Something bad was happening. Something *really* bad. There was no outward sign that Mr Cabot might be home: no Lincoln parked in front of the house, no CAD Co. truck either.

Ignoring SJ's tantrum, Hedda turned a page of her tabloid. I watched her carefully from where I lurked in the bushes, impatient for an opportunity to slip by her. The ladder I'd built was gone. All the fence posts hauled away. Getting to SJ would require that direct approach I'd thought of the last time I was here – *through the door, up the stairs, blast the lock!*

I was no longer worrying about telling SJ who she really was. All I wanted now was to know what was wrong with my friend.

The telephone rang inside the house and Hedda moved swiftly through the screen door to answer. I crossed the street in four strides, the stump-filled yard in three, pausing just long enough to kick off my trainers at the door.

Ignoring the smell of my socks, I was through the

door and up the creaking, groaning stairs in seconds.

An old-fashioned keyhole lock . . . *WHAM!*

A brass knob . . . *BAM!*

A heavy-hinged door . . . *SLAM!*

That was what I *could've* done. It was what I *had* done at the CAD Co. building. Only, that hadn't felt so great.

Instead, thinking fast, I scrabbled in my pocket, yanking the wire spiral out of SJ's notebook, as well as the corkscrewed wheel spoke from the Knucklehead. It took a few tries: a twist here, a bend there, a hook, a crook, a prayer . . . then *CLICK!*

I'd made a fretwork-and-filigree skeleton key and fitted it to the lock.

I opened the door and ducked fast, dodging the alarm clock Sarah Jane had just sent flying. Glancing at the scattered gears and bells and cogs, I grinned.

'Hey! You've got your own mad skills. Stop copying mine!'

'Ledge! It's you!' She was across the room and hugging me before I knew what hit me, squeezing me to death in the doorway to her disaster of a room. SJ had pulled apart her bed, her desk and her bookshelves too. Broken stuff lay everywhere. Though, the two Captain Marvel comics I'd given her rested in mint condition on her nightstand. At least she hadn't torn The Big Red Cheese to shreds.

'I'm sorry, Ledge! It's monstrous! Totally catastrophic!'

'It was just an alarm clock, SJ –'

'No! You don't understand!' SJ pushed away from me, leaving a damp stain of tears on my shoulder. 'Daddy had security cameras in his office!' Her voice dropped quieter and quieter as she spoke. 'He saw us there, Ledge. He saw *you* there! He knows we were the ones who broke in. He knows everything! And he is *mad* . . .' Her last word came out a whisper.

There wasn't enough thin Wyoming air in the room. I couldn't breathe. My fingertips were tingling. My lips felt numb.

Somehow I managed to say: 'How mad, SJ?'

Her eyes rolled wildly and she shook her head. 'Try

exploding-sun, comets-hitting-earth, end-of-life-as-we-know-it mad! He's gone, Ledge. He's taken all his workmen and all his wreckers. He's gone to your uncle's ranch – he's going to tear everything down!'

'But . . . he can't do that! At least, not yet, right? Autry still has time. He's in Cheyenne. He's getting the money to –' I stopped. Looking at SJ's face, I could see none of these things meant anything. Mr Cabot was on a rampage.

I turned from the room, ready to fly to the ranch as fast as my feet would carry me. But Sarah Jane grabbed my shirt.

'Ledge! There's no way to stop him. It's too – it's too . . .' SJ sniffed and stammered, unable to finish. What had she been about to say? That it was too late? Too dangerous? It didn't matter.

'You don't understand!' I said, pulling away. 'There's no one there, SJ. No one who can *do* anything.' Not even the twins would be there to protect their home from Cabot, not if they'd struck out far, hunting for Eva Mae's tall-tale treasure in the outer edges of the Flying

Cattleheart. Sure, invisible Samson might be able to tie Noble Cabot's shoelaces together, or try to scare the workman with his shadow. But what good would those things do against bulldozers?

'I have to go,' I said, knowing the fate of the ranch would be left to a three-legged dog if I didn't. Beneath my skin, the ants were seething. I wanted to take Noble Cabot's entire house down then and there. I could do to Sarah Jane's dad what he was about to do to my uncle. What he'd already done to the T-shirt shop in town. What he was planning to do to the five-and-dime, and the salvage yard too.

And I didn't need a bulldozer or a wrecking ball to do it.

'Ledge, no.' Sarah Jane whispered my name like she knew what I was thinking, her voice pulling me back from the brink, back from a dangerous ledge I hadn't even seen myself nearing. I knew I could make the choice to be like Mr Cabot. Or I could choose another way.

The Ledger Kale way.

'I have to go,' I said again.

'He's my dad, Ledge.'

'So?'

'*So* – I'm coming with you!' Sarah Jane wiped her eyes and shoved her feet into her shoes. I stood in my socks, itching to go as I waited for SJ to lace up her green Converse low-tops – the same ones that had tangled with my running shoes on my very first day in Sundance. The day all this started.

'Fine,' I said. 'But if you can't keep up, you'll have to *catch* up.' Turning, I shot through the bedroom door, then stopped – or would have, if my sock-feet hadn't sent me sliding right into Hedda the Horrible, who stood at the top of the stairs. Hedda held her broom in one hand and her rolled-up tabloid in the other, and she glared at me as if I were a bug she'd like to flatten.

A headline spiralling round her paper caught my eye, one worthy of *The Sundance Scuttlebutt*:

MARS NEEDS HOUSEKEEPERS

Apparently, Hedda was looking for a new job . . . on another planet.

I couldn't push past her – I didn't want to knock the woman down the stairs – and I didn't have time to talk my way around her either. Backing up, I slipped on one of SJ's pencils. With a sudden inspiration, I bent to pick it up.

I shoved the pencil at Sarah Jane, then fished one of the loose notebook papers from my pocket and pushed that at her as well.

'What do you want me to do? Take notes?'

I grabbed SJ's arm and pulled her close, whispering in her ear exactly what I wanted her to write. She looked at me like she thought I'd cracked my last marble, but didn't waste time asking questions. Sarah Jane wrote quickly, pressing the paper against my back. Then she handed me what she'd written, watching as I moved towards Hedda, holding out the piece of paper. Careful not to look at it myself.

'Have you read today's headline?'

Hedda's brow furrowed as she glanced at the words:

THE MOTHER SHIP IS HERE FOR YOU

Eyes round, Hedda dropped her newspaper and

broom. Her hands flew to her heart and fluttered there nervously. Then she lit down the stairs, collected her purse and left through the front door.

'Where is she *going*?' SJ asked, bewildered.

'She's either leaving town, or looking for the landing site,' I answered with a shrug. Sarah Jane stood up taller, eyes dancing.

'That's the power of the press!'

'No, that's the power of Sarah Jane Cabot,' I replied. But I didn't have time to explain more. Not right now.

I pulled Sarah Jane down the stairs and out the door, nodding to the tall birch tree beside the house as I crammed my feet back in my trainers. For what it was worth, I'd kept my promise to Uncle Autry: I hadn't put one shoe inside the Cabot house.

Chapter 34

Speeding from the Cabot house, I wasn't super-sonic, but I was close. I'd never run so fast in my entire life. If I'd been running against Ryan, I would've beaten him easily. But there was more at stake now than a half-marathon, a time to beat, or a trophy. This race had to count – *really* count – and I was glad I'd trained so hard for it. If only Dad could see me now!

Sarah Jane matched me stride for stride, as if she and I had been running in sync together all summer rather than constantly tripping each other up. We passed the *Welcome to Sundance* sign still swinging from one bolt in the wind. With a *snap!* and a backward glance, I repaired the sign – no problem. If only I could snap my fingers and do the same for Willie's, the salvage yard and the Flying Cattleheart. But I knew there were some things I couldn't fix – and I was reminded of it again when we reached the ranch's towering steel gate.

The gravel road cresting the ridge was brutally gouged and furrowed. A parade of heavy equipment had left thick tyre treads in the red soil, flattening the tall grass and wildflowers, squashing grasshoppers, butterflies and tiger beetles in its path. Warm wind mixed diesel fumes with the smell of crushed sage, creating a pungent mix that made my stomach churn.

Suddenly, the ground rumbled, quaking hard enough to make me and SJ stagger and clasp hands as we tried to keep our balance.

'Ledge! Is it an earthquake?' SJ was breathless. I couldn't answer – I didn't know. On the other side of the ridge, thick billows of dirt and dust rose up in grubby clouds. The tremor only lasted seconds, but it shook me to my core.

I'm here too late, I thought. *The demolition's started.*

Up and over the ridge we went, panting as we reached the slope on the other side. Sarah Jane clutched a stitch in her side but didn't ask to stop. Dust hung thick over the basin of the ranch. I couldn't see what was happening below until we drew closer. Then details of the scene came into sharp focus.

At first even I had trouble reconciling what I saw with what I remembered the ranch to be. For Sarah Jane, the disconnect between the old landscape and this new one was even harder to fathom.

'Ledge! When did your uncle get the *moat*?'

I was having trouble with that one too. Between the time I'd left the Flying Cattleheart and now, the path of the river had altered. Now, instead of burbling around the far side of the Bug House, the cascading waters rushed rapidly through a deep gully that wound round the O'Connells' log house. The 'moat' trenched through Rocket's garden, then doubled back to snake in front of the conservatory, resuming its course on the far side of Cam Beacham's lucky-glove cottonwood.

The last person to move the banks of that river –
the *only* person – was Grandpa Bomba. But these days
Grandpa Bomba couldn't move his own *chair*. Still, there
was no other explanation. Somehow, Grandpa must
have found the strength . . . or borrowed a lion's share.

The resounding bark of a dog yanked my attention
away from the wayward waterway. Following the sound
west, I saw Mr Cabot climbing down out of his truck
on the other side of the current, silhouetted against a
settling haze of dust. Leaning on his cane, his shape was
unmistakable, and his yellow CAD Co. hard hat glinted
in the sun like a hazard beacon.

Mr Cabot moved to stand in front of the Bug House,
quickly joined by a company of slack-jawed workmen
and a sloth of heavy equipment as every engine went
quiet, one after the next. Mr Cabot appeared to be waiting for a barrier to be removed, or some high-noon face-
off to end.

'Daddy! Stop!' SJ cried as she and I changed course,
leaving the gravel road and cutting across the field
towards the conservatory – towards Mr Cabot, two

bulldozers, three trucks, an excavator and a digger. There was a spot where Grandpa had made the banks of the gully too narrow, the water flowing mostly underground. It was a small breach in the defences, but one that had allowed the wreckers, and now us, to cross over.

Hearing his daughter's cry, Cabot turned. I could see Bitsy, all three feet planted like a not-so-misfit guard dog in front of the glass-roofed barn. Hackles raised. Teeth bared. The dog that I'd seen licking crayfish and teaming up with tarantulas looked ready to chomp the seat right out of Noble Cabot's trousers.

But Bitsy wasn't alone in her fight. Two other figures had inserted themselves between Cabot and the conservatory, standing their ground against seemingly impossible odds. Just behind Bitsy, Grandpa Bomba stood in Cabot's way, looking stronger than I'd ever seen him. His old muscles were as withered and wrinkled as ever, but he no longer looked like a man knock-knock-knocking on the door of heaven.

The third figure was Samson – flesh and bone and fully visible.

Half kneeling next to Grandpa Bomba, Samson's whip-thin frame was tense as he held fast to Bitsy, the late-afternoon wind lashing his long hair into his eyes. Samson looked just as he had in my earlier there-and-gone visions, only now there was no trace of transparency on him. He'd shown up completely – stepped up completely – making Grandpa and Bitsy stronger.

Down on one knee, Samson held Bitsy back with one hand as she barked and lunged at Cabot and his men, showing them what kind of dog she could be, stalwart as ever, even if she was down one leg. With his other hand, Samson held fast to Grandpa's arm in a way that made me wonder if it was Samson supporting Grandpa Bomba, or the other way round. My cousin's face was gaunt and focused. Giving his strength to Grandpa was taking everything out of him – not just his invisibility. The bugs inside the conservatory had a rag-tag team of unlikely champions.

The Goliath beetles, stick insects and butterflies had no way of knowing that their safely controlled and protected environment was about to come crashing down, sending them out into a world they weren't prepared for, or one that might not be prepared for them.

I knew exactly how that felt. I also knew what it meant to have people standing up for me.

'Daddy, stop!' Sarah Jane cried again, grabbing her father's hand as she reached him, still struggling to catch her breath.

'Sarah Jane! You shouldn't be here!' Cabot's face twisted as he pulled his hand free. He looked at me and his face turned purple. I thought his head might be about to explode. Then shouts rose from behind us, and the girls appeared at the top of the north ridge. The twins must have spotted the cloud of dust and felt the earth rumble too. Now Marisol and Mesquite were headed towards the Bug House as well, their backpacks bumping heavily behind them. Fedora ran out ahead – her own Kale-family speed genes kicking in. Despite everything,

I smiled. Wait until Dad saw that! Fe's feet were a Road Runner blur!

'Daddy, this is crazy!' Sarah Jane clung to her father. 'There are amazing things here. Wonderful things. What you're doing will make the worst, most wrong sort of headline!'

Cabot dropped his chin to his chest, his shoulders heaving. I stood back, waiting to see what he'd do. Close by, Grandpa and Samson watched and waited too. Bitsy stopped barking. Cabot's workmen shuffled their feet and tipped their hard hats back. All eyes were on Noble Cabot.

Mr Cabot stood still for so long, I thought the Bug House might be saved. I waited for him to toss up his hands and turn to go. Instead he raised his cane and brought it down again in one swift slicing motion.

He'd given his men the signal to proceed.

The workmen adjusted their hard hats and fired up their equipment. The deafening rattle of tracks, drive trains and hydraulic cylinders hammered my eardrums. The demolition crew moved towards the conservatory, grim-faced, the noise of their machinery drowning out the shouts of the twins as they drew nearer, and muffling SJ's cries to stop.

Maybe Sarah Jane could stop her father the same way we'd deflected Hedda. I dug into my pocket, pulling out SJ's loose notebook papers, only to have the wind scatter them from my hand. I realized quickly that it didn't matter. We didn't have a pencil.

As the bulldozers and excavators lurched slowly towards the Bug House, Grandpa used the last of his strength – the last of Samson's strength – to shift earth and rock one last time, churning half a dozen monumental boulders up from deep in the earth to try to block the wreckers.

Bitsy barked again. But in the noise ringing and grinding from the bulldozers as they began the new task of pushing Grandpa's boulders out of the way, her woofs and howls went mute.

Moments later, Grandpa Bomba crumpled like an empty hessian sack.

Barely catching Grandpa as he caved in, Samson let go of Bitsy. The big black dog lunged straight for Mr Cabot. Sarah Jane's dad was doing what he could to push her into one of the trucks, trying to remove her from what was about to become a dangerous mess of fallen wood and steel and glass and flying bugs. As Bitsy nabbed Cabot's trouser leg, I ran to help Samson pull Grandpa out of the path of an oncoming bulldozer.

I glanced up in time to see Gypsy poke her head out the door of the Bug House, a giant, iridescent blue-green butterfly stealing a secret ride in her curly hair. It was strange that Gypsy hadn't noticed it. Gypsy usually saw everything.

Seeing the heavy equipment coming towards the conservatory, Gypsy slipped back inside, but not before the enormous butterfly took flight, its wings beating slow and steady like an inhale . . . exhale. My own breathing slowed as I watched the bug land on the wooden beams

just above the exterior door. The thing was awesome –
sis boom bah *beautiful*.

I swore under my breath, wishing Gypsy had stayed
safely outside with the big-honkin' butterfly. But Gypsy
had told Autry she'd watch over the Alexandras – no
matter what. She was keeping her promise. She should've
been saving her own skin.

Grandpa had fallen. The Bug House was about to.
Samson and Bitsy had done everything they could. Now
it was my turn. Made wrong or made right, it didn't
matter.

I had to act.

Chapter 35

THERE WAS MORE AT STAKE THAN the Bug House now. More than Autry's livelihood or home. The workmen hadn't seen Gypsy. No one knew she was inside.

I took a deep breath and held it, watching the bulldozers push aside Grandpa's uprooted boulders one by one. Then I dropped into a crouch, about to begin an all-new race. Splaying my fingers against the ground, I prepared to start blasting booms and buckets into bits, to pull apart bolts and washers and gaskets and valves. I'd stop Cabot. If I had to, I'd fight him bolt and nail for the King of Damage crown.

My fingertips and palms began to prickle, to creep

with that oh-so-familiar savvy itch. Then fear returned, marching through my brain on a thousand tiny feet. What if I lost control? I pictured myself toppling the conservatory the same way I'd pulled down the barn, doing Mr Cabot's dirty work for him. Crushing Gypsy in the process.

Closing my eyes, I bowed my head, wondering . . . praying . . . demanding to know: dear God, what *had* I been built to do?

Something whispered against the fingers of my right hand. I opened my eyes. Gypsy's Queen Alexandra was there, fanning me with its wings. I startled, but tried not to move, not wanting to injure it. The butterfly only stayed for a second before it took off and flew away.

I stood and shook my head to try to clear it. To move beyond my fear. I didn't have much time. Already, the wreckers had shifted half of Grandpa's boulders and they kept moving . . . moving closer. There were only three boulders left to push away.

I had to think through my choices – quickly. I was beginning to suspect that, for me, *choice* might be the key to scumbling. Racing here from Sundance, my feet had been on autopilot, but my brain had been in overdrive. Breaking the twins' bikes, asking Winona to let me help her rebuild the motorcycle, putting a twist in the windmill, bending Sarah Jane's initials into the fence . . . all those things had been choices, not reactions. Every time I'd made the *choice* to do something, my scumbling had got better. I'd controlled my savvy instead of letting it control me.

Now it was time for me to step up, just as Samson had. To show the world who Ledger Kale really was . . .

Not the kid his dad wanted him to be.

Not the kid his mom *made* him be.

No Cowboy. No Sledgehammer. Not *defective*, either.

Only two boulders left . . .

Soon, one.

I knew I was going to have to Bust! Things! Up! But now I knew too, just as Winona had known, that sometimes things have to come apart before becoming something different – something better.

I crouched down again, letting the fear beneath my

skin subside as I looked at SJ and her dad. I thought of the birch tree that protected their house; Cabot had chopped down every tree in their yard but that one. I pictured the birch trees in the glade above us and remembered climbing them, always secure up in the branches. And as a bulldozer pushed Grandpa's last boulder aside . . . as the excavator smashed into the outer door of the conservatory . . . I imagined a picture of my own.

And turned my savvy loose.

Within seconds, everything began to change. Workmen leaped from their seats as their trucks, bulldozers and diggers started rattling apart. Panicked, one man clung tightly to his steering wheel, even as the roof over his head pulled away, twisting in a warp and stretch of metal. But Marisol and Mesquite were next to me, ready for action.

'We've got your back, Ledge.' Marisol punched me on the left shoulder, dropping her heavy backpack.

'We'll take care of the crew,' Mesquite added,

smacking me on the right and dropping her pack too. 'The wreckers are yours!' For the first time, I was glad to have the twins by my side.

The two girls levitated the frightened worker up and out of his seat even as it began to jerk and bump beneath him. As they set the man on the ground, his scuffed white hard hat fell from his head and Fedora shot after it like a kitten chasing yarn.

Nabbing the hard hat, Fe ran it straight to me. Resting grubby fingers on my shoulder, she crouched to whisper in my ear:

'Keep safe, Ledger! Use your head – wear a hard hat!'

Even as I stayed fully riveted on my task, I could feel Fe jam the workman's helmet on to my head and kiss the top of it. Then she ran to join Samson where he knelt supporting Grandpa's failing body.

I wanted to cry out to Grandpa to stay strong a little longer, but I was barely hanging on to my savvy as it was; I couldn't take the chance of letting a fraction of control slip.

I focused on the roiling pieces of the wracked and ruined equipment. Watching as those pieces began to morph and change. As they began to fuse together into a growing grove of metal trunks and branches – branches that sprouted leaves of glass and wire and shattered bits of mirror. Mirror that reflected the real me, doing what I was made to do.

I sculpted trees around the Bug House; each one reaching high and lofty. Each one its own strong, protective column. Its own graceful sculpture. Soon there wasn't a single bolt or spring or wire that hadn't become a part of my metal forest.

The wind whipped the scattered pages of Sarah Jane's notebook off the ground. Some of the papers flew high. Others smacked into the trunks of the new trees, looking just like the peeling bark of her mother's birches.

For this moment at least, the spiders and beetles and bugs inside the walls of the conservatory were safe, and the world's largest butterflies still had their home away from home. Only the outer door and the entry-way had been destroyed; the interior door still held strong. There was nothing more Mr Cabot could do. Most of his crew had run away, or hunkered down, crouched low and cowering behind the one truck I'd left standing – the truck where Mr Cabot had shoved Sarah Jane. Only now SJ was halfway out of the truck and cheering.

Mr Cabot hadn't budged. Still as a statue himself, he stared at the towering, sculpted trees that had once been his demolition fleet.

Slowly, I stood up, the metallic taste I was beginning to like melting away like a sliver of hard candy on my tongue.

'Mighty fine scumbling, Ledger. Mighty . . . mighty . . . fine.' Grandpa's voice was so weak it barely reached me. As I turned his way, he held up a hand and smiled. I smiled back, tears burning my eyes. Then I pulled off the hard hat Fedora had given me and dropped it on the ground.

Marisol and Mesquite turned towards Mr Cabot, who took a nervous step back. I expected the twins to polish him off, to pick him up and shake him before dropping him in the river, letting him splutter and splash down the water's brand-new course.

Instead, the twins dug deep into their backpacks and pulled out heavy handfuls of lumpy, golden rocks. They piled them, crystalline and sparkling, into Mr Cabot's arms before he could refuse their hard-earned riches, every last piece of what they surely believed to be Eva Mae Ransom's long-lost treasure.

I was stunned. Had Uncle Autry been wrong? Because it looked like Grandpa's story might've been true after all. Maybe the twins' attempts at helping me had improved their karma after all.

'Is it enough?' Marisol asked, swiping at her tears.

'Enough to pay off everything Papi owes you?' Mesquite added, wiping her nose on the back of her wrist. 'It's got to be worth a lot. It's got to be!'

'Take it!'

'Please!'

The twins pushed everything they had at Mr Cabot, every last rough nugget from their backpacks. A few more from their pockets.

Unable to hold any more of the brassy yellow stones in his arms, Mr Cabot hunched forward, removing his hard hat with his one free hand and allowing Marisol and Mesquite to fill it. He looked slowly from the twins to me – then to Gypsy as she stepped out of the conservatory and began to twirl in delight beneath the sculpted trees.

'Come, Sarah Jane,' he said at last, his voice unsteady. 'We're done here.' Cabot nodded at the remaining workmen and they hopped into the back of the CAD Co. truck without delay. SJ didn't resist when her dad steered her back into the cab. But as Mr Cabot started up the engine, SJ cast one long, last look my way – part apology, part thanks – and I wondered if any piece of what had just happened would make it into the next edition of her paper.

'Wait!' I called, rushing to grip the edge of Mr Cabot's open window, hopping next to the truck as it rolled forward.

'You have to tell her!' I said to him. 'You have to tell her *everything*.'

Cabot hit the brakes long enough to turn and glance from me to the brand-new forest of glass and metal trees. His mouth worked like he was chewing beef jerky. Then, almost imperceptibly, he nodded. Without another scowl or glower, he took his daughter's hand and spun the truck round to drive her home.

As I turned to watch the truck *thump-bump* carefully over the narrowest crack of the rushing gully, I felt a wave of relief. And not only because Mr Cabot was leaving.

I was relieved to see the minivan parked under the windmill and Mom and Dad standing on the other side of the river, looking for a way to cross. I'd never been so glad to see my parents in my life. But . . . had they seen me? Had they seen what I'd *done*?

Catching sight of Mom and Dad now too, Fedora bounced on her toes, hollering: 'Mom! Dad! Look what Ledge can do! He can build things up!' With her motorcycle helmet bobbing, my sister shadowboxed the air above her, shouting: 'Build! Things! Up!' And as Dad helped Mom step carefully over the pinched canal, he held his own hand high, punching the air. Giving me a big thumbs-up.

Waiting for Rocket and Uncle Autry to return to the ranch, Dad and Mom swung into action doing the things parents always do: making calls, feeling foreheads, furrowing brows and shooing the dog off the bed. I brought Grandpa's colourful afghan blanket in from outside and spread it over his frail frame. It was the first time I'd set foot inside the O'Connells' house all summer, and it felt in a small way like I'd found a port, won a race, crossed a threshold after a long, uncertain journey, stepping into a place where I fully belonged at last.

As tough as rawhide and more stubborn than a two-hundred-year-old mule, Grandpa wasn't finished drawing air into his lungs yet.

'I don't think I ever finished my story . . .' he mumbled as we tucked knitted zigzags in around him.

'Shh . . . Grandpa, it's okay,' Mesquite replied, floating him a drink of water.

'You weren't telling us a story,' Marisol added gently, patting Grandpa's wrinkled hand. 'Just rest.'

'No, no . . .' Grandpa coughed. 'I have to finish my story.'

'Which story, Grandpa?' I asked.

But it was Samson who answered, his voice husky. 'He wants to finish the story of Eva Mae El Dorado Two-Birds Ransom.' Samson sat next to Grandpa: jeans, T-shirt, long hair shadowing his own tired eyes. He looked like any regular sixteen-year-old boy. I blinked at him again and again, waiting for him to disappear. But he didn't and I was glad.

'Come close, children . . .' Grandpa coughed again and we all leaned in, seeing that Grandpa still had the tail end of a tall tale left to tell, and knowing he wouldn't part from this earth allowing a story to go unfinished.

'Where did we leave off?' Grandpa wondered, his words a coarse-gravelled whisper.

'I remember! We left off at the part about the treasure!' Fedora called out as she and Gypsy each took hold of one of Grandpa's hands. Leaning closer, Fe whispered,

'We found it, Grandpa! We found her treasure. It was here all along, just like you said.'

'Of course it was, my dear Fedora,' Grandpa croaked as he tried to chuckle. 'Eva Mae's treasure is *still* here . . . here now . . . sitting all around me.'

Chapter 36

FOR BETTER, WORSE, OR DIFFERENT, SOMETIMES when things go back to normal, normal simply isn't *normal* any more. Mom and Dad ushered me and Fedora home just as the summer heat peaked and school supplies showed up in every store. I'd scumbled my savvy better than anyone could've expected after such a disastrous, stinking start, and Mom and Dad agreed to let me return to school on savvy trial-probation. Everything should have returned to normal . . . felt normal . . . been normal. Instead, everything was the same, but also completely different, like I was looking at things with all-new eyes.

I'd been back at Theodore Roosevelt for six weeks before I stopped waiting for Mom to put her savvy whammy on me every day before school. She even let me choose to avoid the barber shop, allowing my hair to grow *past* my ears and get good and shaggy instead. Mom let me pick out my own school clothes too. In fact, after coming home from Wyoming, I got to pick a lot more things for myself – like whether or not I wanted to keep running.

I did. And I tied with Ryan in the boys' cross-country time trials to boot. But I also chose to take another art class – and signed up for shopcraft.

Sometimes I missed being surrounded by the sensational. I missed it so much I sent Sarah Jane my address in Indiana, asking for a subscription to her paper. She'd written back right away, saying she was so happy she planned to *kiss* me the very next time we met. My face burned as I read the message and my palms began to sweat. I carried that letter in my pocket every day, even after the folds in the paper began to tear.

After that, a new edition of *The Sundance Scuttlebutt*

385

arrived every week like clockwork. I brought the papers to school to share with the guys, laughing my head off as they believed all of SJ's awesome stories like gospel. But I made a mistake when I showed them SJ's letter. By the end of that day, Big Mouth Brody had told the whole school there was a girl in Wyoming who wanted to pucker up to Ledger Kale. When I found out he'd spread the rumour, every locker door in the eighth-grade hallway flew off its hinges.

I was prepared for the lecture I was bound to get at home when I fessed up. But whatever Mom and Dad had to say got cut off by a rumble in the floorboards and a phone call from Uncle Autry. After Autry's call, no one cared too much about my savvy flub.

Grandpa Bomba's death left the ground shaking beneath our feet for days. After the day he moved the river, he'd lived on longer than anyone expected, spending his final days on the ranch, just as he'd always wanted, and slipping away peacefully in his sleep.

We made it to Grandpa's funeral on time and in

one piece. This time, when Dad pushed the minivan to its limits along the interstate, there was no parade of problems to slow us down. Though, Dad and I did have to miss the father-son half-marathon to get there.

'I know how hard you've been training, Ledge,' Dad said as we packed for our trip back to Wyoming. 'Are you disappointed?'

'It's okay, Dad.' I shrugged, remembering my last run from Sundance to the Flying Cattleheart and knowing that I'd already run the race of a lifetime.

'There's always next year.' Dad scrabbled my scruffy hair. Then he added, 'If you want – if you're not too busy sculpting benches into boats, or transforming time clocks into tyrannosaurs. I never meant to push my dreams on you, son.' He smiled and held up his fist. After a pause, I bumped it with my own, tears welling up when Dad wrapped his other arm round me and pulled me into a tight hug.

October had painted the leaves of the birch trees golden, and joined with the autumn wind to carpet the glade at the Flying Cattleheart. Small puffs of clouds crossed the huge Wyoming sky in herds, like ghostly buffalo flying overhead.

I held Fedora's hand tight through the funeral. I even let her wipe her nose once on my sleeve. Fe didn't wear a helmet any more – not since the day Mr Cabot tried to destroy the Bug House. She no longer spouted safety quotes, either. My sister's second-grade teacher may have been a stickler for safety, but her *third*-grade teacher was a science nut. Now Fe was building vinegar-and-baking-soda volcanoes, turning potatoes into batteries, and playing with magnets – though the broken jackalope magnet from Willie's Five & Dime was still her favourite.

Standing near us at the funeral, Great-aunt Jules whispered loudly to Aunt Jenny behind a lacy, sodden kerchief.

'I daresay young Ledger turned out to have some talent after all! Those are fine trees he built to protect Autry's conservatory. Trees like that aren't built every day, you know. The boy's an artist!' Then, issuing two *tisks* and a *tut* as her eyes fell on Gypsy, Aunt Jules added, 'Is it true nothing happened on Gypsy's birthday, Jenny dear?'

Aunt Jenny smiled and said nothing, ignoring Great-aunt Jules with perfect poise. I smiled too. From what I'd heard, nothing usual *had* happened on, or since, Gypsy's birthday earlier that month – nothing but a trip to the eye doctor and a brand-new pair of sparkly purple glasses, her vision test coming back a wild blue yonder from clear, crisp twenty-twenty.

Aunt Jules had said I was an artist. But she hadn't been the first to see it. Somehow I suspected there were still surprises around the blurry corners of Gypsy Beaumont's savvy future.

Gypsy stepped forward, barefoot as usual, holding the peanut-butter jar that had tormented me all summer. After a nod from Aunt Jenny, she removed the last jar's lid completely. I almost cried out as Gypsy let loose the music that had been trapped for years. Everyone had agreed to let it go . . . for Grandpa.

As Grandpa's body was lowered into the ground,

plumes of earth shot skyward across the basin of the ranch. Rocks shifted and jumped like popcorn. Clefts and canyons formed, then snapped together, and the river shimmied and splashed, its banks heaving and yawing to follow yet another brand-new course . . . all while the final trumpet from Grandma's jar called Grandpa Bomba home.

After the funeral, everyone gathered at the house – O'Connells, Beaumonts, Kales and more – to celebrate Grandpa's life with every story that could be remembered, and more than a few made up on the spot.

Marisol and Mesquite kept everyone fed by levitating buttered rolls, lemon bars and little smoky soya sausages over people's heads and dropping them on to people's plates – a potluck falling from the sky, piece by piece. The twins blamed grief for making them *accidentally* rain a handful of pepper down on Great-aunt Jules. But no one seemed to mind when the old woman sneezed three times and vanished in her typical time-bending conundrum. Still shaking pepper out of her hair, she bumped into Rocket when she reappeared fifteen minutes later, red in the face from rushing to catch back up with the rest of us in the present.

Rocket was still clean-shaven, but something else about him was different now too. He no longer stood with his hands jammed in his pockets or tucked under his arms. He looked confident – grown up at last.

Rocket and Winona had driven straight through the night to get back to Wyoming from Gold Beach, where the two of them had been sightseeing by motorcycle along the Oregon coast. I'd cheered when I heard about Rocket's trip. He'd managed to get himself off the ranch at last, and he'd taken a mighty fine travelling companion too.

Inside the house, Rocket and Winona stood chatting with Fish and Mellie and Mibs and Will and another woman with blonde hair and a long fringe. She looked just like an older version of the girl in the bubblegum photo that had once been stuck to the dash of Rocket's truck.

'Gypsy!' I stopped my cousin as she danced past me with a plate of rainbow-sprinkle cookies. 'Is that Bobbi

Meeks?' I pointed at the blonde woman standing with the others. Gypsy squinted through her sparkly glasses, frowned, then pulled the frames down to the tip of her nose to look over the plastic rims.

'Oh, yes! Rocket dated her when I was little, but she's married to someone else now. She wasn't at Fish's wedding because her little girl was sick. See! That's her.' I watched as Bobbi bent down to lift a tiny child who'd been clinging to her leg, hidden in the folds of her skirt. Resting her daughter on her hip, Bobbi rubbed the child's back. She laughed with Rocket and Winona as the other two couples moved to another group – Mibs blushing as she showed off a new diamond on her ring finger. But even from across the room, I could see the white scar that lined the back of Bobbi's hand like a firework burst.

'You said Rocket still had one last thing to learn about scumbling,' I said after seeking out Uncle Autry. 'He figured it out.'

'He did, did he?' Autry squinted at me, then turned to watch Rocket pretend to capture Bobbi's daughter's nose inside his fist, making the little girl squeal and giggle. I saw the way Rocket and Bobbi smiled like old friends, and the way Rocket turned to kiss Winona's hair and laugh.

'I think he just had to learn to make some choices,' I said.

Autry looked back at me and raised his eyebrows, encouraging me to continue.

'Rocket made the choice to stop being scared,' I went on. A knowing smile spread across my uncle's face as the green beetle on his bolo tie shivered its wings in a little dance. 'Rocket made the choice to show himself and go out into the world. And . . .' I hesitated, looking again at the scar on the back of Bobbi's hand. 'And maybe the choice to forgive himself for things he didn't mean to do.' I nodded then, still watching my oldest cousin. 'That's good.'

'It *is* good, Ledge!' Autry thumped me on the back. 'And it was about time too. I needed Rocket's house! We've got researchers coming and going! Entomology students rotating through from all over – Arizona,

Illinois, Maryland, New York . . . Our butterflies have everyone buzzing!' Autry thumped me again, then winked.

As the adults all ate and talked inside, Tucker and Fedora fled outdoors to play with Bitsy. I followed them through the screen door, stopping when I found Samson sitting on the porch next to Grandpa Bomba's empty armchair, looking like he wished he could turn into a shadow, or blend into the wood of the log house like a moth.

'Hey,' I said, not accustomed to having Samson there in the flesh to talk to. Samson was still solid, A-to-Z, soup-to-nuts visible for all the world to see.

'Hey,' he said back.

'Can you believe there really was gold buried here after all?'

A small smile played across Samson's thin face.

'Er . . . I probably shouldn't tell you this, but the treasure the girls found was pyrites, Ledge. Fool's gold.' Samson looked sheepish as he cast around for any sign of Fe or the twins. 'Don't ever tell the girls, but Autry got five kilos of the stuff from the five-and-dime. He bought every last piece Willie had. Then he gave it to me to bury someplace where the girls were sure to find it.' He smiled again as if enjoying the memory of having done something unseen.

My mouth fell open. 'But Mr Cabot took it all! He had to know it wasn't real treasure – he's got a whole collection of rocks and minerals. He knows the difference between gold and pyrites, easy. Marisol and Mesquite must too!'

Samson shrugged. 'Maybe it was treasure enough.'

I sat with Samson a while longer before I slipped away from the gathering. I was itching to be someplace else. I had to see a girl about a letter.

I changed out of my good Sunday church trousers into sweatpants and laced up my running shoes. I was up the gravel road and over the south ridge before anyone could call after me, headed towards Sundance. But just before reaching the highway, I heard a sound and turned.

'Bitsy, no! You can't –' But I stopped before I could finish telling the dog she couldn't come. Her eyes were

395

bright, her tongue lolling from a wide doggy grin. With only three legs, Bitsy was keeping up fine. And even Bitsy deserved to get off the ranch now and then. So, this time, I let her tag along, the two of us proudly running our own misfit marathon towards town.

We didn't stop at Neary's Auto Salvage Acres. But I grinned when I saw that the foreclosure notice was gone and that Neary's sign had been freshly repainted to read: *Neary's Auto Salvage & Sculpture Garden*. I grinned even wider when I saw Winona's scrap-metal bear statue sitting by the sign. The rebuilt Knucklehead hadn't won the top prize in the motorcycle show in Spearfish, but it had earned a white ribbon. Unlike the five kilos of pyrites and the bundle of donor money from Cheyenne that had saved the Flying Cattleheart, a white ribbon wouldn't have paid off Mr Cabot. Yet Rocket had sent a postcard telling me that Gus and Winona had somehow managed to pull the place out of foreclosure. He just hadn't told me *how*.

Moving on, I ran past the gas station and the CAD Co. building. Sheriff Brown's truck was parked in front of the *Welcome to Sundance* sign. I offered the sheriff a quick salute as he handed a speeding ticket to a tourist. Then Bitsy and I pushed our lazy lope into a quick-getaway sprint, running past the open door of *Noble and Willie's Five & Dime,* before heading up the hill.

Reaching the Cabot house, I stopped short, trying to catch my breath as I picked my jaw up off the ground. Mr Cabot had decided not to rebuild his fence. But he had added something new to the yard – something big. Suddenly I knew exactly how Gus and Winona had paid off Mr Cabot. For there, in the middle of the lawn, opposite the protective limbs of the tall white birch tree, stood the greatest of Winona's sculptures: the mythical jackalope she'd been working on when I met her, its branching antlers gleaming in the sun. I liked the newest addition to Mr Cabot's collection.

I smiled as Bitsy sniffed the crazy sculpture, then looked up as an iridescent blue-green butterfly the size of a dinner plate stopped to rest on the tip of the jackalope's right ear. The escaped Queen Alexandra's Birdwing opened and closed its enormous wings slowly. Making me smile even wider.

I pulled a handful of small bolts out of the mailboxes across the street in one quick, easy motion and pitched them up to rap against Sarah Jane's window, hoping that if Hedda the Horrible hadn't yet left for outer space, she wouldn't come running. As I waited for SJ to appear, I bent to pick up the car antenna that had shot off Mr Cabot's Lincoln months before. It had hidden itself in a crack between the path and the grass. Now, quickly and deftly, I reshaped it.

'What's your damage, Cowboy?' Sarah Jane demanded as she opened her window and leaned out, her hair hanging down in one long braid, her green eyes sparkling. She pretended to sound tough, but she was grinning.

'No damage today, SJ,' I called back. 'Just this!' I held up my creation – a carefully sculpted antenna-wire flower – trying not to come off looking and sounding like a besotted buffoon. I wondered if this was the part

398

when SJ would come down and kiss me, just as she'd written in her letter. Josh had told me what to do when this moment came. I had to act cool. I couldn't freak out, geek out, or run screaming.

Sarah Jane disappeared from the window. My heart began to pound, waiting for her to come down and . . . and . . .

Maybe I should *run*, I thought. I could always lie to the guys and say I didn't.

Only Sarah Jane didn't come down to give me that kiss she'd promised in her letter. Instead, reappearing in her upstairs window, she dropped a single sheet of paper. I watched the paper whip and flutter to the ground, not sure if it was safe to read. It might tell me that Bigfoot was standing behind me . . . or that SJ was going to give me *two* kisses now, not just one.

'Oh, go on! Be a man, Ledge! A few alphabet bits don't scare you, do they?'

I swallowed, then bent and picked up SJ's paper. On it she'd written six words:

You shouldn't believe everything you read.

After that, I didn't know *what* to believe, aside from the fact that Sarah Jane and I were friends. The only kiss I got that day was the one in the tall tale I told the guys back at school – and that one would have made one super-duper, *humdinger* headline.

Acknowledgements

Many thanks to Lauri Hornik and the dedicated people at Dial Books for Young Readers and Penguin Young Readers Group. Thanks too to Chip Flaherty and my pals at Walden Media, especially Deborah Kovacs and Kellie Celia, who are always ready with a cheer. Additional thanks to the folks at Writers House who keep my stories moving around the world. I'd be lost in the jungle without my fabulous agent, Daniel Lazar, and missing the masterful email haiku of his assistant, Stephen Barr.

To my family and friends, who all thought I fell in a hole while writing this book, thank you for your patience. Mom, Dad, Michelle, Luca, Phyllis, Christine,

Rose—I love you all. Andy, you deserve a medal. Sean, your support and insight were brilliant and invaluable, as always—you and I learned long ago that not everything that comes apart is broken.

To the many people who took the time to answer my questions about butterflies, motorcycles and more . . . I'm grateful. A special shout-out to Arthur Plotnik, whose book inspired me to take chances (and gave me the word *scumble* in the first place), and to the lovely and talented Laura Resau and Sarah Prineas, who have both given me so much. Counting down to lunch, Sarah. Yup, yup, yup!

Finally, for sticking with me, putting me up, sending brownies, listening to me cry, laughing with me and helping me find this story, my editor, Alisha Niehaus, deserves big hugs, and even bigger boxes of chocolate— or better yet, more lavender air, black truffle explosions and smouldering cinnamon sticks.

Bright and shiny and sizzling with fun stuff . . .

puffin.co.uk

WEB FUN

UNIQUE and exclusive digital content!
Podcasts, photos, Q&A, Day in the Life of, interviews
and much more, from Eoin Colfer, Cathy Cassidy,
Allan Ahlberg and Meg Rosoff to Lynley Dodd!

WEB NEWS

The **Puffin Blog** is packed with posts and photos from
Puffin HQ and special guest bloggers. You can also sign up
to our monthly newsletter **Puffin Beak Speak**

WEB CHAT

Discover something new EVERY month –
books, competitions and treats galore

WEBBED FEET

(Puffins have funny little feet and
brightly coloured beaks)

Point your mouse our way today!

It all started with a Scarecrow.

Puffin is seventy years old.
Sounds ancient, doesn't it? But Puffin has never been
so lively. We're always on the lookout for the next big
idea, which is how it began all those years ago.

Penguin Books was a big idea from the mind of
a man called Allen Lane, who in 1935 invented
the quality paperback and changed the world.
**And from great Penguins, great Puffins grew,
changing the face of children's books forever.**

The first four Puffin Picture Books were hatched in 1940 and the
first Puffin story book featured a man with broomstick arms called
Worzel Gummidge. In 1967 Kaye Webb, Puffin Editor, started the
Puffin Club, promising to **'make children into readers'**.
She kept that promise and over 200,000 children became
devoted Puffineers through their quarterly instalments of
Puffin Post, which is now back for a new generation.

Many years from now, we hope you'll look back and
remember Puffin with a smile. **No matter what your age
or what you're into, there's a Puffin for everyone.**
The possibilities are endless, but one thing is for sure:
whether it's a picture book or a paperback, a sticker book
or a hardback, **if it's got that little Puffin
on it – it's bound to be good.**